Also By Dave Zeltserman

Fast Lane
Bad Thoughts
Small Crimes
Pariah
Bad Karma
Killer
Caretaker of Lorne Field
Outsourced (2011)
Essence (2011)

Praise for *Small Crimes*:

"There's a new name to add to the pantheon of the sons and daughters of Cain: Dave Zeltserman."
—*National Public Radio*, Top 5 Crime and Mystery Novels of 2008

"A thing of beauty: spare but ingeniously twisted and imbued with a glossy coating of black humor."
—Maureen Corrigan, *Washington Post*, Best Books of 2008

"Zeltserman's breakthrough third crime novel deserves comparison with the best of James Ellroy."
—*Publisher's Weekly*, starred review

"A Jim Thompson mentality on a Norman Rockwell setting . . . *Small Crimes* is a strong piece of work, lean and spare, but muscular where a noir novel should be, with a strong central character whom we alternately admire and despise."
—*Boston Globe*

"*Small Crimes* is one of the finest dark suspense novels I've read in the past few years."
—Ed Gorman

"*Small Crimes* has plenty of crime, but obsession, hubris, and evil, pure and impure, are at the heart of this vivid noir."
—*Booklist*

"A dark masterpiece."
—*Crimespree Magazine*

"Zeltserman masterfully controls the action, offering dark noir fiction in the best Jim Thompson tradition."
—*Lansing State Journal*

"The characterization and mental torment are reminiscent of the insightful psychological thrillers of Jim Thompson. Stunning stuff."
—Cath Staincliffe, *Tangled Web*

"Zeltserman creates an intense atmospheric maze for readers to observe Denton's twisting and turning between his rocks and hard places. Denton is one of the best realized characters I have read in this genre, and the powerfully noir-ish, uncompromising plot, which truly keeps one guessing from page to page, culminates with a genuinely astonishing finale."
—David Connett, *Sunday Express*

"This loamy smorgasbord of salvation and revenge has both a violent and comic edge, marking Zeltserman as a name to watch."
—*Crime Time*

Praise for *Pariah:*

"A doozy of a doom-laden crime story that not only makes merry with the justice system but also satirizes the publishing industry."
—*Washington Post*, Best Books of 2009

"Darkly enjoyable . . . clear, crisp prose; his fearless portrait of amorality; and his smart plotting . . . what a fine addition to the local literary scene he's become."
—*Boston Globe*

"Pariah is a terrific blast."
—*Metro* (UK)

"Zeltserman, writing in the pitch-black comic tradition of Jim Thompson or Charles Willeford, deserves to stand in such

exalted company."
—Chauncey Mabe, *Palm Beach Arts Paper*

"With this book Zeltserman entrenches his position as the ranking neo-noirist, putting a contemporary spin on a tradition that goes way back to Thompson and James M. Cain."
—Roger Smith, *Crime Beat South Africa*

"It's the kind of book that is going to spoil whatever I read next, as it's going to be found wanting compared to this."
—*The Bookbag*

"Pariah is sure to catapult Zeltserman head and shoulders above other Boston authors. This is not only a great crime book, but a gripping read that will crossover to allow greater exposure for this rising talent."
—Bruce Grossman, *Bookgasm*

"Pariah is one of the most crazed, hilarious, bitter, brutal novels this side of those composed on violent wards."
—Ed Gorman

"Sheer astounding writing."
—Ken Bruen

"Pariah is my pick for crime novel of the year. Tough, relentless, and packed with blunt force trauma, the book uses a Whitey Bulger-inspired premise as the framework for a disturbing and darkly satirical study of a psychopath."
—*Hard Feelings*

"This is a masterpiece."
—Seymour Shubin

"This book just sucked the air right out of me. It's more than

great noir. This book has teeth that bite and claws that catch."
— Corey Wilde, *The Drowning Pool*

Praise for *Killer:*

"Spare prose and assured pacing place this above most other contemporary noirs."
—*Publisher's Weekly*

"With graphic imagery and exciting twists, this novel is impossible to put down and has a surprising ending. A brilliant read."
—*Aberdeen Press & Journal*

"This novel is everything hard-boiled fiction should be—compact, direct and disciplined, and concerned with humans rather than stereotypes."
—Mat Coward, *Morning Star*

"*Killer* is a major novel of crime."
—Ed Gorman

"The whole book is told in tightly controlled prose that's perfectly suited to the subject matter. *Killer* is another bang-up job from Zeltserman, and a noir novel in the grand tradition. Don't miss it."
—Bill Crider

"Dave Zeltserman's *Killer* is simply one of the best crime novels I've read. Not in a long time, not in ages, not this year, but ever."
—Juri Nummelin, *Pulpetti*

"[Zeltserman's] story telling is very straightforward, not weighing down the story with too much style, but sticking to the substance and delivering a hard-hitting work every time. With

Killer, he has done the same again."
—Iain Wear, *thebookgag.co.uk*

"Read the book, amici. It's a very good one that will rock you in the last few pages."
—Charlie Stella

"To put it simply, *Killer* is a brilliant character study that will rip the literary rug right out from under the reader's tightly-curled toes."
—Corey Wilde, *The Drowning Pool*

"In a nutshell: Superbly written with a real twist in the tale, *Killer* is a novel which will appeal to lovers of crime fiction and the general readers alike."
—*RobAroundBooks*

"Highly recommended . . . Zeltserman's choices and the way he links them feel exactly right. He times the revelations and the peeling away of the past to enhance events happening in the present."
—*NextRead*

21 Tales

Dave Zeltserman

A NEW PULP PRESS BOOK
First New Pulp Press Printing: October 2010

ISBN-13 978-0-98284360-4

Printed in the United States of America

Visit us on the web at www.newpulppress.com

To my wife, Judy

These stories were written between 1992 and 2006. In the early nineties cell phones weren't ubiquitous and we had VCRs instead of CD players, and it was tempting when putting this together to update some of my early stories to reflect these technology changes, but I resisted the temptation. I did use the opportunity to smooth out a few bumps here and there, but these changes were minor. Outside of "Danny Smith", my shortest story, these stories are arranged in the following groups: My Bogusly Autobiographical "Life in Writer's Hell Stories", The Weird, The Hardboiled, The Manny Vassey Stories, and The Brutal. "One Terrific Apartment" is fantasy, the rest of the stories in this collection are either crime, suspense or noir, and are populated by desperate criminals, con men, psychos, dangerous women and losers. There's betrayal, deceit, and treachery on these pages, and occasionally more enlightened behavior, such as self-sacrifice and courage. A few heroes emerge, not many, but a few.

As a kid I used to read all of the Alfred Hitchcock paperback collections I could get my hands on. I loved the twists and surprise endings in the better stories of these, and I've always tried to write the same sort of stories I used to love so much as a kid: stories that are fun and exciting and with plenty of twists, as well as endings that catch the reader by surprise. What can I say, at my core I'm a pulp writer. I hope people enjoy these.

—Dave Zeltserman

Contents

Danny Smith

This is my shortest story. A mere 247 words long. My goal was to write a story in under 250 words that not only had a full arc, but was a satisfying read. You can be the judge for whether or not I succeeded.

I can't get Danny Smith off my mind. . . .

He was a good-looking kid. Well-mannered, soft-spoken, just an overall good kid. Only twenty-four years old. Six months ago he hired me to find his birth parents. You see, he was adopted, had great parents, but he wanted to know his roots. There was something familiar looking about him, made me think I had seen him before. The reason for that was his birth dad turned out to be Sam Lombardo, top guy in the Boston Mob. It didn't take me too long to find that out. It turns out Lombardo had a one-night fling with a dancer, never knew he had this other son. When I told him about Danny, he told me what he would do to me if this kid ever bothered him.

That was six months ago.

Two weeks ago I heard Lombardo was on his death bed, dying of congestive heart failure, and word was he was going down fast. His goons brought me to see him. Lombardo wanted to know about Danny. I thought he just wanted to make peace with his son before he died.

A week ago Danny's parents called me. They were frantic. Danny had disappeared. They had no idea where he was.

Three days ago I heard through the grapevine that Lombardo had found a heart donor. A good match, too. Transplant looks like it's going to be a success.

I can't get Danny Smith off my mind. . . .

My Bogusly Autobiographical "Writer's In Hell Stories"

"More Than a Scam", "Flies", and "She Stole my Fortune!" represent my bogusly autobiographical stories—stories with just enough similarities with my own life to sound as if they could be autobiographical, and all dealing with a writer struggling to break in (these were written before Small Crimes *was bought by Serpent's Tail). But even with the bogusly autobiographical nature of these stories, they're all completely fictional. Still, whenever one of these would come out, I'd get concerned calls from family and friends wanting to make sure my wife was okay. Trust me, she's fine. Nothing to worry about.*

More Than a Scam

The inspiration for this story were the ubiquitous Nigerian email scam letters I was receiving daily. At first I was planning to do the same as my story's hero, namely record a correspondence with one of these scam artists, but instead I decided to go in another direction. "More Than a Scam" received honorable in the 2003 edition of Best American Mystery Stories.

It really all started with the email I received. The message was marked "Urgent/Confidential" and was from one Celestine Okiti, who claimed to be a senior accountant with the Nigerian Federal Ministry of Finance. The gist of the email was that ten and a half million dollars was sitting in a Nigerian bank account and she was looking for a partner to pose as the next of kin of some dead foreign contractor so she could get the money out—and that my cut would be four and a half million dollars, minus expenses.

Of course, it was a scam. It was too silly to be anything else, and besides, I had read about this years ago. The "pigeon" who went for his four and a half million cut would be asked to put up some money to show good faith and to cover the expenses. It was a pretty simple and childish scam, one that makes you wonder how anyone in the world could fall for it, but still, I was fascinated by that email. It got my mind spinning on different crime story scenarios.

I guess I should tell you a little about myself so that this makes some sense. My name's Dan Wilson. I'm thirty-eight, live in a suburb near Boston, been married ten years, and have a pretty boring job processing insurance claims. In order to keep my sanity I write crime stories in my spare time. Usually I write hard-boiled PI stories, sometimes crime caper stories. I've had limited success. I've sold a couple of stories to print magazines and have given away a fair number of them to online Internet magazines.

I sat for a good two hours staring at Celestine Okiti's message, playing out different story ideas in my mind. The one idea I kept coming back to was responding to her email message, pretending to be a pigeon, and then writing up the exchange of emails as a story. I didn't do anything, though, at least not then. By the time I gave up it was one in the morning. I didn't want to wake Cheryl so I slept in the guest room.

The next morning as I sat drinking coffee, my mind raced with different possible Nigerian bank scam stories. I didn't notice Cheryl had come into the room until she sat across from me with her yogurt and newspaper. She seemed too absorbed with the newspaper—and I guess I was too deep into plotting my story—for us to say much to each other. After I finished my coffee I headed off to work.

After three days of working out different scenarios in my mind, I decided on a plan of action. Instead of replying back to the email as a "pigeon", I would instead create my own scam. I have written stories with a roguish conman named Pete Mitchel. For the hell of it I decided to use his identity. I created an email account for Pete and wrote an email back to Celestine Okiti, telling her how fortuitous it was that she had contacted me, that I worked in the office of a large construction company, and that a Nigerian national died on the job several months ago and seven hundred and twenty thousand dollars in death benefits were sitting there waiting for a next of kin. I told her that I was planning a trip to Nigeria to find someone who could pose as the dead man's next of kin, but Celestine could save me the trouble. I further explained that I wasn't greedy, that ten percent, or seventy-two thousand dollars, would be all I wanted.

I sat in front of my computer for several hours with my email message typed out, trying to decide whether to send it. Of course, the scam letter they sent to me had been sent to thousands of other addresses, probably from a purchased email list. They'd have no idea whether or not an email was originally sent to a Pete Mitchel, nor would they check. As I was trying to decide what to do with the email, Cheryl walked into the room and interrupted me. She told me it was late, that she had to get up early the next day, and asked if I'd be quiet when I went to bed. She looked tired, a little worn out. I told her not to worry, that I'd sleep in the guest room again. After she left, I stared at the email message for another thirty minutes, and then sent it.

I didn't get a response for several days. I must've checked my email a few hundred times before I found a reply from Celestine Okiti. She thanked me for the opportunity that I presented, but insisted that her opportunity was urgent and was far more lucrative. She wanted me to contact her right away so that I could reap my four and a half million dollars, minus expenses of course.

I had already worked out in my mind what my next step would be if I heard back from Ms. Okiti. First, I used a travel web-site to book a flight to Nigeria for my fictitious Pete Mitchel. I then sent her back a reply stating that I knew her proposal to me was a scam, but that I considered it good fortune that she had contacted me when she did, possibly saving me from a trip to Nigeria that I wasn't anxious to take. I told her, though, that time was running out for me to collect the insurance money and that I had booked a flight for the following week to Nigeria so that I could find a local who could pose as the dead man's next of kin. I passed along all the flight information, and told her if she changed her mind she could let me know, but that time was running out.

I didn't expect a reply to my email. I guess I must have been feeling a bit queasy about the whole thing and at a subconscious level had decided to put a stop to it. I was more than a little surprised when I got a terse reply back from Ms. Okiti to fax her a copy of the dead man's death certificate and the insurance policy.

The insurance policy was easy. I was able to get a fairly realistic policy printed up in no time. The trick was filling in all of the contact information and then blacking it out with a pen. As far as the death certificate, I found samples on the Internet, and then used a graphics package on my computer to create a fairly realistic looking one. It took some time, but I was happy with the results. I faxed both of them to the number I was given.

Over the next four days we went back and forth over a number of issues until we were able to settle things. First, Celestine Okiti wanted to pay me my ten percent cut after she received the insurance money. I flatly refused, reminding Celestine Okiti that she and her associates were scam artists, hardly to be trusted. With the deadline of my booked flight approaching, she finally gave in. The next issue was how my ten percent was going to be sent to me. They wanted to send a check and I wanted them to wire the money to a bank account that I had opened for Pete Mitchel (I had obtained a fake driver's license for Pete Mitchel which is actually quite easy to do in Massachusetts, and had used it to open a bank account). Since they gave in on the other matter, I gave in on this one. I rented a mailbox in Pete Mitchel's name and sent Celestine Okiti the address.

During those four days, I guess I must have been acting somewhat manic. I could tell Cheryl knew something was up, but I didn't want to tell her anything. She'd think I was nuts and wouldn't be at all happy with what I was doing. She tried a couple of times to ask me what was keeping me so occupied, and I just told her that I was working on a new crime story. I could tell she was annoyed, but she left it alone.

To be honest, I never expected them to send a check. Even when I called up the store where I rented the mailbox and was told that I had a letter waiting for me, I still didn't believe that they would send me a check. But when I picked up the letter and opened it, there it was. A check for seventy-two thousand dollars made out to Pete Mitchel. I drove home and put the check in my desk drawer. I then sent Celestine Okiti an email message, telling her that after the check cleared I would send them the necessary documentation to collect the insurance money.

I had a restless night as I tried to decide what to do. The next morning, though, I drove to Pete Mitchel's bank and deposited the check. Over the next couple of days, Cheryl made comments about how quiet I had gotten. I couldn't tell her about what had happened, so I told her I had some stuff going on at work.

After I heard the check had cleared, I transferred the money to a Swiss bank account I had opened up. I also destroyed Pete Mitchel's email account. I kept the email messages, though. I was still planning on using them for a short story.

Things pretty much settled back to normal after that. About a week later I had gotten home early from work and was sitting at my computer when the doorbell rang. There were two black men standing outside my door. My guess was they were Nigerians. They were both tall, thin. Both were wearing slacks and polo shirts. Either one or both of them had on a heavy, musky cologne. The smell was overpowering. Both of them looked angry.

"We're here for our six hundred and forty-eight thousand dollars, Mr. Mitchel, or should I say, Mr. Wilson," the one closest to me said.

So they had tracked me down. They must've been waiting at my rented mailbox and followed me home after I had picked up the check. I looked at the two of them scowling at me and I just started laughing. "I can't believe you fell for my scam," I told them. "Especially since it was so much like your own scam, using the same next of kin angle. Jesus, how stupid can you be?"

They both looked stunned. I watched with amusement as my words seeped in and the anger in their faces boiled into pure hatred. It was shining in their eyes. "We want our money, now!" the same man demanded, his voice rising.

My neighbor, Carl Moscone, had opened his door and was staring at us, making sure everything was okay. Moscone is a retired Boston Cop. He's a big man, almost as wide as he is tall. I waved at him. The two men on my doorstep noticed him also.

"You're not getting a dime," I said, still laughing softly. I couldn't help it. "You know, at first I was just playing around, seeing if I could get enough emails to get a good crime story. It never occurred to me that you would actually send me any money. But now I'm having fun. And I'm going to have even more fun spending your seventy-two thousand dollars. First thing I'm going to do is buy my wife a very expensive mink coat. Every time she wears it I'll think of the two of you standing there looking like saps."

The two men were aware of Moscone staring at them. It seemed to effect them. The man closest to me asked in a low voice how I would like it if he called the police. That just made me laugh harder. The harder I laughed the more infuriated they both got, but I couldn't help it. It took a few moments before I could talk.

"I'll call them for you right now if you want," I said when I could. I had to wipe tears from my eyes I was laughing so hard. "I'll show them all the emails that went back and forth between us. I'll explain to them how I decided as a lark to see if I could scam you instead, and how you actually fell for it. I'm sure they'll get as good a laugh out of it as I am. You want me to call them?"

Neither of them said anything.

All of a sudden the amusement had dried up within me. "Get out of here," I said, now dead serious. "If I see either of you again I will call the police."

"It is not over," the one closest to me said. "We will get our money." And then they both turned and left. I watched as they got into their car and drove away, then I went next door and shot the breeze with my neighbor. He asked about the two men.

I told him they were scam artists who struck out with me, and left it at that.

The next day I had a bunch of issues pop up at work. It took me until seven that night before I had them under control, and I didn't get home until eight. When I opened the door I couldn't help noticing how quiet it seemed. I called out for Cheryl and got no answer. There was a light on in the kitchen. I walked in and saw the butcher knife lying on the counter top. Its edge faced me and I could see a red smudge running along it. Then I spotted the severed finger. It took me a moment to realize what it was. I don't know why. I guess it looked like a finger, but it just seemed odd lying there. It was placed on top of a note. The note was written in small, neat letters, and informed me that if I wanted to get my wife back without any more missing parts I had better pay them the money I owed them. The note ended by asking if I was still laughing. I picked up the phone and called the police.

The detective looked incredulous as I told him the whole story. I showed him all of the emails—the ones I had received and the ones I sent. I didn't leave anything out. I told him about the fake documents I created, the bank account for my fictitious Pete Mitchel, the rented mailbox, the seventy-two thousand dollars, I told him everything. When I was done he had me tell my story to another detective, and after that to an FBI agent.

It turns out the police found Cheryl less than three hours after I had called them. It was probably due to a combination of the Nigerians being sloppy, since this was most likely their first kidnapping, and not considering that I would call the authorities. In any case, my neighbor Moscone had written down their license plate number from the day before, and they had used the same car for the kidnapping. The police found them in a small house in Chelsea. They had hacked Cheryl into pieces and were in the process of packing the pieces into boxes when the police broke in. I guess they were planning on mailing Cheryl back to me, piece by piece, after I paid them their money.

At the time the police didn't tell me anything, and I didn't find out about Cheryl until the next day. That night they took me in for more questioning. I was asked several times if I wanted a lawyer, and each time I declined. At one point I was asked if I'd be willing to take a lie detector test. I told them I would. They then left me alone for several hours. I was then brought to another room, hooked up to a polygraph, and questioned. I answered each question truthfully, and they seemed satisfied with the results.

I think it was past nine o'clock the next morning when I met with the District Attorney. He looked uncomfortable as he told me about Cheryl. It was the first I heard of it and it took a moment for it to register. When I finally made sense of what he was saying, I just started sobbing. I couldn't help it and I couldn't stop myself. I just sat there sobbing uncontrollably, sobbing until it felt like my chest was going to break apart.

In the end the District Attorney decided not to press charges against me. While I acted criminally in trying to defraud the Nigerians, it was hard to muster much sympathy towards them. He was also convinced that I didn't intend for any harm to come to Cheryl. When the Nigerians were arrested they had confessed fully and bitterly, explaining why they had hacked my wife to pieces. The D.A. decided not to hold me criminally negligent, even though in his opinion I acted stupidly. We agreed that I would turn over the seventy-two thousand dollars to a local youth group. I think it really got to him the way I reacted when I heard about Cheryl. He knew my reaction was genuine, he knew I wasn't faking it, but he completely misunderstood the reason behind it.

I was lucky to pass the lie detector. I was lucky that all they were trying to do was verify my statement, and I had been completely truthful with my statement. If they had had some imagination I would've been sunk. To be honest I never expected the Nigerians to send me any money. Up until the point where they told me they were mailing me the money, I was just playing around. But from that point on I guess my mind was spinning with different ideas of how I could make it more than a scam. I knew that they wanted to send a check instead of wiring funds to my bank so that they would be able to follow me when I picked up the money. And I saw the Nigerians watching my mailbox when I picked up the check. I saw them when they were following me home; I even slowed down several times so I wouldn't lose them. And I had no intention of spending any of that seventy-two thousand dollars on a mink coat for Cheryl. I told them that to infuriate them, to give them ideas. And I found reasons to stay late at work to give them time to do what they were going to do.

The thing of it was Cheryl and I had drifted apart over the years. We didn't really talk much any more, and we didn't really like being with each other. It had been over a year since we'd had sex, and even longer since I cared about it. A divorce would've been costly and unpleasant. So while I had to give up the seventy-two thousand dollars, I was paid six hundred thousand dollars from her life insurance policy. Her parents are now suing me for it, claiming I negligently contributed to her death, but my lawyer doesn't think they have much of a case. I'm not worried about losing the money.

No, the D.A. wasn't even close to understanding why I broke down the way I did. It had nothing to do with Cheryl's death. It just hit me all of a sudden as to what I had done and what I had become. It took me a while to get used to it. But I'm fine now.

Flies

We had a dead mouse in our basement, and the inspiration for this story came from the swarm of flesh-eating flies that came afterwards. And like my noir hero in this story, I hate those damn flesh-eating flies!

As I was trying to figure out how to finish the paragraph I was working on, a fly flew past my ear and another two landed on the monitor in front of me. Carol found it pathetic the way I reacted to flies, but I couldn't help it. Flies unnerve me. I knew I wouldn't be able to get any work done knowing they were buzzing around, ready to land on me at any moment. This specific type of fly I recognized. Larger, sort of greenish, with a big head. We were once infested with them. It turned out we had a dead mouse in the basement. According to our pest control person, these were flesh-eating flies, and any time you had a dead mouse you'd end up with hundreds of these.

By the time I grabbed and rolled up a magazine, the two flies on the monitor were gone. I slowly walked around the room until I spotted them. Two on the window panes I got with the first strike. Another on the wall required three swings before I hit it, and the damn thing left a red smear behind. I was thinking how I was going to have to use some disinfectant to clean off the mark when I noticed Bowser standing in the doorway with his head cocked to one side, staring at me. Bowser was a white Bull Terrier, and as bullheaded as they come.

"It's not my fault," I told him. "It was her decision."

He just stood staring at me, letting me know that he wasn't going to let go of his grudge. Watching him, I felt myself losing my temper.

"This is your doing, isn't it?" I yelled at him. "About all these bloody flies! You got into the basement again, didn't you?"

As he realized my discomfort, he started chortling. Anyone who's ever had a Bull Terrier will tell you that they do chortle. A soft wheezing-type noise. Unmistakable. After that, he sniffed in disgust and scampered out of the room.

Bowser was ostensibly my dog. Carol had bought him for me when I decided to try writing full-time, thinking that an author should have a dog like a Bull Terrier lying by his feet. He was really Carol's though. Any time he could he would plop down next to her, or when she was in the kitchen, squeeze himself between her and the cabinets. Me, he would tolerate. I was good to rub his belly or give him food from the table, but that was about it. I had the basement door closed. How he ever got down there was beyond me, but he was a bright dog and somehow had figured out a way.

I knew I'd have to go down to the basement and take care of what he had left behind, otherwise I'd have flies bothering me all day. There was no way I'd be able to get any writing done with flesh-eating flies buzzing around my ears. I started to get up, but felt my strength drain out of me. I just didn't feel up to it. Later, after I rested a bit, I would take care of it.

We still had a dirt floor in the basement and I think that was how we were getting mice. Not that we were getting a lot of them. A few here and there, but enough to be a nuisance. I had bought the materials so I could put down a sub floor and pour a layer of cement over it. Carol had laughed when I told her I was going to do that, but I don't see what was so funny about it. Maybe I don't work much with my hands, but I'm capable, I can read how-to books as well as the next guy. In fact, I was planning to take a break from writing in the next day or two so I could put down the new flooring. Get my hands dirty for a change.

I got the disinfectant and scrubbed the red spot on the wall until it was gone. Then I picked up the dead flies with tissues and flushed them down the toilet. As I sat at the computer, I tried to get my mind back into writing. I was a hundred and eighty pages into my novel and I had to push myself to get it done. I'd been struggling with the damned thing for almost two years.

When I quit my job two years ago to try writing full-time, Carol at first was supportive. Before that I had worked eighteen years as a software engineer, writing short stories whenever I could squeeze in the time. Mostly crime fiction, a few sci-fi and fantasy stories. I was starting to get published in magazines and was also achieving a few other successes. One of my stories made honorable mention in a best mystery fiction list, another was picked up by an anthology published by a large New York house. After eighteen years of pure drudgery developing software, I got lucky. A startup I was working for got bought and I made some pretty good money with my stock options. Not enough to live extravagantly, but enough to quit and give writing a shot.

Carol's support faded quickly, though. It was as if I was always in her way. I tried to hang out mostly in my study, but it didn't matter. Any little thing I did would get on her nerves. If I went into the kitchen to get something to drink, next second she'd be standing behind me, exasperated that I was interfering with her making dinner or whatever. If I tried helping out by cleaning up something or tidying up, she'd be ready to explode because I wasn't putting things in their proper place. It went on and on like that. Eventually she started finding reasons to be out of the house. One of those reasons was David Bryce. Supposedly he was just a friend, someone to play tennis with, or to accompany her to a new restaurant. After all, I would be too busy with my writing and she wouldn't want to disturb me. I guess it was possible they were just friends, at least at first. Bryce is a good-looking man, and Carol, quite frankly, isn't at all attractive. She's one of those nondescript women. Looks no different than any one of a hundred women you might find on the street.

The real bone of contention between us came six months into my full-time writing gig. I had spent eighteen years dreaming of the day when I would have the time to focus on my writing. I guess Carol spent a lot of those eighteen years dreaming of when she would have the opportunity to travel. And not just to Disney World, or even Hawaii, but to more exotic locales like Africa, India, and Bangkok. I don't know why she was so hung up on those places, especially Bangkok, but she was. She knew I had no interest in going to any of those places, but she didn't care. Actually, I don't think she even wanted me to go with her. I think she preferred that I would tell her to go off with Bryce if she wanted to, but I wasn't going to do that. As it was, all the pressure and stress she put me under affected my writing. I was originally hoping to get my book done in six months and that was now dragging out to over two years and with no end in sight. And she let me know about it. God, did she let me know about it.

Last week it all came to a head. She was sick of me, found me repulsive, and would rather be touched by a corpse than by me. As if that came as any surprise. After all, she had stopped having sex with me over a year and a half ago. Not that we ever really had much before then.

So there she is, yelling at me, telling me how absolutely nauseated she is at my very sight—

Damn it! More buzzing! Four more flies this time. How am I going to make any progress with this going on? I had kept the magazine by my feet, and now have rolled it up and am hitting those flies one by one. This time around it was easy. All four dead in less than a minute.

So where was I? That's right, Carol's telling me how she's going to divorce me, and how she should be entitled to most of the money. While I might've earned it, she was the one who had to put up with me all these years. Put up with my neurotic behavior, my craziness, my poor hygiene, and the list went on and on. A lot of it was just meant to hurt me, especially the poor hygiene part. She knew I took great care in my appearance. Nevertheless, though, she was serious about the divorce. Now the idea of her walking away with more than half the money was laughable, but even losing half of my money would mean I'd have to give up my dream of writing—and I never even had a shot, not a fair shot anyway, not with all her sniping and bitterness. If I lost that money, I'd have no choice but to go back to the drudgery of writing software. Or worse. With all the work they're outsourcing these days, I didn't even know if I could still get a job as a software developer. Especially after being out of it for two years.

I begged her to reconsider. She'd been talking all this time about traveling. I got on the phone right in front of her and bought her a roundtrip ticket to Bangkok. I asked her to go on her trip, take a month, see some of the places she always wanted to, think things over.

That was a week ago. Her plane to Bangkok left three days ago. And well . . .

Bryce stopped by earlier today looking for Carol. I told him she went on a trip by herself. He didn't seem to believe me, so I gave him the flight information. Let him check for himself. If he asks around he'll find out that a woman matching Carol's description boarded the plane and used Carol's passport. Of course, sometimes people disappear in Bangkok. It's been known to happen. Sometimes they just never come back.

As I said before, Carol is nothing special to look at. Could be any one of hundreds of other slightly dumpy women in their late thirties. If you try hard enough you can find one of them willing to fly to Bangkok for free. One of them that looks enough like Carol where she can use her passport and get away with it. It will cost you, quite a bit actually, but still much less than what I would've lost in a divorce settlement. At least now I have a chance of finishing this book. If only these damn flies would leave me alone!

More flies! I had no choice. I had to take care of what Bowser had left me in the basement. This was the third time he had done this. That's the thing with Bull Terriers, they're tenacious, and they can dig like hell. Smart too. He knows exactly what he's doing to me. I wish I could figure out how he keeps getting into the basement.

I spot him now, staring at me intently. Damn, that dog can hold a grudge. "Look," I yell at him, "it wasn't my fault. Can't you understand that?"

He doesn't want to listen. He turns around, looks over his shoulder, grinning sardonically. Who would ever have thought a dog could grin sardonically? Well, this one sure as hell can.

As he walks away I yell at him. "Four feet's not enough for you, huh? How deep do I have to dig this time? Damn it, how deep?"

She Stole My Fortune

Like my noir hero in this one, I had all these publishing deals in the works that seemed imminent, then they all fell apart. Things worked out in the end, but this is one of those stories that helped me work out some issues.

"She stole my fortune!"

The first few times I had said that, Susie rolled her eyes and showed me the little condescending smile she uses when she thinks I'm acting childish. This time she showed the same condescending smile, but it seemed strained. She was finally beginning to realize that I meant what I was saying.

"Come on, all Barb did was swap fortune cookies."

"She had no right doing that." I felt a hotness flush my face. "The waiter put that cookie in front of me for a reason. Your idiot friend had no right taking it. Everything has gone to shit since she did!"

"You're acting insane," Susie muttered.

I was livid. I couldn't speak, I could barely look at her. She knew better than to say that. Her words must've slipped out, but she had no right. No fucking right. I caught a quick glimpse of her face, pale now, an anxiousness ruining any attempt she had at looking unconcerned. I turned on my heels and got the hell out of there.

Driving to McGinty's, it was like I was on autopilot. I didn't even realize where I was going until I got there. Still too angry to do much of anything else, I took a seat behind the bar and ordered a black and tan. As I cooled off, I regretted the way I had acted. It wasn't Susie's fault about what happened, and besides, she's been a rock in my life, by far the best thing that's ever happened to me. I shouldn't have treated her like that. It's just that the whole damn thing frustrated me to the point where I could barely breathe, let alone think straight.

Joe had taken my order. After letting the beer settle, he brought over my drink. Half a pint of Bass with another half a pint of Guiness layered on top. I guess the type of drink that shows indecision. You just can't make up your mind what you really want.

"So Dan, how are things?"

I took a sip of my beer, met Joe's eyes for a moment before looking back down. "I've seen better days," I said.

"Sure you have." He thought I was joking. He waited for me to say something. When I didn't, he added, "You must've signed your book deals by now."

"The deals died on me. All of them stillborn."

"You're kidding?" There was a long silence where I could sense him standing there, but I just wasn't in the mood to look up. Then, his voice oddly formal, he said, "Sorry to hear that. Look, the drinks are on the house tonight."

I nodded, felt him walk away. I could understand his discomfort, especially after the way I had been celebrating the last time I was in. After fourteen years of struggling as a wannabe writer, it finally looked like I was going to make it. I had an Italian publisher telling me they were going to send me a contract for two of my books, a midlevel US publisher interested in a third, and the kicker, HarperCollins all but promising to buy my latest. All of this happening within a two week period. When I had gotten the call from the editor at HarperCollins last week, I left work and went straight to McGinty's and bought drinks all around. There was no way I could've stayed at work after that. I was on just too big a high. For fourteen years I'd been trying to make it as a writer and it finally looked like it was going to happen. All those years of squeezing in whatever time I could to write my books, all the rejections, one publisher after the next telling me my writing was better than good, but just too dark for them. Waiting year after year for that one break. For that one crack so I could squeeze through. And then three deals all but done. One right after the next. Floating on Cloud Nine? Fuck no, not even close. Stratospheres higher than that. Way up in that rarified air.

After McGinty's, I went home to pick up Susie so I could continue the celebration, and of course, Barb had to be there. *Come on, honey, Barb's depressed about Tom, couldn't she join us?* I was in too good a mood to turn Susie down, so we all went out for Chinese food.

During dinner I was mostly in a good mood. Barb has a way bringing me down, but not that night—at least not for most of it. After we ate and the plates were cleared away, the waiter dropped off fortune cookies in front of each of us. Before I could move, Barb had snatched my cookie and replaced it with her own.

"Maybe some of your luck will rub off on me," she said.

I sat there annoyed, but forcing a smile.

She cracked open her cookie, and laughing that grating horse laugh of hers, read the fortune. "*Years of hard work will soon lead to fame and fortune.*" Turning to me, she snickered, "Ha! Jeeze, sorry Dan, it looks like I stole your fortune."

I opened the fortune cookie she had left me. *Humility is a valued teacher.* I didn't even understand what the fuck that was supposed to mean, but then again, why should I? That fortune was meant for her, not me.

Two days later I got an email from the Italian publisher that he was going to have to pass on my books. It seemed that he had a falling out with the translator he had lined up and had no one else to work on them. Then the next day another email from the midlevel publisher. He was cutting back on his crime fiction list and would have to pass on my book. That afternoon I got a call from the editor at HarperCollins. The book I had sent him was a crime caper with outsourcing as an integral theme. The editor was having second thoughts whether the subject of outsourcing would still be topical by the time the book came out. I sat and listened as he convinced himself to kill the deal. At some gut level I knew there was nothing I could do about it, no way to talk him out of it, and I knew why. . . .

Joe interrupted my thoughts, asking if I'd like another black and tan. I was about to tell him sure, but instead changed my order to a pint of Guiness. My indecision was gone. With a clarity of thought I knew what I had to do.

The next few days were rough ones. I couldn't help feeling antsy. Susie sensed my uneasiness, but misunderstood the reason for it. Still she tried her best to be supportive, telling me over and over again that I'd find new book deals to replace the ones that had fallen apart. I played along. I knew what she was saying was shit, but it wouldn't have done any good to let her in on what I was thinking.

Finally Thursday came. Somehow I made it through the day at work without jumping completely out of my skin and got home a little after six. The next three hours were murder as I waited for Barb to call Susie. She always called Susie after her Thursday's *Men Are Bastards* support group meeting, usually with half a bottle of wine already in her.

The phone rang a little after nine. I let Susie pick up, but could tell quickly from her end of the conversation who she was talking to. I then waited twenty minutes before signaling to Susie that I was heading off to McGinty's for a couple of beers. She nodded back, somewhat distracted.

I went to McGinty's and had a couple of pints of Guiness. Checked my watch, saw it was quarter to ten. By this time Susie would've gotten off the phone. I threw a twenty down for Joe and headed off to Barb's apartment building.

Ten minutes later I parked my car on a side street, trying as much as I could to keep in the shadows. A couple of days earlier I had taken a hammer from my tool chest and left it in the trunk of my car. Now I had the hammer inside my jacket and was headed towards Barb's apartment—a ground level unit with its own private entrance. Using the spare key she had left with Susie, I let myself into her apartment.

She was sitting on the sofa wearing a nightshirt that barely covered her chubby thighs. A bottle of wine next to her was three quarters empty. She blinked a few times before she recognized me and then asked what I was doing there, her words slurred by the wine.

"There's something I have to do," I told her.

Her eyes narrowed as she looked at me. "Why are you wearing gloves?"

I didn't answer her. Annoyed, she asked, "Susie know you're here?"

I nodded.

"What happened, is she worried I'm going to hurt myself? Jesus, she shouldn't take me so seriously. Especially after my Thursday night meetings."

"That's not why I'm here." I let out a heavy sigh. "I've got no choice, Barb, I have to reclaim my fortune."

She stared blankly at me before her mouth twisted unpleasantly. "You're not making any sense."

"Sure I am. You fucked everything up when you stole my fortune."

The unpleasantness had spread to the rest of her face. "I don't know what you're talking about. But I don't think I want you here."

"This will just take a minute." I stopped for a moment so I could gather my thoughts. Somehow I had to get through to her. I don't know why, but it just seemed important for her to understand. "Do you have any idea what fate is?" I asked.

She didn't say anything. Just stared at me dumbly. Her complexion had always been too pasty. Still, before Tom had split on her you could argue that she was kind of cute. Not now though, not with the extra weight she had packed on, not with how fleshy her face had become, like several layers of stucco had been slapped on. I could barely make out her eyes buried under all that extra flesh.

"Let me explain," I continued after realizing she wasn't going to answer me. "Fate is something real, something tangible. Kind of like a wave, or maybe more like a wind current."

"I don't know what you're talking about, and I don't really care, either. You're giving me a headache."

"I've got to explain this to you, Barb. When you swapped fortunes with me, you caused whatever wind current I was about to ride to bend around me instead. Unless I find a way to bend that current back to me I've got no chance of being published. I'm sorry, Barb, but I've got to reclaim my fortune."

She sniffed, her expression more petulant than anything else. "I'm calling Susie and telling her that you're here bothering me."

She reached for the phone. I moved quickly then, slipping the hammer out from under my jacket and swinging hard as I reached for her. I caught her on the side of the head. The way her eyes rolled up in their sockets she was probably dead then. The hammer, though, got stuck in her skull and it was a struggle to get it out. After I did, I hit her a few more times. There was no doubt she was dead by the time I left.

When I got to my car, I wrapped the hammer in an old towel and tossed it and the gloves into the trunk, planning to find a dumpster later. I guess on the way home I must've been driving erratically. A cop pulled me over. After he shined a flashlight in my face, he took a step from the car and had his service revolver out and pointed at me. I hadn't realized it at the time but some of Barb's blood had sprayed on me. I guess I had felt the stickiness but thought it was sweat.

The cop's voice cracked as he ordered me out of the car, and then to put my hands behind my head. When I did, my hands were jerked behind my back and handcuffs slapped on.

The next few hours are pretty much a blur. I know they obtained a search warrant and found the gloves and hammer. I remember sitting in an interrogation room when a detective dumped the stuff in the middle of the table, all of it in evidence bags. I remember him and another cop yelling at me, trying to get me to tell them who I had killed. I didn't say a word, but they found out soon enough. They had called Susie and she must've realized I had taken Barb's key. Anyway, before the night was over they found Barb's body.

Susie divorced me before the trial. When the trial came, I ignored my lawyer's advice and pled guilty. I didn't see much point in doing anything else. After all, they caught me red-handed, or, to be more precise, red-faced.

That was fourteen years ago. I have eight minutes to finish this up before they take me out of my cell and prepare me to die by lethal injection. The warden is now standing to my left, frowning as he tries to look over my shoulder to read what I'm writing.

In an hour and eighteen minutes I'll be dead. The most famous prisoner to be executed by the State of California. Everything I told Barb about needing to reclaim my fortune turned out to be true. Thanks to my notoriety, my books went from gathering dust in my closet to being published, with three of them ending up on the NY Times bestseller's list. After that I became a hot commodity, signing whatever book deals I wanted. The last fourteen years I've worked nonstop, writing thirty-seven books. The last one I finished only a couple of hours ago, giving me only that much time to squeeze in my one nonfiction piece. Not really a confession, more an explanation. While I've hinted in some of my novels about what happened with Barb, I've never really given a full explanation before.

Early on, after my first six books started making money, Barb's family sued me for damages. The jury awarded the family five million dollars, probably figuring that was more than I was ever going to make. By the time my twenty-fifth book hit the best-seller's list I had made ten times that, but it was too late then for their lawyer to go back and change the jury award.

Even though Susie remarried, I've tried transferring my money to her, but she won't take it. I can't really blame her. It would've been nice, though, if she could've talked to me one last time, or at least acknowledged one of my letters, but I understand why she hasn't.

Only four minutes left. The warden's now tapping his foot, his face folded into a scowl as he stares at his watch. Damn, I just didn't leave myself enough time to do this properly. My one nonfiction piece and it's going to be a fucking hack job.

Two weeks ago the Governor of California offered to commute my sentence to life if I'd publicly state remorse for murdering Barb. I turned him down, not out of principle, but for the simple reason that the well has run dry. I'm out of ideas for novels. To be honest, the last four were derivative of earlier works. Critics noticed and commented on that. Anyway, I could tell the Governor was disappointed by my refusal. You can take a lot of flack executing a bestselling author.

Out of time. The warden's indicating for me to wrap things up. I raise my index finger pleading for one more minute. He doesn't like it, but he nods, and then asks me if it was all worth it.

He's a decent man. For his sake I try to keep the smile off my face as I tell him it wasn't. But come on, thirty-nine books on the bestseller's list? Twelve of them made into movies?

Was it worth it?

Losing Susie, my freedom, my life. Just to get my books published?

Fuck yeah.

The Weird

The stories grouped in this section all have some element of weirdness to them. Maybe something supernatural, maybe sci-fi, maybe even dark fantasy, or in one case, just very weird human behavior.

Closing Time

This was my first story to appear in Alfred Hitchcock Mystery Magazine. The concept for this one: a guy spending a night buying drinks in a Dublin Bar. Anyone who thinks Alfred Hitchcock doesn't publish dark nasty crime fiction needs to think again!

When I walk into Donlan's there's a loud chorus of "Dev", just as the bar patrons used to yell "Norm" in the old sitcom *Cheers*. These days I am going by the name Devlin Smith. Over the years I've gone by a number of different names, which is important in my line of work. My current business card reads: *Devlin Smith— Dealer in antiquities and rare objects*. While the name's phony, for the most part the rest of the card's correct, although you could argue how rare the objects really are that I collect.

Anyway, I acknowledge the greeting with the same sort of wave the aforementioned Norm used to give. I even look a bit like Norm these days, although I'm quite a bit taller. About six and a half feet, topping out at three hundred pounds.

Jack already has a pint of Murphy's waiting for me. "Right on cue, Dev," he says as he hands me the glass, a genuine smile stretching his lips.

"Now what in the world would make me miss my night at Donlan's?" I answer back. "And you better start pouring more drinks. Round for the house on me."

Another cheer roars through the pub. They know that I'll be

buying rounds all night. I take a sip of the Murphy's, grateful that Jack had poured me the ale instead of waiting for my order. I'd been hankering all day for a Jameson's, and that wouldn't have done me any good. Alcohol has always been my downfall. If I started with whiskey this early who knows what trouble I'd get into? Better to stretch the night with Murphy's and finish off with a couple of Jameson's. Much, much safer that way. I really do enjoy my nights at Donlan's and it would be a shame to lose them over a sloppy night of drinking. I let out a sigh of relief that Jack had been looking out for me, and say a silent prayer for him.

Katy's working the tables and stops by to give me a wink and a smile bright enough to blind. "Howya doin', Dev?" she says. It's great to have ya here, ya know?" She's a little thing, barely able to fill out a size two pair of jeans. But as cute and perky as any I'd ever seen, and I've seen many, trust me. Blond hair, blue eyes, slightly upturned nose, and that perfect Irish skin.

"Seeing you makes it all worthwhile," I tell her. "Screw all this. Let's say you and me get married after your shift and I'll show you how well I'm really doing."

She giggles at that, her face blushing a perfect amount of pink. "Ah, if only you weren't joking me," she says, and then grabs a tray of drinks and squeezes by, turning back to give me one last wink.

I take another long drink of my Murphy's and am surprised to see the pint glass already empty. Jack has another glass waiting for me. I make a mental note to slow down. I remember other times where I had screwed things up because of alcohol. Then I stand for a moment soaking in the atmosphere of Donlan's, and smile broadly at all the beaming faces that are turned my way already smiling at me.

Four months earlier I had business up north and stopped off afterwards in Dublin for what I thought would be a couple of days rest and relaxation. Then I found Donlan's. Now Dublin is a city of over a hundred bars, many of them these days trendy, loud, with music blaring, and filled with well-dressed, beautiful but basically plastic people. I can have fun in places like that, and usually in my own way find them rewarding, but Donlan's was something special. Genuine salt-of-the-earth types. Good wholesome people. So I stretched my vacation from a few days to four months. Well, sort of, because in a way I'm always working.

I squeeze through the bar area, getting numerous slaps on the back. Donlan's seats forty, another thirty can crowd by the bar. These days the place is stuffed to the rafters since word got out about that generous Yank from Brooklyn buying rounds all night long. Still, as I look around I notice most of the faces, the regulars still fighting their way in each night.

In reality I'm not from Brooklyn, not even from North America, but I guess I developed that heavy accent from the years I spent in New York. Anyway, I saw no reason to correct these people's impression. With some amusement I've noticed an Irish brogue slipping into my speech patterns recently. If I stay here long enough, next place I go all the locals will assume I'm Irish.

Gerald Herrity, an eighty year-old duffer who could barely keep his false teeth in his mouth, starts to get up from his barstool to offer me his seat. I place my arm around his shoulder to keep him where he is. "I don't mind standing awhile," I say to him. He flashes me a drunken grin, his eyes already glazing from the alcohol, and then raises his shot glass for a salute.

I raise my own pint glass, and with some alarm notice the glass is again empty. Another mental note to slow myself down. I catch Jack's eye and he starts pouring me another draft.

A thin, fiftyish year-old man with a shock of white hair is making his way over so he can pump my hand.

"Devlin, an honor to be able to spend the night drinking with the likes of you."

I like the guy. He's a writer from Galway, been coming to Donlan's the last two weeks. Probably made the trip to Dublin on word of my nightly buying routine at Donlan's.

"Pleasure's all mine, Ken."

Jack works his way through the other patrons so he can hand me a fresh pint and I indicate to him from this point on to make the switch to Jameson's. He gives me a wary eye but acknowledges my request. I turn back to this Galway writer of all things criminal and dark.

"I finished your wonderful manuscript," I tell him. "A thing of pure beauty. I loved every second of it." And I'm not kidding him. I really did.

"Now if I can only find a publisher with the bollocks to print it," the Galway writer tells me, smiling somewhat bitterly. He finishes his Jameson's in a gulp. I signal to Jack with four fingers to bring us a couple more apiece.

"I don't understand why they wouldn't," I say.

"Too dark and violent for them, I guess."

"To me it could be even darker." I finish the last of my Murphy's and take the shot glasses from Jack, handing two of them to Ken. I hold one of my shot glasses up to the light and study the amber beauty of it. My hand shakes slightly. Deep down I know I'm making a mistake, but I've had the taste of Jameson's on my tongue all day.

"As much as I love your manuscript," I tell the writer, "you could make it even darker. Screw them. You need to make it even more over the top, more violent. I can give you some ideas I have about what more you could do with your hero."

"You mean my anti-hero. There's no hero in this one."

"Sure. Whatever." I spot Mick. I've been counseling him every night for the last three weeks about a problem of his and am anxious to talk more with him. I slap Ken on the back, leaving him nodding, thinking over what I said.

Mick's looking glum. I can almost feel the lump in his throat. When he sees me he tries to smile but it doesn't stick.

"I don't think Cara cares for me," he tells me.

Katy's walking by. I ask if she can bring a tray of Jameson's. Knowing the shape Mick's in, he's going to need them.

"Mick," I say to him. "I've seen the two of you. I know about these things. I've been the same place you are now. Trust me, okay?"

We stand together silently twiddling our thumbs until Katy brings over the tray. After a few more shots each, I ask him if he's been calling Cara and telling her all the things I've told him to tell her.

"I have," he admits. "Although it don't seem right."

"Sometimes you have to let them know you won't take no for an answer. Trust me, Mick. I've been there."

With some disbelief, I realize the tray is loaded with nothing but empty shot glasses. Fortunately Katy is within earshot. I signal for a fresh tray. After she brings it over and Mick and I have a few more shots, I explain to him that sometimes actions mean more than words.

"Mick, I can see in her eyes how she feels about you. Sometimes a girl's just shy. Sometimes you need a boy to act like a man. Are you a man?"

Mick shoots down another tumbler of Jameson's, his jaw hardening. He nods.

"Well, goddamn it, show her you're a man," I tell him. "Go straight to her apartment now and give her what she's been wanting."

Gawd, he's drunk. In the state he's in I doubt he could get it up. More likely he'll end up beating her to death. Still, Mick takes a deep breath and then clenches his jaw even tighter. I give him a slap on the back and send him on his way.

Of course I'm laughing on the inside. I saw the way Cara had looked at him in the past. No interest whatsoever. Still, this is what I do.

I can feel someone staring at me, feel the hotness of it. I turn and see Katy, her eyes now narrow and beady as she looks at me, her mouth scrunched up into some sort of hurt look. All the cuteness and perkiness has been bled out of that tiny little body of hers. "I overheard you talking to Mick," she says, her voice cautious, controlled. "I don't think that was good advice at all. Someone's going to get hurt."

I finish off the last of the Jameson's. How many does that make? Eleven, twelve? I've lost count. "Don't worry, Darling," I tell her. "Everything will work out as it should."

For a moment I'm lost in thought. I'm thinking about the events that are going to unfold between Mick and his darling Cara, about whether he'll end up beating her to death or whether she uses that gun I had sent to her. Then my mind drifts to other bar patrons I had counseled at Donlan's and the violent ends they have recently met. There was George O'Halloran, suspecting his wife of cheating on him, and me telling him about it all being hogwash and convincing him where and when he should surprise her, all in the name of romance. And then there was Seamus, a disillusioned young man needing some meaning to his life. The advice I gave him over two months about how he could make a difference in Belfast, and only a few short weeks later his corpse being returned back to Dublin for a proper burial. And there were others, maybe not making as big a splash, but the damage still done. You see I'm always working. Even when on vacation, I'm always working. Always collecting. . . .

I'm laughing now, silently, but uncontrollably. I mean it's all so goddamn funny. I notice Katy now, her mouth twisted into a look of pure horror, her face utterly drained of blood. I don't get it. Why that reaction, just from a few uncontrollable belly laughs?

"Looksh, darling—" I realize I'm now slurring my words. Then I stop dead, also realizing what she has noticed. What the whole bar has noticed. Cause Donlan's is now dead as any morgue. For a long ten-count utter complete silence. Then you can hear all of their bloody hearts beating like crazy.

What they're all staring at, wide-eyed and open-mouthed, is that I had slipped up and had given myself away. My hoofs are now visible, and my tail, red as any flame and sharper than any dagger, has ripped through my pants. As I said before, alcohol has always been my downfall. With Pontius Pilate it was wine, with the Pharaohs it was mead, with the Tsars it was vodka. So it has always been. And, as I am sure, so will it always be. As much as I have enjoyed my nights at Donlan's I have to face facts that the place was now lost to me.

Since it no longer matters, I give up all pretenses and show them who I really am in all my glory. As my body expands, as my clothes rip from me, some of the bar patrons swoon, and I'm sure some probably expired right then and there. I let loose a laugh, but it's hollow. I know I'm going to miss the place.

As I leave for the last time, I try to cheer myself up, remembering reading in People Magazine about a trendy new bar opening up recently in Los Angeles. A place that's a magnet for Hollywood's rich and famous. While I know it will be no Donlan's I take solace that in my own way I'll make it my home.

I turn, give Donlan's one last nod, and disappear into the night.

Dave Stevens, I Presume?

I wrote two endings to this story: the one that Alfred Hitchcock ended up using which made this more a hardboiled story with an interesting metaphysical twist, and my original ending which brought the story more into horror. Both endings are included here.

The bar seemed pricey for Wichita, but they had the brand of gin I liked and they allowed smoking, and after a long day on the road I figured I deserved to indulge myself a little. I was on my third martini when I noticed her, and she was certainly worth noticing—brunette, mid-twenties, slender, and a very nice figure which the miniskirt she was wearing didn't do much to hide.

I don't think I was so much staring at her as gazing in her direction, but the look she gave me turned me straight around. If I weren't a little high from the martinis I would've put two and two together faster when I caught her out of the corner of my eye making a beeline towards me. Before I knew it she was next to me, tossing her drink in my face. I made the mistake of letting go of my glass to reach for a napkin and my seven dollar Bombay Blue Sapphire martini was left dripping down my neck also.

"You dirty rotten bastard," she forced out in a breathless tone, her small hands clenched into fists. "I hope you rot in hell."

She then turned on her heels. I sat silently and watched as a hundred and five pounds of pure fury stormed out of the bar.

Then I mopped up my face as best I could, silently cursed Dave Stevens, and signaled to the bartender for another drink.

"That was quite a show," the bartender said as he raised an eyebrow. He was a big man, mostly bald, with way too much flesh on his face—almost like a couple of extra layers of stucco had been slapped on. He tried giving me a smile, but there wasn't much life to it.

"I never saw her before," I told him.

"I would've bet otherwise."

I didn't bother responding. What would've been the point? Somewhat reluctantly, he poured me a fresh martini. I could tell he'd rather have me leave his establishment than sit there at his bar, but hell, it wasn't my fault that gal threw her drink in my face, and then my own. I just had the bad fortune of looking exactly like Dave Stevens.

If this had been the first time something like that had happened to me it probably would've left me stunned, but it wasn't the first time. Far from it. So I sat glumly drinking my freshly made martini and over the din of voices and ice clinking in glasses and other bar noises I could make out the faint rumbling sound of the universe laughing over the cosmic joke that it had on me.

And it was a good one.

Given how poorly I always did with women, it surprised me how often something like this did happen to me. But this Stevens guy has something I don't—charisma, extreme confidence, animal magnetism—I don't know exactly what, but he has no trouble breaking hearts and inspiring violent passion in the girls he dumps. In contrast, the few girlfriends I've broken up with over the years couldn't have cared less.

I finished the martini and asked the bartender for another. As I sat there waiting for it, I thought of Dave Stevens, something I hadn't done in almost two years. While he might look exactly like me there's something special about him that women gravitate toward. There's no denying that. One of these days I'll meet up with him and see if I can find out what it is. Maybe also knock out a few of his teeth in the process.

My own name is Andy Lenscher. For seven years I sold copier machines in the Mid-Atlantic, and during that time somehow ended up shadowing Stevens. I'd be sitting in a bar in Reston, Virginia or Scranton, Pennsylvania, or wherever, and invariably run into one of Stevens' pissed-off and furious ex-flings. As best I could figure out, he sold women's undergarments in the same cities that I sold copiers. I know some of you are probably thinking that this is going to turn out to be one of those split personality stories where in the end I realize I am in fact Dave Stevens. Nope, no such luck. This is just one of those fluky coincidences where the two of us kept traveling in the same cities, and I always had the misfortune of being several months behind him and paying the price for his bad behavior.

During those years I was yelled at, bitten, kicked, spat on, and punched by some very attractive women I'd never seen before. At first I tried to explain myself to these women, but of course it turned out that I also sound exactly like Dave Stevens. I learned the best thing to do was to keep quiet, try my best to protect my vital organs, and hope their rage would blow over quickly. After one of them tried to run me over in a downtown Bethesda crosswalk, I put in a transfer to another sales district. The problem was my company didn't want to move me—I was too valuable where I was and had too good a rapport with my customers. They dragged their heels and five months later I was shot at outside a motel in Pittsburgh. Whoever it was missed, but that was the final straw. I quit my job and joined up with a competitor who was able to offer me their Midwest district.

That was two years ago. The Midwest was far less lucrative than my old territory and I made about half the money that I used to, but at least I didn't have Dave Stevens to worry about.

At least until those two drinks were tossed in my face.

With a sick feeling in my gut I realized Stevens must have

switched territories also—probably for his own safety. Once again I was shadowing the sonofabitch. And once again the cosmos was having a good long laugh at my expense.

I didn't sleep much that night. After Wichita, I was going to be driving north to Topeka, then Lawrence and Kansas City, and all I could think of was running into more ex-flings of Stevens'. As it was, I was wide awake at six-thirty when the alarm went off. I showered and dressed quickly, and after checking out of my motel, found a roadside diner where I ordered corned-beef hash and poached eggs. I didn't have much of an appetite, mostly pushed my food around the plate, but the three cups of coffee helped. The waitress, a motherly type who looked like she could be anywhere from sixty to eighty, gave me a concerned look.

"What's wrong, hon?" she asked. "You hardly touched your food. Anything wrong with it?"

"Everything's fine. I guess I'm just not as hungry as I thought I was."

She gave me a sympathetic smile. "Hon, you should try to eat. And if you want to tell me what's troubling you, I'm all ears."

There was nothing but genuine concern in the smile she gave me. That's the thing with Midwesterners, most decent Salt o'the Earth types you'll ever run into. But how in the world could I tell her, or anyone else for that matter, about Dave Stevens?

"Nothing more than I got a long day ahead of me," I told her. "But I'll make more of an effort." I took several bites of the hash while she stood and watched approvingly. The bill for my food came to five dollars and seventy-four cents. When she turned to take another customer's order, I dropped twenty dollars next to my plate and left the diner.

I had several sales calls to make before leaving Wichita. It was at the first one, The People's Credit Union of Wichita, that I spotted her. I had an appointment to talk with the operations manager about switching their business to us, but I stopped dead in my tracks when I saw her. According to the plaque on her desk her name was Lena Hanson and she worked as a loan officer. She was sitting down so I could only see her from the waist up, but that was enough to know she was the most beautiful woman I'd ever seen or was ever going to see. For a long moment I stood there lost in her golden hair and green eyes and perfect soft lips, watching as she absent-mindedly chewed on the end of a pen.

She sensed that I was staring at her. As her eyes caught mine, at first there was nothing but a slight frown, then I could see the recognition hit her.

Dammit, she knew Dave Stevens. Dammit!

I wanted to bolt, pretend I never saw her, anything as long as I wouldn't have to stand there and watch her hate me—or at least hate the person she thought I was. But I couldn't move. It was like my legs had turned into bags of wet sand and I had no strength to move them. So I stood frozen, dreading what was coming, but unable to look away. The hatred never came, though. As the recognition drained away, it was replaced by something more like surprise, maybe even fear. She seemed to freeze up, her color dropping several shades. Then, looking around to see if anyone was watching us, she stood up and came out from behind her desk. As I looked at her I realized she was even more beautiful that I had at first imagined. Her body was damned near perfect. Thin, athletic, but with all the right curves. And those legs, Jesus, I felt my mouth grow dry as I looked at those legs.

Moving cautiously, she walked over to me, stopping about two feet away. "How . . . what are you doing here?" she asked, her voice barely above a whisper.

There was a faint smell from her, something like magnolia blossoms, at least that's what I would've imagined magnolia blossoms to smell like. I wouldn't have been able to move away from her if my life depended on it. Not if you'd put a knife to my throat. Over the pounding in my head, I heard myself telling her that I had to see her, that I couldn't leave things the way we had left them before.

Fear flickered for a moment in those heart-stopping green eyes. "Meet me tonight at Maloney's. Seven o'clock. We'll talk then."

She glanced around to check whether anyone had noticed us, and then walked back to her desk. She seemed like some fragile, beautiful porcelain statue as she sat staring intently at her hands folded in front of her, her face tense, unmoving. I watched her for a long moment and then turned and left the office. I didn't stop until I got into my car.

I sat there feeling shaky inside. After taking a few deep breaths, I called the manager at the credit union whom I was supposed to meet and told him I had to cancel our appointment. He didn't much care. There was only a small chance he would've switched his business, anyway. After hanging up, I closed my eyes and thought about Lena Hanson.

I had never pretended to be Dave Stevens before. I didn't intend to with Lena either, but the words just came out of me. Of course I could've gone back in there and told her who I really was, but I didn't. I had to meet with her. I had to somehow have a chance with her. The thought of doing anything else was suffocating. Later I'd figure out a way to set things straight between us, but until that time I would be Dave Stevens. I had no choice.

With the way I was feeling I knew there was no point in going through with any sales calls, so I cancelled the rest of the ones I had that day. I couldn't keep from thinking about Lena, about the fear I saw in her eyes. I got the sense that she wasn't so much afraid of Stevens as she was of being seen with him. Then it hit me. It was only a hunch, but in my gut I knew it was more than that.

I drove to the public library. While they only kept a week's worth of Wichita Tribunes on the shelves, I was able to access all the old copies I needed online. After an hour and a half of searching I found what I was looking for. Five months earlier two hundred thousand dollars was reported missing from the credit union Lena worked at. I found more stories about the missing money over the next few weeks worth of papers, but what it came down to was that they had no leads or suspects.

I sat for a while thinking it over. Then I found a yellow pages, copied down the numbers of the motels in the area, and went back to my car so I could have some privacy. I went through the list of phone numbers, calling each motel and telling the clerk that I was Dave Stevens and thought I might have left my Rolex in my room the last time I was there. The first eight motels had no record of a Stevens ever staying there, the ninth confirmed that I'd been there five months earlier. The desk clerk I spoke with gave me the date Stevens checked out—the day before Lena's credit union had reported the missing money. He insisted that no Rolex had been left in the room. I told him I'd probably misplaced it somewhere else and thanked him for his time.

So there you had it. Five months ago Stevens had convinced Lena to rob her credit union, and then skipped with the money leaving her high and dry. No wonder she reacted the way she did when I showed up there.

As the magnitude of what I was getting involved in fully hit me, I started to panic. I'd never broken the law in my life—never even come close, and here I was getting in the middle of a two hundred grand robbery. As far as Lena was concerned I was the guy who planned it and I was the guy with the money. I took out my Palm Pilot and brought up my schedule from five months earlier and saw that I had sales calls in Topeka at the time of the robbery. Topeka to Wichita is only a little over two hours. I could easily have traveled back and forth between the two cities. If Lena accused me of being the guy she robbed the credit union with there would be no way of me proving otherwise.

I decided then to leave Wichita. I'd follow through with my sales calls in Topeka, Lawrence, and Kansas City, and then I'd quit and find a job in another part of the country. Maybe California.

After twenty minutes of driving hard, I was past the city limits and hitting the cornfields. Miles and miles of cornfields as far as the eye could see. As I drove, though, I couldn't get rid of the shakiness inside, and I couldn't keep from thinking of Lena. About thirty miles from Topeka I stopped at a roadside diner, but I just didn't have much of an appetite and left most of my food untouched. I had a couple of cigarettes and then continued driving. By four, I pulled into a motel off the highway a couple of miles outside of Topeka.

I sat in my car feeling too weak to move, as if all the strength had been bled out of me. I just kept thinking of Lena, of how damn beautiful she was. It was as if her image had been burnt into my brain. I was thirty-two, and so far my life had been nothing but one restless moment after the next. I think that's why I ended up in sales, so I'd always be on the move, always trying to outrun my restlessness. I know this will sound sappy—after all, I knew almost nothing about Lena and only saw her for at most a minute—but I couldn't keep from thinking that she was the person I was meant to be with, that somehow she could bring me some peace. And hell, if she could fall for Stevens, then why not me? I thought through a dozen different scenarios where I'd convince her to join me out in California. Nothing quite clicked, but I realized I couldn't just give up. At five o'clock I was still sitting in my car. I made the only decision I could make, and headed back towards Wichita.

I drove like a madman, my hand aching as I gripped the wheel. As I approached Wichita County, I called information and got the address for Maloney's. A quarter to seven I pulled into its parking lot. From the outside the place looked like a dive. A drab concrete one-story structure with a lone neon sign out front. I waited in the car and watched as Lena pulled in a few minutes before seven. I felt my heart jump as I watched her get out of her car and enter Maloney's. She had changed her clothes and now wore a pair of jeans and a tee shirt. She was breathtaking in it. I followed her into the place.

Maloney's was as much of a dive inside as it was out. The smell of stale cigarettes permeated the place and there were just enough overhead florescent lights to keep the room mostly in shadows. About a half dozen guys were sitting at the bar, nobody at any of the tables. Lena jumped a bit when I took hold of her elbow, but she let me lead her to one of the tables in the back where we'd be able to talk without being overheard.

"What next?" she asked.

"Let me get us some drinks. What do you want?"

She shrugged. "I guess a beer."

I went to the bar and got two drafts. When I returned to the table, Lena was watching me intently. Her skin had lost most of its color.

"You were watching me from the parking lot when I pulled in, weren't you?"

I didn't say anything. Instead, I looked away from those mesmerizing green eyes and took a long drink of my beer.

"Why'd you let me walk in here?" she asked.

Confused, I asked, "What else was I going to do?"

She shook her head, smiling over some private joke. "Again, what next?"

As I watched the anxiety tighten the skin around her eyes and mouth, I wanted to end the charade and tell her who I really was but I didn't see how I could do it without her either walking out on me or not believing me. So instead I kept the lie going, mumbling something about how she was all I'd been able to think about the last five months. I felt a hotness flushing my face as I added, "I couldn't just leave things the way we ended them before."

The anxiety in her eyes was too much for me. I reached out to take hold of her hand—anything to try to comfort her, but she jerked back from me and knocked my beer over.

"That was an accident," she said.

"I know, don't worry about it."

"I'll get you another one."

"You don't have to—"

She didn't bother listening to me. As I watched her walk back to the bar, I felt sick inside. I decided enough was enough, I'd tell her the truth and let the chips fall where they may.

When she brought me back another beer, I looked away from her as I drank down half of it. "I'm not who you think I am," I told her. I tried to make eye contact, but couldn't quite do it. Self-consciously, I wiped a sleeve across my face. "I'm not Dave Stevens. I know I look like him, but I'm not him." I paused, and then forced myself to meet her stare. "I know about the two hundred thousand you two stole. I'm not going to say anything to anyone about it."

She sat quietly, her eyes narrowed to thin slits as she stared at me. I waited for her to say something, but nothing came.

"I don't know why I pretended to be Stevens before," I said after a while. "When I saw you I guess I went kind of nuts, and, well, from your reaction I knew you knew Stevens. It just happened, I'm sorry."

Still nothing from her. "I know this is going to sound crazy," I went on, "but things could work out with us. Besides, you can't stay in Wichita. Sooner or later someone's going to find out about the money."

I realized I was slurring my words. My eyes had gotten so damn heavy. I put my elbow down in the middle of the spilt beer so I could support my head.

"So what if someone did," Lena was saying, her voice barely above a whisper. "You were the one who stole it. No one can connect me to it."

I had gotten so damn tired. I could barely keep my eyes open. The next thing I knew the side of my face hit the table. Then blackness.

Consciousness flickered on and off for the next few minutes. At one point I remember two guys dragging me to a car. Lena was saying something about me having too much to drink, but that she'd take care of me. I tried to say something but nothing audible came out. Then the world disappeared and the next thing I knew I was being bounced back and forth. I was still mostly out of it and it took a while for me to realize that I was sitting in the passenger seat of Lena's car. As she drove, a smoldering intensity burned on her face.

Lena noticed me. Her lips twisted into a thin smile. "You're finally conscious, huh?" she asked.

I was being jostled back and forth in my seat like a rag doll. Whatever I'd been drugged with, I still didn't have the strength to talk or even hold myself upright. From what I could tell we were on a dirt road.

"I don't know what type of game you thought you were playing, but it wasn't very bright of you to give me a second chance," she said.

In the moonlight her face looked so pale and grim. I couldn't keep my eyes open any longer. I let them close.

Next thing I was aware of was a clapping noise, mixed in with someone yelling over and over again "wake up". I realized Lena was slapping me in the face. When I opened my eyes, she pushed something hard and cold against my temple.

"You should be able to move by now," she said. "Get out of the car."

"Lena, this is all a mistake—" I had to stop for a moment, my throat feeling as if I'd swallowed a handful of sawdust. "You don't have to do this. . . ."

"Shut up!" She pushed the gun barrel harder into my temple. "If you don't get out now, I'll kill you right here and leave you for the crows and raccoons."

I caught a glimpse of her face. There was nothing beautiful about it anymore. Instead it had been transformed into something hard and violent. With some effort I opened the car door and got to my feet. Lena followed, keeping the gun trained on my chest.

"Start walking," she ordered.

We were on some sort of path. I could barely lift my feet, and moved about as fast as if I were wading through a pool of molasses.

She said, "I have to admit I'm curious. How'd you do it, Dave?"

"I don't know what you're asking. And I told you before, I'm not Stevens—"

"You don't want to tell me, fine, you can keep your secret. But I would've thought you had more brains than to show up the way you did. Especially after last time."

My eyes were starting to adjust to the moonlight. I could make out what looked like a small structure up ahead.

"Where are we going?" I asked.

"You should remember this place. This is where we said our last goodbyes."

As I got closer to it, I realized the structure was the remains of a shack. We walked past it, and that was when I saw the well.

"Lena, please—"

"Shut up!"

The base of the well was stone, maybe two feet high. She backed me up until I was against it.

"Do me a favor, Dave, this time die like you're supposed to," Lena muttered half under her breath. With her arm outstretched, her gun was only inches away from me.

In the moonlight I could see the knuckles on her gun hand turn white. I could see my death shining brightly in her eyes.

Something happened then. I'm not sure what the noise was— an animal howling or maybe a groan of some type—but whatever it was, it seemed to come from deep inside the well and it distracted her for a split second which was long enough for me to grab her gun hand.

My muscles were still rubbery from whatever she'd drugged me with and she fought with a manic intensity, but I was still able to slam her gun hand down against the base of the well and the gun tumbled down into it. We both froze waiting for the sound of a splash, but there was nothing. It just disappeared as if it had fallen into a bottomless hole. I faced Lena then. The pale grimness faded from her eyes and mouth. She started to look more like she had when I first saw her. Beautiful, vulnerable. . . .

"Dave," she said, her voice a breathless whisper, "let's forget this. We can still work something out."

I hit her in the jaw and knocked her out cold. After lowering her to the ground, I searched through her pockets and found my cell phone on her. Then I called the police and told them a woman had tried to kill me and that there was a dead body in a well. My phone had GPS tracking and I gave them my coordinates. The person I spoke to told me that officers would be right out.

It took longer than I expected for the police to show up. While I waited Lena started to come to. I flipped her over and sat on her. As she realized what was happening, she started swearing at me but I ignored it. When she heard the police sirens she struggled harder and I saw the same brittle grimness from before come over her face.

"You're making a big mistake," she forced out in something that was more of a hiss than a human voice. "We can still split the money instead of both of us going to prison."

I ignored her and pushed down harder to keep her on the ground. When I heard car doors open and slam I yelled where I was and kept yelling until I saw two wide-eyed state troopers come through the woods. They both had their guns drawn.

"Help!" Lena yelped, her voice mostly a hoarse whisper at this point.

"Move slowly off her," one of the officers warned me.

I shook my head.

"My name is Andy Lenscher," I said. "This is Lena Hanson. Five months ago she stole two hundred thousand dollars from the People's Credit Union of Wichita. She killed the man she stole it with. His body's in the well."

The two officers exchanged glances. One officer kept his service revolver trained on me while the other flashed a light down into the well.

"There's something down there," he said, his face as white as the moon.

While we waited for the emergency workers to come I told the two officers the whole story. They looked skeptical but they put Lena in handcuffs. I could tell from her expression that for the first time she realized I wasn't Dave Stevens.

It didn't take long for the emergency workers to get Dave Stevens body out of the well. While his face was mostly rotted away, there was enough left for me to see the resemblance. One of the EMT workers noticed it too and remarked to me about it. I asked him why I didn't hear the gun splash when it dropped in there.

"Well's bone-dry. The gun must've landed on him."

I thought about the sound that distracted Lena enough to keep her from killing me. I know it probably didn't come from the well. It probably came from an animal in the woods, or maybe it did come from Steven's body adjusting a certain way. But as I looked at him, I'd like to think that it was some kind of cosmic settlement for all the grief he had caused me. That somehow he saved my life.

As they carted away his corpse, I nodded farewell to Dave Stevens.

Alternative ending (starting from the point where Andy is being backed against the well):

The base of the well was stone, maybe two feet high. She backed me up until I was against it.

"Do me a favor, Dave, this time die like you're supposed to," Lena muttered half under her breath. With her arm outstretched, her gun was only inches away from me. In the moonlight I could see the knuckles on her gun hand turn white. As she pulled the trigger, I fell backwards. She ended up taking off a chunk of my shoulder instead of shooting me in the chest like she intended.

I tumbled in the air for what seemed like an eternity. The well must've dried up years ago, and when I hit the bottom I hit hard ground. My legs were twisted behind me in a way that shouldn't have been physically possible, but other than the throbbing in my shoulder I felt nothing. I knew I was paralyzed from the waist down. Then the stench overwhelmed me. It was the most godawful thing I had ever smelled. Even though I was in shock I knew what that smell was. I fished a book of matches out of my pocket, lit one, and there he was waiting for me. Even with his face mostly rotted away, there was enough of him left for me to notice the resemblance.

"Dave Stevens, I presume?" I asked the decomposing corpse. Then putting everything I had into it, I punched what the flies and other insects had left of his face. His head broke off and skidded along the dirt floor of the well before bouncing off the wall and rolling back toward me. I think that was when I went insane. I started laughing like a madman, laughing long after the match had burnt out, long after the cosmic joke that had been pulled on me made any sense.

View from the Mirador

This story was inspired by a trip to Acapulco. While the tone of the story has an almost old-fashioned cheery quality to it, this may be one of the sickest stories I've written.

The maitre d'hotel ran to greet Oscar Heile. "It is good to see you!" the maitre d'hotel exclaimed as he pumped the fat man's arm. "We have been so worried!"

A great wave of relief had broken over the maitre d'hotel's face, leaving a joyful smile. "And who could blame us?" he asked as he walked with Heile to the Mirador's entrance. "For eight months you have been a fixture here. Every day, every show you are here. We always have the very best table set aside just for you. And then what happens? You disappear for six whole days! Not a word! The cliff divers look up and see your empty table and they are heartbroken. We all are heartbroken!"

Heile smiled apologetically, his lips almost lost on his large, pink face. "I am very sorry," he said stiffly. "But unfortunately, personal business kept me away."

The maitre d'hotel, now beaming from ear to ear, gave Heile a clap on the back. "You are here now. That's all that matters." He turned and motioned to a waiter standing a few feet away. "Almondo, show Senor Heile to his table."

The waiter, a small thin man with slightly stooped shoulders, approached and bowed politely. "It is very good to see you, Senor

Heile," he said, a wooden smile intact on his face. "Please follow me." He escorted Heile to the table on the second level that for the last eight months had been reserved exclusively for the fat man. The best spot from which to watch the cliff divers.

Heile waited until he had squeezed himself into his chair before asking the waiter whether Sunday was his day off.

Almondo nodded. "Normally, yes. But how could I not come today worrying about you?" He gave Heile a sly wink. "The two ladies behind you were very mad that I would not give them your table. But I held it for you, hoping you would come."

Heile glanced over his shoulder and saw two ladies glaring at him. They were both young, beautifully sculpted, obviously part of the jet set Acapulco crowd. One was honey-blonde and wearing a wide-brim gray hat, the other was a dark brunette with very rich red lips.

Almondo smiled slightly at him. There was no warmth in his eyes. "I will get you your champagne right away, Senor."

Heile nodded. "Bring a bottle to the ladies," he commanded. He watched uneasily as Almondo walked away. All he could think was damn him! Damn that little man to hell! The last six days had been torture for Heile. And it was all Almondo's fault. All because Almondo thought he saw something.

Oscar Heile shifted uncomfortably, feeling a queasiness stir in his stomach. Almondo had been his waiter for eight months and like everyone else at the Mirador had treated him with genuine warmth and adoration. Until a month ago. . . .

It was after Roberto had made a successful dive from the one hundred and thirty-five foot cliffs that Heile had momentarily forgotten himself. For a split second he had let his true disappointment show on his face, and during that split-second he noticed Almondo staring at him. He could see the little man's face grow dark and he knew the little man understood everything. Understood why Heile had become a patron of the cliff divers. Understood what Heile was waiting for. Since then all genuineness in the waiter's manner faded. His civility became a facade and his dull black eyes masked something Heile dreaded.

Those dull black eyes were the reason Heile stayed away for six days. The thought of facing them became unbearable. But staying away any longer became even more so. Heile fidgeted uneasily and took out a handkerchief to mop away dampness that had formed over his upper lip. Somehow he had to ignore those dull black eyes. Somehow. . . .

The four divers appeared on the rocks opposite the cliffs. They spotted Oscar Heile and began to jump up and down and wave wildly at the fat man. Heile acknowledged their attention with a short embarrassed wave back. Champagne was brought to his table. Dom Perignon 1986, a very good and very expensive champagne. Later, he would give the signal, and as had become the custom, Almondo would pour him a single glass.

He heard a low murmuring from behind and saw that champagne had been delivered to the two ladies. They were talking to Almondo, and Heile knew what they were asking the little waiter and what he was telling them. That Heile was immensely wealthy.

Heile gave the women a polite nod and introduced himself. "Please accept the champagne for any inconvenience I may have caused," he added, smiling demurely. From the corner of his eye he noticed Almondo staring vacantly at him before turning and walking away. The two women's faces were brightly lit. The honey-blonde remarked that the divers seemed to be good friends of his. "They were waving right at you," she said, awe-struck.

"We have become very close," he explained. "I have bought them many shots of tequila."

"I certainly hope they haven't had too many today," noted the dark brunette. She picked up her champagne glass, drank, and slowly licked her red lips. "The waiter mentioned you have a spectacular villa in the Las Brisas area?"

Heile nodded. Normally, a man like him would have no chance with two women like these, but money was the great equalizer.

Even though layers of soft pink flesh hung loosely from his body, looking as if they could be torn off as easy as meat from a roasted chicken, he knew these two would be available to him. The thought of his grossly obese body sandwiched between their slender firm flesh seemed obscenely ludicrous. He would get little satisfaction from it, but it would be expected. "Just a small villa of twenty-two rooms. I would be honored to give both of you a private tour later," he offered.

He noticed the divers had jumped into the water and were swimming towards the cliffs. He felt a rush of impatience. The two ladies told him they would love a private tour. "Tonight then," he said, bowed courteously from the neck, and hurried his gaze back to the divers.

He tried to enjoy himself, but he couldn't—not with the unsettling feeling that Almondo was staring at him. He was afraid to look around, afraid he might catch the little waiter's eyes. It seemed so unfair. He had finally found a way where he could appear normal—actually be respected and admired—and also satisfy his morbid perversity. The dives were so dangerous! From one hundred and thirty-five feet into at most eight feet of water. And that was only when the tide was rolling in. Eventually there would be an accident, but in the meantime, each successful dive would be a delightful tease, building the anticipation. And when the fatality came, so would come the incredible release. And the fatality would eventually come—it would have to with all the alcohol Heile was inducing the divers to drink.

But how could he enjoy himself with Almondo sneaking around, spying on him, acting as if he were some kind of fiend? Heile felt a hotness flushing his cheeks. It was so damn unfair! Before coming to Acapulco he lived a hellish existence, last trying to satisfy his perversion in Los Angeles. The movie showings he attended there did nothing but fill him with loathing, what with the operators and other patrons leering at him, considering him as one of their own. He had tried buying his own movies, but had always been overcome with a paralyzing fear that he would somehow be discovered. In Los Angeles he was nothing but a freak, in Acapulco he was normal—at least until Almondo had to think he saw something.

He felt a presence and noticed Almondo standing next to him. The waiter was gazing at the cliffs. "I have bad news for you, Senor Heile," he said, his lips twisted up slightly. "This is the last day I will be able to wait on you. Tomorrow you and I will be very far apart. That is why I had to come tonight."

Oscar Heile looked up, his mouth opening dumbly. An incredible wave of joy welled up within him, almost making him burst out in tears. "I will miss you," he said when he could finally talk. Then he pointed at his empty champagne glass. "Tonight I will drink in your honor."

"Certainly." The waiter nodded, picked up the glass and filled it, his back partially turned to Heile.

Oscar Heile sat back in his chair. The oppressive black cloud Almondo had brought had finally lifted. For the first time in a month Heile felt happy—truly, completely happy.

He noticed the divers had finished their swim and were now climbing the cliffs. Roberto was already halfway up. The diver disappeared in a part of the rock formation where Heile knew a bottle of tequila was hidden. When Roberto reappeared, he turned toward the fat man and started waving his arms over his head, indicating through a private signal how many shots of tequila he had just downed. Heile counted eight waves. A burst of adrenaline nearly floored him. Eight shots of tequila! Roberto had only before worked up to six! He had added two more shots in honor of Heile's return.

Oscar Heile felt dizzy. His hand shook as he reached for the champagne. Eight shots! He still couldn't believe it. Today could be the day. In his excitement he took most of the champagne in a single gulp and then stared at the almost empty glass, confused. It had an odd bitter taste. All at once it was like a hand gripped his heart and yanked. The champagne glass dropped from him, shattering onto the terra-cotta floor. The hand once again gripped his heart and almost ripped it out.

He turned helplessly. Almondo was staring at him, his eyes shining defiantly. Heile knew the waiter had poisoned his champagne. Those black shining eyes were telling it all, damning Heile, damning him to hell. . . .

The honey-blonde jumped up and screamed that Heile was having a heart attack. Heile opened his mouth but only a sick gurgling came out. One tremendous pull yanked at his heart and he fell out of his chair.

A crowd gathered to watch him die. His eyes fluttered from one face to the next. All he could feel was envy. Then, as the last few convulsions rocked his body, he wished more than anything he had a mirror.

Almost Human

This is one of my very early stories, and "Almost Human" is every bit as much noir as it is science fiction.

Robert Danby watched as the holographic image of his wife's head formed in the glass compartment. As it crystallized, the facial expression of the holograph suggested disorientation. Within seconds the expression changed, the disorientation shifting to fear.

"It's so lifelike," Danby uttered softly. "Nothing at all like the emulograms I've seen before."

"Uh huh." I nodded. "The ones you see in stores are fairly crude. They duplicate a few movements and phrases, but they don't really act or sound like the real thing." I compared the alpha waves generated by the emulogram to those measured from his wife. They were an exact fit. "Right now," I continued, "its audio and visual inputs are being blocked. When I turn them on it will act and sound just like your wife. It will emulate her exactly. Are you ready?"

He gave me a short, determined nod. I activated the sensory inputs and voice circuits. As the visual came on, the pupils within the holographic eyes contracted, as if they were adjusting to the light. One of the many things about emulograms that fascinate me.

Its eyes focused on Danby, and as they did, shock and confusion flickered in them. "Robert," it pleaded, its voice cracking, "What's happened to me? Where am I?"

"N-Nothing's happened to you, Marcia, everything's just f-fine." He turned to me, his face ashen and bloodless. "I don't think I'm up to this," he whispered. "I didn't expect it to recognize me. I just don't know. . . ."

I turned the emulogram off and Marcia Danby's image faded from the glass compartment. "It can be disconcerting," I said, offering my most compassionate smile. "Why don't I handle the interrogation myself?"

Danby was shaking his head. "How did it recognize me?"

"It's a precise emulation of your wife. It will appear to act the same, think the same, and have the same memories as Marcia."

"It seems like such a violation of a person's privacy. I just don't know if it's right."

"Look," I softened my voice. "All that is is computer circuitry and lasers. There's nothing human there. Nothing at all. And it's the best way to find out if your wife is planning to kill you. The only alternative I have is placing her under surveillance, which would be kind of foolish when we have this option."

"It's not as if I have any real evidence," he explained, smiling weakly. "It's just a feeling I have. Sometimes, out of the corner of my eye, I catch her looking at me a certain way and . . ." He let the sentence die and held out his hand to me. "You're the expert," he acknowledged sheepishly. "You go ahead and do what you think's best."

We exchanged handshakes. "Maybe you could get out of town for a few days?" I asked. "Better safe than sorry."

He gave it some thought but shook his head. "No. Forget it. Just prove I'm acting crazy, okay?"

He was looking a little green around the gills, trying his damnedest to smile. "Don't worry about this," I assured him. "We'll clear it up soon enough." I watched as he left and then reactivated the emulogram. As its sensory inputs turned on its eyes searched the room before settling on me. In a hushed voice it asked what was happening to it.

"You're not Marcia Danby," I explained. "Last night a sedative was slipped into her food. While she was unconscious I made a holographic portrait of her and performed a mind scan and took alpha wave measurements, all of which were fed into a computer. You're the result of it. A simulation of Marcia Danby. An image of a disembodied head floating in a glass emulogram box."

As it processed the information, its facial muscles relaxed. "That's all I am?" it asked.

"That's all. You're not human, you're not real. You're only software. You're an it."

It winced as I said "it". Usually the direct brutal approach was best with emulograms to help them orientate themselves, but this time it didn't seem right. "Please," it asked. "Don't call me that. Could you call me Marcy?"

"Sure," I said, nodding.

"What can I call you?"

I was going to say something flippant, like "God" or "Your Creator", but its eyes stopped me cold. They touched me. "Paul Sanders," I said.

"Paul." It gave me a slight smile. "I like that. Hello, Paul. Please tell me what's happening?"

"I'm a private investigator. Robert Danby hired me."

"I figured that much." Its smile weakened. "What reason did he give for hiring you?"

"Maybe you could tell me?"

It started to say something but stopped itself. First helplessness and then resignation washed over the holographic image, leaving the eyes blank and distant. "I'm not sure," it said. "But I think I have an idea."

"He suspects his wife is planning to kill him," I said.

There was almost no reaction, but if the holographic image had included a neck it probably would've nodded. "I'm sure he would say that, and to be honest, if I had the guts I think I'd even try to. At this point I'm almost desperate enough to try anything."

"What is Marcia Danby desperate about?"

"About Robert," it answered softly. "What do you know about him?"

I accessed Robert Danby's file from the Federal Database. "He's a wealthy man, over fifty million in accounts and has property holdings of over—"

"Yes," it interrupted, "Robert is extremely wealthy. But what else? What did you think of him?"

I muttered something about him seeming sincere. I had an EMV running—a polygraphic analysis of the emulogram's eye movements. Lying causes spikes to be drawn. The line being displayed across the monitor screen was flat.

"He can come off as sincere when he wants to. He's learned how a normal person's supposed to act."

"What do you mean?"

It was studying me, its face dead white. Finally, its cheeks sucked in and expanded the way a person's would when blowing out a lung full of air. "It doesn't matter. You wouldn't believe me."

It shut itself off from me after that. I couldn't get it to tell me anything more about Robert Danby or Marcia Danby's desperation or why it thought I was hired. The information was there, I could see it in its eyes, but I couldn't pull it out. I tried all the tricks, inducing exhaustion and fear and anything else I could think of to break it down, but none of it worked. At two in the morning I gave up.

I tried to get some sleep. Hell, I could've tried to swim the Atlantic with my arms tied and had better luck. Marcia Danby's holographic image raced through my mind. I couldn't block out the desperation in its eyes. Or the funny sad smile it had. Or the way it looked at me when it didn't realize I was noticing. It wasn't the way Danby had explained it, not hate or murder but something on the opposite end of the spectrum. I lay awake for the full duration sweating through my underwear because I couldn't get a by-product of lasers and computer circuitry out of my head. It was a hell of a note.

I was awake at six when the alarm went off. As I entered my basement where I keep the emulogram lab, Marcia Danby's holographic image lit up. "Paul!" it shouted, a broad grin breaking onto its face. "I've missed you! I don't think I've ever felt lonelier in my life!"

"I could've turned you off," I explained, ignoring its eyes. "But I wanted to give you a chance to think." I sat at the computer with my back to the emulogram. After about a minute it asked what I was doing.

"I'm making your twin. Right now I'm designing a filter that will screen out most of Marcia Danby's inhibitions. About seventy percent worth. When I'm done you'll have company in the emulogram box across from you. And it won't hold back information from me."

"I'm not trying to hold anything back from you," it said in a hurt voice. It hesitated. "I'm just not sure what to do."

"Yeah, don't worry about it. Marcy 2 will be ready in a few minutes." I glanced over my shoulder and saw the holographic image struggling to keep its composure. It's a funny thing when emulograms cry; they don't shed any tears. It's as dry as sand.

"Paul?" it asked.

"Yeah?"

"Could you please turn around?"

"I'm busy." The filter was complete. The alpha waves and mind scan were fed through it, creating a slightly skewed version of Marcia Danby. If I did my job right the filter would act as a kind of truth serum to the new emulogram. With a soft mechanical hum, the emulogram processing finished and Marcia Danby's image appeared in the second emulogram box.

"That's me without any inhibitions?" Marcy asked.

"Without most of them. If I filtered out all of them it would only utter gibberish. The way it is, it should tell me whatever's on its mind."

Marcy greeted Marcy 2 with a queer smile. "Hello sister. Welcome to the wonderful world of emulograms." The new emulogram's eyes shifted wildly from Marcy to me. "What's happened to me?" it cried, its voice cracking into a harsh whisper. "Why do I feel so strange? Why can't I feel my body? Please! Help me!"

Marcy explained calmly. "You're just like me, sister. Nothing but a simulation of Marcia Danby." And then to me, "It's too bad I didn't have a chance to put some makeup on before you made your holographic portrait. My eyes could use it, huh?"

"Don't worry about it," I said. And there wasn't any reason to. Marcia Danby had an almost unnerving beauty about her and it had transferred intact to the emulogram. Makeup wasn't needed. I turned to Marcy 2. "Why does Robert Danby think his wife is planning to kill him?"

"He doesn't think that." Marcy 2 scrunched her face. "Are you a private detective?" it asked. I nodded. "You look like Robert," it observed. "You're about the same height and body type." All at once it broke into a sharp, hysterical laugh. "I know why he hired you," it gasped, its eyes shining.

"Why?"

It stopped laughing. "He's going to kill me," it said, its mouth gaping wide open. "He's going to use you to kill me. And he's going to kill you too. He's evil. He's not like other people. You have to stop him! Please, you have to—"

Panic had set it. I turned off its voice circuits. Marcy 2's lips continued working, fighting uselessly against the imposed silence. Marcy was watching intently, its brow furrowed in concentration. "What's going on?" I demanded.

It looked at me, a softness melting its eyes. "She's right. I didn't want to admit it, I tried to convince myself there was something else behind Robert hiring you, but there isn't. Robert is not really human."

"Yeah, what is he?"

"He's a sociopath. He has no conscience. Over the years I've realized it's all an act with him. But the act of pretending he's human has been taking its toll. For the last year I could see the stress building up. I know he's looking for a way out."

"I still don't get you." But I did. My knees felt weak. A dull numbness began to throb in my temples.

"He's hired you because he plans on your body being identified as his. He's going to kill me so that there are no loose ends and probably also because he's been looking forward to it."

"This is crazy," I muttered, or at least I muttered something like that. With my Class 1 private investigation license I had full database access rights. I pulled up Danby's will and started reading it. "It wouldn't make any sense," I said. "His will leaves everything to Marcia Danby and . . ." The numbness spread across my temples. "An addendum was added two weeks ago," I continued, the words echoing thinly through my head, "which leaves the full estate to Karen Barwood if Marcia Danby is also dead."

"I never heard of her," Marcy said.

I accessed Karen Barwood's file and photo from the Database. She was a knockout. Blond, twenty-four, starlet material. "She lives in San Diego," I read from her file.

"Robert travels all the time to Los Angeles on business."

An icy coldness replaced the throbbing in my temples. I shook my head to get it out. None of it made any sense. It was impossible, it couldn't—

"He's probably planning to kill us in an explosion," Marcy continued. "That way the bodies wouldn't be identifiable. Then he and Karen Barwood would disappear with the money."

"Look, it couldn't work," I explained. "The DNA results would prove I'm not him. This just couldn't happen." I still had the EMV running. There was no indication of deception, only anxiety. On a hunch I pulled up the files on the County Coroner's office.

There was no reason for it, it was just a crazy hunch, but staring right at me was a fifty thousand dollar transfer from Danby to the Chief County Coroner's private account. I told Marcy about the transfer.

The phone rang. It was Danby. It was urgent that I come to his house right away. He felt it was a matter of life and death. As I hung up, I felt my heart drop to my feet.

"You've got to stop him, Paul." The holographic face was frozen white with fear. "If you don't he'll kill us both."

I didn't say anything.

"You need to do it now. Before he realizes you're on to him."

I found myself nodding. Marcy was right. I knew it as well as I knew anything. I understood what I had to do and Marcy could see the understanding in my eyes. "Be careful, Paul," it said, and then it hesitated. "I wish I could somehow kiss you good luck. I wish more than anything." And then it—she didn't say anything more. She didn't have to.

I glanced over at Marcy 2. The holographic image was still contorting its mouth wildly, desperately trying to break its silence. I tried reading its lips and got something like Please Don't Let Me Die. As I left the house, I took an eight inch carving knife from the kitchen.

Danby met me at his front door. Small beads of sweat dampened his forehead. "Am I glad you're here!" he exclaimed as he led me into his house. "Marcia will be back in a few minutes and I have to show you something I found in the basement."

Yeah, I knew what he had waiting for me. I closed the front door, and as I did, I edged the knife from my sleeve into my hand. "Mr. Danby?" I asked.

"Yes?" As he turned to face me I pushed the knife into his throat. There was a short gurgling noise, and I pushed harder using all my weight, sending Danby flat against the wall. Confusion drained from his eyes leaving an awful dullness. He was dead. I let go of the knife but Danby stood erect, the knife pinning him to the wall.

I was shaking all the way home. Shaking like a damn junkie. I knew I did what I had to, but I couldn't get the image of Danby's eyes out of my head. The initial horror followed by that awful dullness. I looked at my hands and saw my knuckles pinched white from gripping the steering wheel. By the time I got home my hands ached.

As I entered the emulogram lab both holographic images studied me. Both sets of holographic eyes followed me as I moved across the room. They were a mirror image to each other. As they noticed the blood on my shirt, their expressions changed, becoming almost machine-like. "You killed him." Marcy stated, with Marcy 2 silently mouthing the same words in unison. Then they both started laughing. One, a crackling laugh like glass breaking, the other noiseless.

My legs felt cold, dead, as if they were disconnected from the rest of me. I had to grab onto a table to support myself. It wasn't possible for both emulograms to behave identically, not with the filter I had built. Unless, and the thought stunned me, how would a sociopathic mind react to the filter? For that matter, how would a sociopath react to an EMV? There was a study done years ago in France and . . .

Both emulograms stopped laughing. Both started talking, their lips perfectly synchronized, asking if I'd figured it out yet. I didn't say anything.

"I think you understand," they both said. "It really wasn't difficult to manipulate Robert to hire you. He is, or was, a simple man. He didn't even have a clue about emulograms until I put the idea in his head. Let me show you the look I'd give him, the one he'd see out of the corner of his eye." The expressions on both holographic images shifted, becoming ones of death. Then a harsh smile streaked both faces.

"You're the one who changed his will," I heard myself saying.

"And you transferred the money to the Chief County Coroner, also."

"Among other things," they acknowledged, their lips moving in unison. "Robert had no idea about any of it, just like he had no idea I chose you from the Database for him to hire. I had to choose you. I had to choose someone physically similar to Robert for my plan to work. By the way, I'm sure at this point Marcia Danby has called the police. Be sure to breathe deeply in the gas chamber. It will be faster and less painful for you that way."

Then they both started laughing. Off in the distance I could hear a police siren. As it got closer, it drowned out the laughter.

One Terrific Apartment

This is the only noncrime story in the collection. Instead "One Terrific Apartment" is a whimsical fantasy about the lengths someone will go to to hold onto a really cheap apartment on Beacon Hill.

The apartment situation bothered Laura—about why Steve refused to invite her to see his place. From what she'd been able to piece together he had an incredible apartment on Beacon Hill. Whenever she found herself obsessing about it, she would squeeze her eyes shut and try to put it out of her mind. Telling herself over and over again that it wasn't worth getting upset about. That Steve needed his space right now and given time he would be more willing to share his life with her. That he wasn't just a jerk.

As the weeks blended into months, it worked on her. "When can I see your apartment?" finally slipped out. He pretended not to hear her and when she repeated the question he made a crack about having to wait until he got his old girlfriends out.

It became almost torture after that. Doubt slowly twisted into her stomach. She became withdrawn, sullen. She stopped eating and started letting her East Boston studio apartment go to pot. "I don't understand why we stay here," she complained one night after they had finished in bed. "My place is a dump." He didn't say anything. She let the silence build and then asked if he was married.

He turned to her, grinning. "Not yet, but you never know

when the right girl's going to come along." He reached over to hug her, but she pulled away.

"When am I going to see your apartment?"

"Soon."

She turned away and started sobbing. The sheets slipped away from her. Steve lay in bed and studied her thin slender back and watched as her shoulders shook convulsively. Her reddish hair flowed like liquid copper down her back. Her crying was barely audible; the sound of a far away storm gathering speed.

"Tomorrow," he promised.

The next morning they cut through an alley on Revere street, then through a maze of brick walkways and cobblestone paths before Steve held out his hand at a brownstone building with large curved bow windows and evilly grinning stone gargoyle heads trimming the front.

"It's incredible," Laura murmured in awe.

Steve led the way with Laura tightly squeezing his hand. Inside, the apartment opened into a large living room, larger than Laura's whole apartment, with polished oak floors, built-in bookcases, and a spectacular stone fireplace. A mantel built with the same stone design as the fireplace ran the full length of the wall. Laura stood in the entrance way staring all around her and then at the intricate patterns molded into the tin ceiling. "Wow," escaped with her breath.

"Eighteen foot ceilings," Steve bragged with a slight smile.

Laura ran into the middle of the room, her face flush with excitement. She spun around slowly to take everything in. "This is so cool," she exclaimed. "You can see the same design in the molding as in the ceiling. The dragons are so neat. And those other things, what are they, a type of ape?"

Steve pursed his lips as if he were deep in thought. "No, not apes. Something not of this world, that's for sure." Directing her gaze away from the designs in the molding, he pointed out a kitchen off to the side of the living room that could've been taken out of Metropolitan Home and asked her what she thought of it. Before she could answer, he added with a sly wink, "Wait 'til you see the bedroom upstairs."

Laura ran to him and pressed herself hard against him. "I love your apartment," she said, and then she gave him a hard, passionate kiss, hard enough to loosen a few teeth.

When she pulled away, Steve cleared his throat and asked what she thought about moving in.

She gave him another long, hard kiss and then broke loose and skipped around the room like a school girl, studying everything one more time. She stopped in front of a three-foot curved sword hanging above the fireplace. The sword had a carved ivory bone handle and was unsheathed. The sunlight from the bow windows glistened off its blade. Laura wrinkled her nose as she studied it. "Of course, if I'm going to move in this will have to go."

"I'm sorry to hear that," Steve said. There was nothing in his eyes, no humor, nothing. The skin around his mouth tightened. "Because the sword is staying where it is."

Laura tried joking. "The things I put up with for love," she sighed.

Steve nodded. He only half-smiled. The skin around his mouth was still pulled tight. "Two rules about living here," he said. "Never leave the front door unlocked. Not even for a second." He paused to rub his chin, then continued, "There's more crime in this area of Beacon Hill than you'd guess. And we're hidden away here. Promise me that."

She did. "Okay," Steve said. "Second, we have central air installed so never open the windows, especially the upstairs' ones."

"Why?"

Steve looked away. "The smog around here. It bothers me. Just promise, okay?"

"Okay, okay, I promise."

•　　　•　　　•

For the first week, Laura would get lost trying to find her way back to the apartment building. It didn't seem to matter how well she thought she had the path memorized; she would still somehow turn down the wrong cobblestone walkway. It was as if things never quite stayed the same, as if the maze of cobblestone and brick walkways leading to the building were always subtly changing. After a while she would find her way back, but only by chance and intuition, things along the path not quite seeming the same. It left her with a vague, odd feeling in her stomach. For the most part, though, she was happy, even though there were other things that bothered her. Small things, for the most part unimportant things. Like Steve acting sort of weird. When they would leave the apartment, he would lock the front door and then go through a ritual where he'd test it over and over again, pulling and pushing on the doorknob. He would make comments about how she had gotten messed up with an obsessive compulsive nut and she would try to smile. And she would listen to the shake, rattle and roll of the locked door as he would pull on it ten, twenty times. It was weird, just like his insistence on keeping the windows always closed. The air around the building seemed fine to her, but he wouldn't budge. To make matters more bizarre, the windows upstairs had been nailed shut.

One morning when Steve had left to play softball, Laura decided the hell with it. She was starting to freak out from his weird behavior and rules. She had to do something about it. As she sat outside by the front door thinking about what to do, she jumped up, her mind made up. Just because he was a compulsive nut didn't mean she had to become one. She left the door unlocked and headed upstairs to the bedroom with a hammer and pulled the nails from the windows. When she was done she opened them wide and leaned on one of the sills. The cool air felt wonderful.

She heard the front door open and then Steve shouting. The sound of his voice was frightening, more like a hysterical scream than anything else. Stunned, she ran from the bedroom to the top of the stairs. Steve stood in the doorway, wild-eyed. "Th-The door was unlocked," he stammered out, his voice choking off into a hoarse whisper.

"No big deal," she started to say. "Nothing happened—"

"Get out of here!" he ordered, barely able to spit out the words. "Get out now!"

She stood paralyzed as she watched him run into the living room and grab the sword. Her body tensed as she half expected him to attack her. Instead he ran around the living room and swung the sword under the furniture.

She raced down the stairs and started screaming at him, following him as he opened closet doors and cabinets and stabbed inside with the sword. "What are you doing?" she screamed. He seemed oblivious to her, his face pale white, his eyes hard and grim, his lips bloodless.

He moved into the kitchen. "Stop it!" she pleaded with him. "Please stop it! You're scaring me!" As he started to open the pantry door, she grabbed his arm. "Stop it!" she screamed, her lungs aching.

Out of the corner of her eye she saw both the axe and the creature. The creature was no more than a foot and a half tall, with a flat grotesque face, blood red eyes and six inch fangs hanging from a muzzle-like mouth. It was wearing some sort of leather armor and was brandishing an axe.

It jumped out of the pantry, its axe aimed to split Laura's head. Steve pushed himself on top of Laura and the creature flew past them, its axe hitting nothing but air.

The creature bounced off the floor and cursed in a garbled baboon-like screeching. Steve lay sprawled on top of Laura. He tried to regain his footing when the creature turned, noticed, and screamed out in delight, then rolled toward Steve and aimed a blow at his neck. Steve twisted enough so that the axe dug into his shoulder instead. With his sword hand, he swung and hit the creature with the hilt of the sword, sending it bouncing away like a bowling ball.

Laura slowly stood up, dazed, and watched as Steve battled the creature. The thing raced around the room as Steve swung wildly at it. During one of the creature's attacks, Steve sliced off its axe arm. The creature cursed bitterly and retrieved the axe with its remaining arm.

Laura grabbed the first heavy thing she saw, a canister of flour from the kitchen counter top. The creature spotted her, twisted its ugly face in delight and rolled under a hair-line miss from Steve's sword. It sprung at Laura, its axe raised and ready to kill. Laura meant to throw the canister at it, but with the shock of the attack, sort of just jerked it forward. The top fell off the canister and flour flew out, hitting and covering the creature. The creature, blinded by the flour, missed and fell to the floor. It sat coughing and spitting and rubbing its eyes before tottering to its feet. As it weaved drunkenly across the floor, Steve split it in two.

Steve stood over it, breathing heavily, his face red. Blood from his shoulder dripped onto the floor. "Sorry about this," he gasped. Laura started crying. Steve staggered to the living room sofa and collapsed onto it.

"Jesus, look at me bleed," he noted with a detached fascination. He gingerly touched his wound and winced. "I'm going to need stitches. Could you do me a favor and get me a towel from the bathroom?"

Laura obeyed mechanically. When she came back she found she could talk. "What was that?" she asked in a weirdly calm voice that seemed to come from somewhere outside of her.

"A kind of troll. Take another look at the tin ceiling."

Laura didn't bother looking. She knew the troll was the same as the ape-like creature detailed in the tin ceiling.

"The things are worse than cockroaches," Steve added. "If you leave the door unlocked, even for a second, they come in. I should've told you, but I guess I was trying to figure out a way that didn't sound nuts."

All at once emotion overwhelmed her. "How can you live here with something like that!" she demanded, her voice shaking uncontrollably.

Steve sat on the sofa and twisted the towel around his wound and pulled tight. "Where else am I going to find a sixteen hundred square foot apartment on Beacon Hill with its own fireplace and private garden for four hundred a month?" he asked. He sat back and rubbed his hand over his eyes. "Just thank god you didn't open the windows instead."

From the corner of her eye she saw the twelve foot dragon with jagged three foot long teeth float past the top of the staircase.

The Hardboiled

A Long Time to Die

"A Long Time to Die" was my first sale. I think this is true for most writers, but there's just nothing like the exhilaration you feel from your first sale. I will always have a warm spot in my heart for New Mystery Magazine, and their editor, Charles Raisch.

Brendan was sitting across from me, smiling like the cat who just swallowed the canary. "My suit's a little tight on you," he said, nodding. "You were always heavier than me, even as a kid. Always bigger than your big brother."

"I-It's okay. I don't—" I fumbled with my beer glass, spilling some of it. He reached over the table and moved it away from me.

"You got to be more careful, Nick," he said.

He stopped a waitress and had her wipe off the table. After she left, he turned to me, forcing a smile again. "Ah, never mind, in a couple of days when I have time we'll go out shopping and buy you your own clothes." He hesitated. "Nick, do you know how much it cost me to have that detective find you?"

I looked away from him. "I'm sorry."

"I'm not complaining, Nick." He grabbed a handful of pretzels. "I promised our parents I'd take care of you."

"I was okay," I said. "I had a job. Almost for two months and . . ."

"Yeah, I know. You had a job frying burgers. I know, it was the longest job you had since Nam. But you can't settle for something like that. I'll get you set up with a real job."

I could tell he was losing patience with me. I didn't want to ask him anything else, I didn't want to get him any madder at me, but there was something I had to know.

"Uh, Brendan," I said clearing my throat, "is Marge still mad at me?"

"That was over three years ago." He took a sip of his beer and held the glass in front of him. A dullness crept into his eyes as he studied it. "It was my own fault, Nick. I shouldn't have left the credit card out in the open. I know it's something you can't help." He stood up. "Got to go answer to nature. You won't run away on me while I'm gone?"

I shook my head.

"Good." He put his hand on my shoulder as he walked by. "Order yourself another beer. I'll be right back."

After he left, I stood up and looked for the exit. I wanted to leave. I wanted to walk out the door and go away, but I couldn't. I'd promised Brendan I wouldn't. The waitress came over. I tried ordering a beer. She started joking with me, but I must've said the wrong thing because she looked at me funny and walked away. It was getting hard to breathe. I felt like I couldn't sit there any longer.

I looked around wondering what was taking Brendan so long. Then I saw him walking back with a small redhead. I turned away, hoping he wouldn't bring her back to the table. No such luck. Brendan clasped my shoulder. "Nick," he said. "I want you to meet a friend of mine, Lisa Chaney."

She moved in front of me and took my hand. Her hand was small, her fingernails painted a deep blood red. She sat down next to me.

"Hi," she said, smiling. "It's nice to meet you." She had the pale white complexion that redheads usually have. Her lipstick—the same blood red as her fingernails—stood out on her skin like a knife wound.

"What's the matter?" she asked. "You know how to talk?"

"Uh, sure—"

Brendan grinned. "I think he's shy."

She reached over and whispered something into Brendan's ear, and he started laughing. He whispered something back. I guess I was watching her and her eye caught mine. I lowered my head.

"What do you think you're staring at?" she demanded angrily.

I realized my head was level with her chest. I turned away.

"Uh, Brendan." It was difficult to talk, everything had become so hot, dizzy. "I-I h-have to go. I have to—"

"I was just kidding you," she said. "Can't you take a joke?"

"Sure he can." Brendan winked at her. "It just takes him a while to get used to people."

"Friends again?" she asked, a thin trace of a smile showing.

"Uh, yeah."

The waitress came over and told Brendan he had a phone call. He left and came back a minute later. "Nick, I have an emergency. I need to go to the police station and see a client."

He took fifty dollars out of his wallet and handed it to me. "This should cover the drinks and a cab ride home. Will you be okay?"

"Don't worry about him," Lisa interrupted. "I'll take good care of your little brother."

"Okay, then." Brendan gave me a funny look and then hurried out of the bar.

"So," she said, cocking her head, studying me. "Brendan said you were in Vietnam?"

"Yeah, I guess so." I turned away from her. "Yeah."

She didn't say anything for what seemed like a long time. I could feel her staring at me. Then, in a tired voice, she said, "Look, I don't see any point in staying here. I think I'm going to head home." I nodded, waiting for her to leave, waiting for her to stop standing over me. Something touched my hand. I looked up and she had that thin trace of a smile again. "Well, are you going to sit here all night?" I let her lead me out.

•   •   •

When we got to her apartment, Lisa took her coat off and I realized then how pretty she really was. She was wearing a tight skirt which outlined slender hips, and the rest of her, her face, her— I turned my head away. I didn't want her to think I was staring.

She moved me into the living room and had me sit on a leather sofa. She then told me we were going to have a little party and she started taking bottles out of the liquor cabinet.

She turned to me, and with disappointment told me she was out of gin and she would have to go get some because that was all she felt like drinking. Right before she left she kissed her finger and pressed it against my lips and told me that when she got back we would really live it up.

I looked around the room and noticed a desk next to the liquor cabinet had one of its drawers partially opened. I got up and looked inside and found a stack of hundred dollar bills. I picked it up and counted five thousand dollars. I put it back and tried to walk away, but I couldn't.

I stood frozen, feeling the blood rush to my face. Hearing it pounding in my ears. Tasting its hotness in my mouth. I grabbed the money and left Lisa's apartment.

Out on the street, I just started walking. I wanted to go back and return the money, but I couldn't. I had to keep moving. A half hour later I came to a bar and went inside.

After three hours of buying drinks and handing out money I had nothing left. I didn't even have any of the fifty dollars Brendan had given me. But for those three hours I had people smiling. I had people slapping my back and laughing with me, not at me. For those three hours I was something other than a dead man. It's hard to explain, but taking the money was something I had to do. When you feel dead all the time and you know there's something that will make you feel less dead, you don't have any choice. And I've felt like a dead man for almost twenty years.

About a month before my eighteenth birthday Brendan killed

a woman in a hit and run accident. He came to me afterwards, begging me that I tell the police I was the one driving the car. After all, he had just gotten accepted into law school and this would ruin his life, but I was still a juvenile so they'd only slap my wrists.

Well, I didn't have any choice. I had to help my brother so I told the police what Brendan wanted me to. The judge though, did give me a choice. I could either be tried as an adult and go away for ten years, or I could enlist when I turned eighteen and serve my country in Vietnam.

When Bobby Johnson heard I had to enlist, he told me he'd go in with me. Hell, hadn't we been best buddies since first grade? He'd be damned if he'd let me go alone and have something happen to me, so we signed up together and arranged to be in the same platoon.

The first week we were over there, a kid ran up to us and pulled out a gun and shot Bobby in the chest. I tried to help Bobby. I tried to keep his blood from pouring out, but after about a minute he wasn't breathing. I got up and ran after the kid. I chased him almost two miles into the jungle before I caught him. And when I did, I stuffed mud into his mouth so no one would hear him scream. Then I took out my knife and skinned him.

From the moment Bobby died it was like I had a blindfold on. I had to keep killing—I had to keep paying them back for him. Later when my tour was almost over, the blindfold slipped off and I realized what I'd done. I realized that for a long time I'd stopped being alive.

I had a ten mile walk to get to Brendan's house. It was hours later when I got there, and I could see a car parked in front of my brother's house with people in it. When I got closer, I could see it was Brendan and Lisa in the front seat and another man in back. Brendan saw me and rolled down his window and gasped, "Nick, what did you do?"

The other man opened his door and pointed a gun at me. "Get in," he ordered softly.

I stood where I was. The man started to get out of the car. Brendan burst out, "For godsakes, do what he wants!"

Lisa looked amused. I walked around the car and got in next to the man with the gun. He was a heavyset man with big ears and not much hair. He poked the gun under my chin. "You stole my money." His voice was raspy, kind of like his throat had been scraped with sandpaper.

"I-I'm sorry."

"He's sorry," the man with the gun chuckled. He pushed the gun into my throat. "What you going to do about it?"

"Brendan," I said. "Could you give him the money?"

That made the man laugh harder. "It don't work that way, smart guy. You stole from me, now you going to pay me back. You got any money?"

I shook my head.

"Then you owe me. I have a job I need help on and you're it, smart guy. You gonna help me steal some money."

"No," I said, shaking my head.

"No?" he raised an eyebrow. "It's okay to steal my money but not someone else's?" Then, low and mean, "You say yes right now or I blow your goddamn head off."

Brendan lurched forward, his eyes wide with excitement.

"Do what he says, Nicky!"

I didn't say anything. The man with the gun growled, "You think I'm joking?"

I shrugged.

"Okay, smart guy," he said. "You don't care about yourself, is that it? What if I take your brother inside and blow his head off instead?"

Brendan was screaming at me. "My God, Nicky. Marge and the kids are home! Please Nicky, try and understand what's happening!"

"I'm sorry," I told him. I turned to the other man. "I guess you better take him inside."

Brendan's jaw dropped. The man with the gun gave Brendan a questioning look, like he was unsure of what to do. Lisa broke out laughing. I slapped the man hard and his eyes went dumb. I slapped him again. Lisa laughed harder. The man's eyes exploded with fury. He raised the gun and I hit him across the mouth with my open palm, splitting his lip. Brendan reached back and grabbed the man's arm, the one with the gun. He shouted at the man, "No, Mike! No!" Then he turned to me. "What the hell—" he choked it off, swallowed and tried again. "Nicky, what are you doing?"

I faced my brother. "You wanted me to steal the money. You had her take me to the apartment so I'd steal the money."

"No, Nicky." He was shaking his head hard like that would settle the issue. The other man had gotten his arm free, but just sat silently holding a handkerchief against his mouth.

"The detective you hired," I said to Brendan. "I saw him six months ago and I saw him other times, too. He was keeping tabs on me until you needed me."

"Oh, boy," he muttered. "Oh, boy. You're confused and—"

Lisa interrupted, her eyes shining. "I thought your little brother would be too dumb to guess what was going on. Isn't that what you said?"

Brendan's face flushed. He glared at her, then turned to me, but he couldn't look me in the eye. "I'm sorry, Nicky. Can we talk?" I told him we could always talk. We drove to Lisa's apartment and during the ride no one said a word.

Inside the apartment, Brendan was grinning and acting like nothing had happened. He introduced Big Mike, the heavyset man I slapped around. He then told me about a client of his, Paul Dreason, who was the top man in the local crack trade. Dreason had five million dollars and Brendan told me we were going to take it away from him.

We sat down and Brendan explained it to me. The five million was sitting in a safe in an empty warehouse waiting for the mob to pick it up. Brendan asked Big Mike to get the blueprints of the warehouse, and then he spread them out, showing me where the safe would be.

I looked at Brendan. "How do you know about this?"

"It's a long story, Nicky. I don't think you'd understand."

I didn't push him on that, instead asked, "Why isn't it being protected?"

Lisa smirked at Brendan. "For someone as dumb as you say he is, he asks a lot of questions."

Brendan's face went white. He turned to her, his lips pressed into a tight smile. "Will you lay off?" he said.

I brought his attention back to me, asking, "What do you want me to do?"

Dropping his hand, he turned back to me. "This is going to be easy, Nick. Big Mike has already put together a bomb that will blow off the safe cover. It works on a timer. All I need you to do is place it next to the safe and carry out the money after it blows open. It won't take more than five minutes."

I stared at him and kept staring until his smile cracked. Then I asked Brendan why he needed me to blow up the safe. Why he or Big Mike or anyone else couldn't do it.

He looked rattled. "I need someone I can trust. And you've been in Vietnam, you know how to handle yourself in difficult situations. I'm going to be in the car driving. And Big Mike needs to be watching the building in case there's any trouble. I need you, Nicky. You won't let me down, will you?"

"No, I guess not."

Relief washed over his face, leaving a broad, wide smile. "Okay, Nicky. Why don't we go home and get some sleep." Lisa grabbed Brendan by the arm and the two of them turned their backs to me and talked in hushed voices. I could see Brendan nodding and then he turned back to me.

"Nicky," he said. "Why don't you stay here tonight. Is that okay?"

I told him it was. "One more thing. . . ." He hesitated. "We have it planned for twelve tomorrow afternoon. We have to do it then. But don't worry, the explosion will just be a little pop, no one will hear us."

I told him I guessed it didn't matter. He smiled, nodding his head. "I'll pick you up at eleven. Don't worry, Nicky. Everything will work out fine. And Dreason deserves this. We're not doing anything bad." He got up to leave. Big Mike joined him, glaring at me as he left. I could see his lip had swelled.

Lisa took me to the guest room and helped me make up the bed. She gave me a funny look. "Yeah, what do you want to ask me?"

"Why did Brendan want me to stay here?"

"Because," she smiled slightly. "I promised your brother I'd make sure you didn't run out on us. But that's not the reason I wanted you to." She started to unbutton her blouse, her flesh warming to a soft pink as she did.

"Are you and Brendan . . ." I didn't know how to finish the sentence.

"Maybe. He's planning on leaving his wife for me after we get the money. Why, does it matter?" She gave me a hard look and stopped unbuttoning her blouse. "I guess it does," she said, softly.

She took hold of my chin and studied me, then nodded to herself. "You do look a lot like your brother," she said. "You're about the same height and have similar features. But you're better looking, you're heavier, more muscular, and you don't have his shifty eyes."

She laughed and walked over to the door. "No," she said. "You got big, dumb eyes, like you don't know a damn thing." Her face softened. "Nicky, it's not too late for you to just walk away. You could leave now and be in another state by tomorrow."

"I-I can't. I promised Brendan."

"The two of us could go, Nicky. We could walk out together. Would you like that?"

"But the five million dollars—"

"Skip it." Her eyes hardened. "You really don't have a clue, do you?"

I shook my head.

"I guess you don't," she said, her voice brittle. "You see, when I'm driving at night and I catch an animal in the headlights, and they freeze and look at me with big, dumb eyes like yours, you know what I do?"

"I'm sorry, I don't—"

"I step on the gas. Have pleasant dreams, bright boy." And she slammed the door shut.

You can't steal five million dollars from the mob and expect to live. It's not that easy. They'd be after you for the rest of your life. And they'd catch you. Brendan had to know that much, and besides, there were too many holes in the way he told it for it to be that way. I took out a pack of cigarettes and lay down on the bed.

Of course, I knew why Brendan needed me. I knew why I had to be the one to bring the bomb into the warehouse. The warehouse had to be rigged with explosives, so when the one bomb went off the whole place would go up in flames.

Brendan and I are the same height and we do look a lot alike. The extra bulk I have would be burned off in the fire and wearing his clothes would cinch it. All that would be found in the warehouse would be a burnt body that would be identified as Brendan's and a pile of ashes that the mob would think used to be five million dollars. That's the only way it could work. Which meant that the money had already been taken out of the safe.

I lit another cigarette and inhaled deeply, letting the smoke fill my lungs. If Brendan had asked me straight out to do it, I probably would've. There's not much for me anymore, and besides, I'm tired of feeling dead inside. But I couldn't do it for him now, not with him acting as if I was dumb. I was sick of acting dumb.

I thought about Lisa, about the way she'd been acting, and decided all she was doing was playing games with me. She could've told me the truth, but she really didn't want me to walk away. If I was as dumb as she thought I was, none of her hints and nudges would've helped me. I guess it was part of her nature. I couldn't walk away from it anyway. I don't have much, but fighting for the little I have could make me feel something. I had to stick around and see if I could feel something.

The next morning Lisa made us pancakes and bacon. While we were eating, she kept giving me nervous glances. Finally, she cleared her throat and told me Brendan had called while I was asleep and changed the plans for midnight.

I didn't say anything. "Well?" she asked angrily. "Do you understand what I said?" I nodded. Her face relaxed. "Your brother asked me to give you some money so you could see a movie or something. How's that sound?"

I looked at the clock on her stove. It was ten thirty. I told her it would be fine, that I'd leave as soon as I finished breakfast. I then slowed down with my eating. Every once in a while I'd glance up at her and she'd give me a jerky smile. I pushed my plate away a couple of minutes before eleven.

Her face turned red and she hollered at me, "You're a real smart guy, aren't you?"

I played innocent and watched as Brendan walked through the door. "All set?" he asked. Lisa shook her head as she walked by me. Big Mike was sitting in the back seat of the car waiting for us.

Brendan and Lisa sat up front. I joined Big Mike in back. Brendan held up a bag, "The bomb's in here, Nicky. It's set to go off at twelve fifteen. You have to be careful with it."

Lisa deadpanned, "Yeah, make sure you don't blow yourself up."

Brendan handed her the bag, "You better hold it," he said, giving her a cold stare.

As we drove, the buildings got more and more run-down. Finally, Brendan pulled up next to a large gray one. Big Mike ran out and about a minute later came back puffing. "It's all ready," he said, lowering himself back into the car.

No one talked. Brendan kept looking at his watch. Finally, he took the bag from Lisa's lap. "It's time," he said. He reached back and handed me the bag. He kept his eyes away from mine. "Okay, Nick. We've got seven minutes. You better get going."

I leaned back in my seat. "I'm not sure I understand what I'm supposed to do. Maybe we better go over it again?"

Lisa gave Brendan a quick sideways glance. "Your brother's a real bright light, isn't he? I think we should just forget the whole thing before he screws up on us. I think we should leave the bag here and go."

Brendan's head snapped as if he'd been slapped. He growled at her, "I think I should knock your damn teeth out!"

"I don't know," I interrupted. "I forgot what I'm supposed to do."

Lisa let loose with a nervous laugh. Big Mike was looking impatient, his ears turning a bright red. "You stupid idiot!" he exploded. He started to pull his gun from his jacket. "Take that stinking bag and go in there before I blow your goddamn head off!"

I swung my right arm and caught him hard with my elbow. His head bounced off the door, making a dull thud. I think he was unconscious, but I hit him again. His gun had dropped from his hand. I picked it up and brought the handle down on his skull. Blood started to spread across his forehead, down into his face.

Brendan's mouth dropped open. Lisa's eyes were sparkling. "Brendan," I said. "I think it would be better if you did it for me."

I tossed the bag onto his lap. He couldn't talk, at least not right away. Finally, he sputtered, "N-Nicky, w-what's going on?"

I reversed the gun in my hand and flicked the barrel across his cheek, drawing blood. "Don't make me shoot you, Brendan. Please, open the door and get out of the car. We don't have much time left."

He hesitated. I flicked the gun again, this time catching a soft spot on his neck. He got out, his legs looking like rubber bands. The bag hung from his left hand. I got out and joined him. Lisa also got out.

"Go ahead," she said to him, her voice shaking with contempt. "Do Nicky's job."

"You stinking bitch!" he swore. He lunged to hit her. I shot him in the hip. Lisa giggled. Brendan turned towards me, his eyes wide with terror. His mouth tried to work, but no noise came out.

"Brendan," I said. "If you had leveled with me and asked me to do it, I would've. But you shouldn't've done it this way. You shouldn't've treated me like I was stupid. There's a difference between being stupid and not giving a damn."

He was wobbling on his feet like a fighter in the tenth round who had taken too many shots to the head. He turned from me, and then staggered back. He pulled a locker key from his pocket and handed it to me. "At the airport, Nicky. Please, forgive me," he half-said, half-sobbed. He held out his arms as if he expected a hug. I pushed the gun into his chest. "We don't have time for this," I said. "Get moving."

He nodded, and turned towards the building. He moved as if he were an automaton, as if his legs were disconnected from the rest of his body. As if he were a corpse. He reached the door, stepped through it, and closed it behind him. The explosion came seconds later. The windows shattered, flames seared through them. There couldn't've been much of Brendan left.

Lisa gave me a funny look, half appraising, half scared. "You're not as dumb as you act, are you? What other tricks do you have?"

I showed her a bare-fanged smile. "Get in the car," I ordered. I pulled Big Mike from the back seat and left him in the street.

Dave Zeltserman

It was going to be a while before he woke up. I had enough time to do what I had to before he talked. As we drove to the airport, neither of us said a word. I found the locker that matched the key. There were two briefcases inside. I opened them. You wouldn't think five million dollars would've been able to fit in them, but it did. I took a large chunk out of one of them and counted half a million dollars. I closed the locker. I put the key back in my pocket.

Lisa grabbed my arm. "Let's take the money, Nicky. We'll get on a plane and go somewhere where they'll never find us. We can do it right now."

I laughed. "Yeah, just the three of us. Just you, me and five million dollars. When were you planning on cutting my throat, the first night I'm asleep?"

She took a step away from me, her face hardening. "That's right, the first chance I get I'm going to cut your throat. And while I'm at it, I'm going to cut out your dirty, stinking heart. You dirty bastard, you dirty . . ." And she started sobbing. I grabbed her wrist and jerked, almost pulling her off the ground. All the way to the car it was like that, me dragging her as if she were a rag doll. Inside the car she started laughing, a weird hysterical laugh, kind of like nails on a blackboard, except much worse.

"You're dumber than I ever gave you credit for," she swore at me. "You're a bright light, alright. A big twenty watt bulb."

It went on and on like that, but I ignored her. I could understand how she was feeling. I drove to Brendan's house. Marge and the kids were out, and I was thankful for it. I left the half million in one of her dresser drawers. Brendan probably had life insurance, but I had to make sure Marge and the kids would be taken care of. I left a note and signed Brendan's name. I found the suitcases hidden in Brendan's workroom. I brought them back out to the car. Lisa was sitting there with hate in her eyes. I put the suitcases in the trunk and got back behind the wheel. "You and Brendan were planning on taking a trip?"

"You were able to figure that out all on your own? You better give it a rest before something inside pops."

She stopped talking. She looked so white, so pale, as if all the blood had drained from her body. After a while she asked where I was going.

"We're going to your place." I could feel her body cringe. "You got bags to pick up, don't you?"

"We don't have to, Nicky." She waited for me to say something, but I didn't. "Please, Nicky. Let's go back to the airport." There was a pleading in her voice. I didn't want to look at her. I knew I'd change my mind if I did.

"Who says," I sneered, my throat beginning to tighten, "that I want to go anyplace with you? Maybe I only want to get you alone. Maybe I want to take my knife and carve you up a little. I had practice with that in Nam, and maybe I miss it."

"If that's what you want, go right ahead. You got all the answers, don't you?" She hesitated. Then in a soft voice. "So I'm just a dirty whore? Nothing but a dirty, lousy, heartless . . ." And she let it die in her throat.

We drove in silence the rest of the way. A cold, harsh silence. It was something like death. I knew what was waiting for us at her apartment. Brendan should've known too, but I guess he just didn't look hard enough. I guess he was too busy being a wise guy.

He should've known the whole thing was too easy, almost like Dreason opened the safe and handed the money right to him. It should've sounded funny to him. And Lisa. He should've known she wouldn't want anything to do with someone like him. He should've known Dreason would be waiting for the two of them to go back to Lisa's apartment. Waiting for them to pick up her bags.

Dreason was only a cog in the drug industry. Someone to hold the money and watch it pass from big shot to big shot. But he saw his chance to walk away with five million dollars.

Brendan would walk through Lisa's door and get his face blown off. I guess Dreason's wallet would be planted on Brendan's body, and he and Lisa would walk away free and clear. He'd have enough connections to make sure Brendan's body would be identified as his. No reason for the mob to ever look for him, not if they thought the five million dollars was blown up and Dreason shot dead. And . . . and a thought startled me. Maybe Lisa never had any choice. Maybe she had to do what she did. She wanted us to go away together, but she must've known that Dreason would know she double-crossed him. She must've known he'd never give up looking for her. She'd always have to . . .

We got to the building. Doubt was working its way into my stomach. I tried looking into her face. It was hard, as if it were chiseled out of marble.

"What are you waiting for?" she asked, her voice defiant, challenging.

"Nothing." I grabbed her and pulled her out of the car. She jerked herself free and walked in front of me, leading the way to her door.

She stared straight through me. "Okay, bright boy. You want the key?" And she held it out in front of me. I reached for it and she pulled it back. Then, she told me everything. She told me about Dreason waiting behind the door, how Dreason promised to kill her if she didn't do what he wanted, how sick inside she'd been feeling. As the words rushed out of her, I realized she wouldn't've let me walk into the warehouse. She would've stopped me.

She gave me an uneasy smile. "Please, Nick," she almost begged. "Don't go in there." Her face was struggling to keep its composure, to hold back a flood of tears. Trying desperately to stay tough, but it wasn't working.

"We can't leave like this." I smiled at her. "He'll always be after us. It has to be taken care of now. Don't worry, it will be alright."

I took out the locker key and folded it in her hand. I still had Big Mike's gun. It was a magnum forty-four. Holding it made me feel like I was back in the jungle. I could feel my smile stretching, freezing into the same mask I used to wear over there.

She tried to reach for me, but her arms fell slack to her side. I took a deep breath and kicked the door open, rolling forwards as the door broke apart. I ended up on my knees with the magnum stretched out in front of me. Dreason was standing there, a shocked expression on his face. I waited just long enough to let him get a shot off before I pulled the trigger. The last thing I saw before the darkness was a piece of his brain splatter across the living room wall. The last thing I heard was Lisa screaming, and then her footsteps running towards me.

I read somewhere that the brain can keep functioning minutes after the heart has stopped. Dreason's bullet had cut my heart in half, so I guess that's true. It's funny though, my thinking now is crisp and clear, not scattered with random images and impulses like I would've thought. It had to be this way. Lisa needed some sort of chance. She didn't need to be saddled with a dead man, and that's all I've ever been since Nam. That's all I'd ever be, and now it's just complete. The body has caught up with the soul.

I know Lisa is no angel. I know she was going to double-cross my brother. But he would've deserved it, so I can't blame her much for that.

No, she's no angel, but she deserves a chance. She did what she could to let me walk free. She tried her best. With the four and a half million that's left she can start over. It's all up to her now.

There is nothing left of me but a few thoughts. And these probably won't last more than a minute. Even though I can't feel anything, I know Lisa is holding me. I know her tears are warming my face. Just for a minute it would've been nice to feel something.

Money Run

This is my first story to appear in Ellery Queen Mystery Magazine. "Money Run" is a fun, light con man story and gives a slight tip of the cap to Jim Thompson's great Mitch Allison stories. It also pulls off not a double or triple cross, but a quadruple cross.

Pete Mitchel sat at the bar feeling sorry for himself. Things hadn't gone as planned. Instead of raising enough money to bankroll his Hollywood scam, he had just enough left to get drunk on. Maybe, he grinned to himself sourly, enough to pass out on. He placed five dollars on the bar and nodded to the bartender, who responded in kind by collecting the money and refilling his empty glass. As Pete nursed his gin, he spotted Warren Langely.

Langely, a thin wiry sort with a deep friendly smile, slid onto the barstool next to him and coughed. "How's it going, Pete?" he asked, clearing his throat. "The baking soda business making any money?"

"Well, you know how it is." Pete could feel his cheeks reddening. "A couple of things crapped out on me and . . ." He let the sentence die in his throat.

"Yeah, I know how it is." Langely ordered a beer and sipped it before shaking his head, his smile growing friendlier. "Man," he said, his eyes slightly amused, "you were supposed to be a bright guy from New York. You're here in Boston less than a month and you're peddling baking soda as coke. Not a very smart thing to do if you ask me."

"I appreciate your concern," Pete murmured. Warren Langely had befriended him when he had come to Boston, setting him on to a couple of ventures that had unfortunately busted out. While Pete liked the small, affable man, he wished Langely would leave so he could suffer his misery in peace.

"Don't you think you're acting stupid? The cops could pick you up for selling narcotics near a public school."

"I'm not selling narcotics, am I? Just a common household product. As best I can see I'm saving these school kids a trip to the market."

Langely gave the matter some thought and then slowly shook his head and chuckled softly. As he studied the foam fading from his beer, his smile became somber. "I gotta tell you, buddy," he said, "I feel bad for hooking you up with those busted jobs. I got a chance to make it up to you. Two grand worth."

Pete turned to his companion, raising an eyebrow. "And how's that?"

"Nothing dangerous or anything. Nothing more than delivering a package to Las Vegas, but it's serious stuff. And serious people. You can't afford any kind of screw up. None whatsoever."

Pete studied Langely through a gin-induced haze; the type a half dozen shots of cheap eighty-six proof rotgut would naturally produce. He could see apprehension in the small man's eyes. Obviously Langely had some doubts whether he could do a simple delivery job. He felt insulted, but the alcohol dulled his outrage. Slowly, he let a smile spread on his face from ear to ear. "You're talking to the right man," he said at last.

The next day Langely brought Pete to a small Italian restaurant in Boston's North End. Pete felt dehydrated from his previous night's drinking. A hard, painful thumping knocked in his head and his tongue felt like a wool sock had been wrapped around it. From his outward appearance, though, it would've been impossible to tell he was suffering. His gray eyes were clear, his rough good-looking features appeared at ease. As usual, his grooming was impeccable.

A nod sent the two men to a private room in back. Sitting alone behind a table for eight was a large man with a severely receding hairline and tiny, dull eyes. Langely quickly ran to the man, dropped to one knee, grabbed the hand the large man waved to him, and pressed his lips against the heavy knuckles.

"Thank you, Mr. Carbone," he said in a hushed, gravely serious tone. "We are deeply grateful for your audience. I would like to introduce you to my friend, Pete Mitchel."

Langely released the man's hand, and Carbone again casually waved his hand, this time signaling for the two men to sit.

"Does your friend understand how important this is?" the large man demanded.

"Yes, Mr. Carbone." Langely's head was bowed in reverence.

"You," Carbone pointed a large sausage finger at Pete. "Do you consider yourself a bright man?"

"Yes, sir."

Carbone sat motionless, staring at Pete, his small black eyes glazing over. Finally, satisfied, his eyes came to life. With a grunt, he lifted a briefcase onto the table and then pulled two envelopes from his inside jacket pocket—one he handed to Langely, the other to Pete.

"There are instructions inside," he said to Pete, his eyes unblinking. "And a bus ticket to Las Vegas. You will deliver that briefcase to the address specified. There will be no mistakes. Swear your life to that."

"Excuse me?"

"I said, swear your life to that."

Pete shrugged. "I swear," he said.

"No," the large man shook his head. "Your life."

"I swear my life."

"Good." A heavy weariness seemed to fall over Carbone's face.

"I take your pledge to heart," he said. And with that, he picked up an Italian newspaper and ignored Pete and Langely.

The abruptness of the large man took Pete by surprise, but Langely was on his feet, profusely thanking Carbone for his generosity. He gave Pete an impatient signal to grab the briefcase and the two of them hurried out of the backroom. When they got to the street, Pete looked inside his envelope and saw that along with the bus ticket and instructions, there were twenty crisp hundred dollar bills. Langely let loose with a short whoop of relief and took a thousand dollars from his envelope. "My commission," he said, a big smile stretched across his face.

Pete laughed. "Not bad for an hours work."

"No, not bad." Langely flashed Pete a sheepish look. "Not bad at all. I hope you keep in mind the promise you made."

"What about it?"

"Well . . ." Langely hesitated. "You can't make any mistakes with this, kid. He's dead serious about that promise."

The muscles around Pete's mouth tightened, drawing his lips into a slight smile. He didn't like what he perceived as Langely's condescending attitude. After all, this was only a delivery job. Any monkey in a suit could do it. "I could end up on the wrong bus and get lost, huh?" he asked.

Langely took a step back and raised both hands in a mock defensive posture. "Hey, don't get mad at me. I'm just pointing out what has to be pointed out. This is serious business. I'm involved too, you know. If anything happens, they're going to be coming after me also."

"Sure." A muscle in Pete's jaw was pulsing like a rabbit's heart. "You're just being helpful."

"Look, if you have any problems give me a call." Langely slowly recited his phone number. "You want me to write it down?" he asked.

"That's okay," Pete said. "I've got it."

"Well, enjoy the sun. Don't do anything I wouldn't do." As

Langely moved away, he brought a hand up as a kind of salute. Pete stood silently until the small man faded from sight, and then crossed the street and entered yet another small Italian restaurant, heading straight towards the bathroom.

He quickly went to work on the briefcase lock. It was easy. Within two minutes he had the case opened and its contents forced a genuine smile. In one corner of the case was a Browning .25 caliber automatic and a silencer. The rest of the case, though, was filled with tens, twenties, and hundreds. Pete thumbed through the stacks of bills and counted thirty thousand dollars. He took a deep breath and closed the case.

His palms felt moist. He rubbed them several times across his pants and took another deep breath before heading out onto the street. With thirty thousand dollars as seed money he should be able to do something. He checked his bus ticket. The trip to Vegas wasn't for three days. That would give him enough time to go back to New York and organize a high stakes poker game. He'd have to kick in about five hundred for fake police uniforms and, of course, take on a couple of partners, but after the game was "busted" his split should at least match the seed money. Thirty grand would probably be enough for a Hollywood scam that had been playing in his mind for years. Right after the delivery to Vegas, he'd head straight to California.

There was a gorgeous redhead walking about thirty yards in front of him. As plans whirled through his head, he found himself absent-mindedly enjoying the soft rhythmic motion of her hips. He was so absorbed by his own thoughts he didn't pick up on the motives of the punk heading towards her. It wasn't until the punk grabbed her handbag, and the woman screamed as the punk hit her, that the scene registered on him.

Pete then moved quickly. Within seconds he had sprinted to the punk, grasping the handbag and holding his briefcase with one hand and using his free hand to reach for an eight inch switchblade to persuade the punk with.

The punk tugged hard on the handbag and then pushed it away using all his weight. Caught off balance, Pete could feel his feet slipping out from beneath him. Next thing he knew, he was sitting on the sidewalk smack in the middle of a puddle. He felt stupid as he watched the punk run away.

The redhead was standing over him speechless. She was wearing a tight fitting business suit that showed off nice curves. Her green eyes were dazzling, but not quite as much, Pete noticed, as the diamond earrings she was wearing. Pete smiled at her. "Are you okay?" he asked.

"I guess I'm a little shaken," she said, color slowly seeping through her ashen paleness.

"How's your cheek?"

"What? Oh." She put a hand up to where she was struck, flinching slightly. "I must've rolled with the punch," she said, smiling. "I think I'm okay."

Pete nodded, returning her smile. He held up her handbag. "I believe this belongs to you, ma'am," he said with the utmost courtesy.

All at once she started laughing—a nice, wholesome, friendly laugh. Pete liked it. He also felt stupid as all hell. "I'm sorry," she said at last, wiping tears from her eyes. "Ha, ha, I'm so sorry. You just look so funny sitting in that puddle. But thank you."

"I'm glad I could be of service," he said gruffly.

"I really am grateful to you for rescuing me." Her dazzling eyes twinkled. "My hotel is less than a block away. Why don't you come with me? We can get your suit dry-cleaned."

She offered him her hand to help him out of the puddle. The beautiful redhead introduced herself as Lauren Hadley, visiting Boston on business. He introduced himself as Paul Michaels. As they walked, Pete laughed and joked with her, all the while trying to estimate the value of her earrings. They looked real to him. His sixth sense told him they were real. He'd get his chance to palm them off her. If they turned out to be cubic zirconium, he'd give them to Toni, his fiancée. If they were real diamonds, he'd sell them and use part of the proceeds to buy Toni a nice pair of cubic zirconium earrings.

By the time they got to her room, Pete was glad she had made the offer. And not just because of the diamonds. His clothes were soaking wet, from the lower part of his back to his thighs. They were uncomfortable and he was anxious to get out of them.

She pointed out the bathroom. "Paul, why don't you change in there. You can take a shower and I'll call the concierge about sending up a man's robe. This place advertises two hour dry-cleaning. You don't mind spending a couple of hours alone with me, do you?"

He flashed her a grin. "You do what you have to do," he said.

"That's awfully brave of you." She took hold of his hands and placed them on the side of her face. The skin felt hot. "I'm still trembling from that mugger," she breathed softly. There was a glint in her eyes.

Pete brought the briefcase into the bathroom and got out of his wet clothes, leaving his wallet, switchblade, and envelope on the vanity. He wrapped a towel around his waist and carried his soiled suit and underwear out to Lauren. As he headed back to the bathroom she called out to him, a warm throaty purr resonating in her voice, asking him not to be too long.

The hotel was a high class one and the room was really more of a suite with a separate sitting area in the bathroom. Pete examined the lock and was satisfied with it. Still, he propped a wicker chair under the door handle. One thing he took a great deal of pride in was his thoroughness. Always one step ahead of the next guy—which was why his recent setbacks had been so tough to swallow. He wasn't used to his plans crumbling apart, and it hurt him deeply.

As Pete stepped into the shower and turned the hot water on, he could feel his body start to relax. Finally, the bad luck had run its course. Things were back to normal. Better than normal.

First two grand for a simple delivery job, then thirty grand to borrow for seed money, and now diamond earrings that were probably worth five grand. And to top it off, an hour or so to tumble around with Lauren's luscious and willing body. Pete smiled, wondering how long it would take for her peaches and cream skin to blush a deep red.

By the time he got out of the shower he was feeling on top of the world. As he reached for a towel, he noticed the bathroom door was missing. He stared at it, unable to comprehend why it was that way, and then a sickish feeling wormed its way into his stomach. He only half glanced at where he had left the briefcase, knowing full well it was gone.

He stood motionless, his eyes narrowed, his features marble hard. Peering out from the corners of his eyes he could see that the envelope was gone but his wallet and knife were still on the vanity. He let another minute pass before reaching for a towel. As he left the bathroom, he could see the bathroom door lying flat in the hallway. It had been taken off its hinges. When Pete had first entered the room, he had seen clothes scattered about and a suitcase next to the bed. They were no longer there. Of course, neither was Lauren.

Pete sat down on the bed, a towel wrapped around him, and tried to think. It was obvious that he had been set up. The redhead and punk had been tipped off about the briefcase, and he, like the first class putz that he was, handed it right to them.

Now he was stuck in a hotel room without any clothes and without any real hope. He wanted to call Toni. To beg her to drive up from New York and rescue him. He wanted to, but he knew he couldn't. It would be tough enough under normal circumstances to explain how he was literally caught with his pants down, but it would be impossible with the way things stood between them. Before he left to Boston, they had had a doozy of a fight—one of their worst. Well, he had really only been a spectator, with Toni screaming enough for both of them.

It had ended badly. With tears streaming down her face, Toni announced their engagement was over. She was sick of his excuses about why they couldn't set a wedding date. She finally realized he was a lousy stinking jerk who had no intention of living up to his word. Then, in dramatic fashion, she stormed from their apartment, her sobs echoing painfully from the hallway. During their five-year engagement it was the first time she'd threatened to break things off, and it had Pete worried.

As much as he hated to do it, he called Warren Langely.

Langely paced the hotel room, his small body moving in short jerky motions. "Less than an hour and you lose the case. Less than a goddamn hour!"

Pete sat silently. Langely glared at him, his eyes burning with anger. "A real smart guy, aren't you? Too smart to listen to me, huh? Well, I'm sorry I insulted you before by trying to warn you to be careful. I guess you showed me!"

Pete met Langely's angry stare. "I was set up. . . ." he tried to explain.

"Don't give me that crap. You screwed up, plain and simple."

Pete shrugged. "Okay, I screwed up. What next?"

"What next?" An indignant snort exploded from the small man. He shook his head with disgust and then curled his lips and let loose with a string of curses. When Langely had arrived at the hotel room, he had brought Pete a soiled work shirt, a pair of worn corduroys, and an army jacket. The clothes smelled heavily of garlic and onions, and itched around the crotch, neck, and armpits. He now listened as Langely compared him to the different anatomical parts of a donkey. He had half a mind to deck the small man, but a sickish feeling deep in his gut held him back.

"Let me explain it to you," Langely seethed. "Mr. Carbone needed a job done outside of the family. You see, if he went to the family with it, he'd have to split a good deal of money with them and he didn't want to. So you screwing up will put him in a very uncomfortable situation. And since I recommended you, I too will be made very uncomfortable. But believe me, not as much as you."

From his outward appearance Pete seemed calm and unconcerned. Inside, though, he was dying. His instinct was to flee, and he would've if he'd had any money. He considered rolling Langely for whatever was in his pockets, but decided against it. He asked how they were going to square things with Carbone.

"I don't know," Langely answered dully. "You meet me at Jack's in two hours and I'll see what I can come up with. And trust me, you better show up."

The small man gave Pete a sullen stare and then left in a huff. Pete sat for a few minutes to collect his thoughts. Fortunately, the redhead left his shoes. Thank heaven for little things, he told himself as he slipped them on.

Jack's bar was a little cubbyhole of a place bordering Boston's Chinatown and theatre district. When Pete showed up there he was still wearing the ratty clothes Langely had brought him, having been too depressed to bother going back to his hotel to change out of them.

The bar was crowded, filled with a mix of hookers, college students, and businessmen. As Pete pushed his way in, he caught sight of Langely. The small man looked in his direction, then left his seat and headed to the back of the bar. Pete followed him. Noises lofted through the air: glasses being slid across tables, a woman shouting angrily, men laughing.

Langely had found an isolated spot. When Pete approached him, he stared at Pete with eyes that were nothing more than cold ice chunks. He spoke in a voice that was painfully low. "I arranged for us to meet with Mr. Carbone tomorrow night. Before that you're going to make it up to him."

"W-What do you mean?" Pete said, amazed to hear himself stutter.

"I've been calling around—" He stopped to let a large, busty woman pass by. "And found you a job." Pete felt something hard and cold being forced into his hand. He looked down and saw that Langely was giving him a gun. "Take it," Langely ordered. Pete obeyed, hiding the gun in his army jacket.

"You're going to hit a local bookie tomorrow," Langely explained. "The mark should be carrying ten grand. You're going to stick the gun in his ribs and free him of his burden. Time and place are written on this paper." He shoved something into Pete's jacket pocket.

"No." Pete shook his head. "I don't do that type of job."

"Is that so? I guess, buddy boy, you're going to have to start learning."

"You don't understand—"

"Listen," the small man's tone was murderous. "You're going to make it up to Mr. Carbone. You're going to show him respect."

"I can't—"

Langely moved within an inch of Pete and poked him hard in the chest. "You can and you will," he forced through compressed lips. "Mr. Carbone's got connections all up and down the east coast. If you ever want to set foot in your beloved New York again, you will show the man the proper respect. You're going to do what you can to pay him back."

"There was thirty grand in the briefcase."

"You broke into it, huh?" Langely smiled, his lean face as deadly as a razor. "So you know Mr. Carbone's not going to be happy only getting back ten grand. But it's the only chance you got."

Pete looked away from Langely, his eyes seeming to focus on some distant point. Slowly, he nodded.

"So you see how it is," Langely said gravely. "Tomorrow night at nine you meet us at the same Italian restaurant." He started to walk away but turned back. "And don't try anything stupid," he warned. "Even if you run to freaking Afghanistan, don't bet Mr. Carbone won't be able to reach you."

It was minutes after Langely had left before Pete moved. Slowly, a smile stretched across his face and he laughed out loud, startling a tired-looking blond a few feet away.

While Langely had been poking him in the chest, he realized how deep the setup was. If Langely had been watching him carefully enough, he might have detected a slight glimmer in his eyes. That was the only indication, though, that Pete gave of his revelation.

He found himself admiring the scam Langely and Carbone were running on him. It was cute. First hand him thirty grand, then take it away, and finally, scare him hard enough to commit an armed robbery.

Of course, they had to soften him up first. It was more than a coincidence that his luck turned sour after he had met up with Langely. He had to be made desperate enough to accept their delivery job.

Pete left the bar and started walking towards the Charles River. The cold night air blew against his face. He felt restless.

The scam had to be an ongoing concern. A game they played on drifters. Find some witless sap and make him dance. They were probably right now having a good, long laugh at his expense. More than anything, Pete wanted to rip them off, and he was willing to bet they still had the thirty grand on them. If it was the last thing he did he was going to take it away.

He had come up to the Charles River. He walked halfway across one of the connecting bridges to Cambridge before dropping Langely's gun into the water.

In order to play along with the scam he would have to come up with ten grand, but he wasn't going to do it with a holdup. His angle was the confidence game, the scam, the rip-off—not guns and robberies. Even though he carried a switchblade, he did it more for show than anything else. If he could flee he would flee. If not, he would show the knife for effect, hoping to scare the son of a bitch away.

As he walked back to his motel, he thought about how he

was going to come up with ten grand, and his thoughts kept centering around Toni.

"You must think I'm stupid, don't you?" Toni demanded, her voice hot with anger. When Pete first called her, her attitude was icy cold, but that quickly melted into a passionate outburst in which she called him every name in the book. Inwardly, Pete felt a great sense of relief. He had fully expected her to hang up on him with frigid indifference. The fact that she was so angry showed he still had her hooked.

Pete was stretched out on the bed. The first thing he did when he got back to his room was dump his soiled clothes into the trash and scrub himself clean. Now, wrapped in a cloth robe, he explained to Toni that of course he didn't think she was stupid. "I think thirty thousand would be a good start for a marriage," he said matter-of-factly.

There was a long hesitation. Then Toni asked him if he meant it.

"Of course I do. It's about time, isn't it? As soon as we get the money we'll stop off at the first chapel we see."

Another long hesitation. "Pete, I don't have ten thousand," she said at last.

"Well, bring what you can. And try to get here by noon. We have a long day ahead of us tomorrow." He gave her his hotel address and phone number, and hung up.

He didn't believe her about the money. Toni worked as a hostess at a club near Times Square, and Pete knew guys were always tipping her fives, tens, twenties, and sometimes even more to take off her clothes and join the other strippers on stage. She never did, but that didn't stop the club's patrons from trying. And they had good reason to try. Toni was a knockout. Barely five feet tall and at most ninety pounds, she had a shape that would make any man fantasize. And with big, brown eyes that could melt butter and a smile that could stop a heart, she was the club's biggest draw. Even though she left her clothes on—as tight fitting as they were—she took home more in tips than any of the strippers. Charlie, the club's owner, liked to brag that Toni added an element of class to the joint.

Pete slowly drifted into sleep with thoughts of thirty thousand dollars dancing in his head.

He woke up the next morning refreshed. Strong sunlight streamed into the room, warming him. It felt nice. He lazily reached for his watch and saw it was ten o'clock. After taking a long, hot shower, he dressed in jeans and a sweater. He would've preferred to put on a suit, but the redhead had taken the only one he brought to Boston. Lying on the bed, he closed his eyes and waited for Toni.

A few minutes before noon there was a knock on the door. Pete opened it and Toni stood in the hallway, eyeing him suspiciously. "If this is a trick," she threatened, "it's all over between us."

He scooped her up in his arms and twirled her around in circles. He felt her body slowly loosening. "It's great to see you," he said, giving her a hard kiss on the mouth and at the same time slipping her pocketbook from her shoulder. "Don't worry, baby," he said, smiling, "I'm on the level with this."

Toni wasn't a morning person. Pete knew she probably got up at six in order to arrange for the money and drive to Boston. She looked worn-out around the eyes and mouth, and it made her look so fragile that it brought a lump to Pete's throat. He gave her hand a squeeze and then took a stack of bills from her pocketbook. When he counted only seven thousand dollars, he glared at her.

"I only had five thousand saved up," she explained weakly. "I had to borrow two thousand from Charlie. He expects fifty percent return." She met Pete's glare. "I had some bad days at the track," she said defiantly.

"Did you drive the Caddy up?" he asked. Toni nodded. "All

121

right." He held out his hand. "Give me the keys. I got some errands to run."

She shook her head. "No. If I give them to you, you're going to sell the car. Forget it."

He turned away, furious that she knew him as well as she did. "Okay, then," he announced in an aggrieved, bitter tone. "If that's how much you trust me, I'll just have to take a cab and waste our money. I hope you're satisfied."

As he stormed from the room, shoving the money into his pant's pocket, he heard the light twinkle of Toni's laughter and then her hands clapping in applause. "Bravo!" she called out after him as he stomped down the hotel hallway, infuriated.

By the time he got to the lobby, he had calmed down. He considered trying to convince Langely and Carbone that the robbery only netted seven thousand, but he was afraid that might tip them off. No, he was going to have to come up with the whole ten grand. He bought a newspaper and thumbed through it quickly before settling on a plan.

The pawnbroker wouldn't budge. "Three hundred," he stated stubbornly. The leather briefcase on the counter was a rich, expensive one, but Pete pointed out it had the initials RT monogrammed on it. "So change your name," the pawnbroker offered in a flat tone.

Pete studied him. A short, stocky man with sagging basset hound eyes. "Two hundred," Pete growled. The man started to remove the briefcase from the counter, and Pete turned towards the door. Before he got there, he heard the man offer two-fifty. Pete turned back and agreed. "You got any overcoats you can show me?" he asked.

The pawnbroker squeezed his way into a corner of the shop and rummaged through a pile of clothes before holding up a full length black leather coat. "It's a size forty-six," he grunted, his bloodshot eyes unblinking as he studied Pete. "It should fit you."

Pete asked for a closer look. The coat was of cheap quality. A couple of months of wear and it would start coming apart at the seams. "How much?" he asked.

"Two hundred," the stocky man said with a straight face.

Pete broke into an incredulous laugh. He took three hundred dollars from his wallet and laid it on the counter. "For the briefcase and coat. Take it or leave it."

The man looked at Pete and then the money. "Sure. Why not?" He shrugged, collecting the cash.

With the coat and briefcase taken care of, the next step was to get a suit, and Pete didn't spare any expense there. He went to an exclusive men's clothes store on Newbury Street and picked out a twelve-hundred dollar gray pin-striped number. He asked the tailor if it could be ready in an hour. The tailor shook his head. "Sorry," he said. "Maybe in three days." Pete showed him a fifty and got no reaction. He angrily added another fifty and the tailor told him the alterations would be completed in an hour.

Pete spent part of the next hour picking out a dress shirt and tie, part of it consulting the phonebook, and all of it amazed at how quickly he could spend money. It was like water through his fingers. He started wondering if it was worth it. What was the point of always knocking himself out chasing after the big score? If he ever made it, he knew he'd be flat broke again a few months later.

As soon as he put on his new suit and felt the precise cut of its material, all his doubts faded. The struggle was worth it. Maybe the money would go like there was no tomorrow, but he'd have a hell of a ride while it lasted.

Pete next started out on a walking tour of Boston's fancier restaurants. He visited almost a dozen before finding what he was looking for—an unattended coat rack. He hung his cheap leather coat next to a rich, expensive one, and then called Toni, asking her to call back the restaurant and have Dr. Robert Tucker paged. Before hanging up, she congratulated him on his recent professional achievement.

A minute after he was seated his waiter came back, and noticing the RT monogrammed on his briefcase, asked if he was Dr. Robert Tucker. Pete nodded, and the waiter, handing him the restaurant's cordless phone, informed him he had an emergency call.

Pete picked up the handset and heard Toni giggling. "Oh, Doctor," she exclaimed, "this jerk I know has been giving me a royal pain in the ass. What should I do?"

"Sounds serious," he murmured. "Take two aspirin and insert them where it aches." He slammed down the phone, muttering out loud about a critical operation, and rushed from the restaurant grabbing the wrong leather coat.

"An honest mistake," he smirked to himself as he slipped it on, admiring how nice it felt.

He walked briskly, waiting until he was a block away before hailing a cab. He had the cabbie make two stops before taking him to the dog track, one at Amalgamated Computers, where he picked up an annual report and other miscellaneous sales brochures, the second at a stationery store.

The Club, a semi-posh restaurant within the track, was a hang-out for the more serious gamblers. Pete pulled aside a busboy and showed him twenty dollars. "Who's stupid and loaded?" he asked. The kid nodded towards a thick-necked man with a deep scowl. Pete took him in with a glance and liked what he saw. The man's clothes were expensive and in bad taste. He had the pasty, surly look of someone who'd been losing badly and was too stubborn to know when to quit.

Pete sat down next to the man and immediately opened his briefcase and started studying reports and jotting down random figures in a notebook. He caught the sap peering at him with a mix of annoyance and curiosity. "You figuring out some handicapping formulas?" the sap asked distrustfully.

Pete laughed. "Unfortunately, no," he said, a big friendly smile stretched across his face. "I have to finish a sales report for tomorrow morning." He stretched out his hand and introduced himself as Robert Tucker. "Vice-President of Sales at Amalgamated Computers," he added.

"The track's a funny place to do work," the sap grunted as he halfheartedly took Pete's hand. He chose not to introduce himself.

"I guess so," Pete shrugged. He took off his leather coat and draped it on the back of his chair. Outwardly he appeared oblivious to the man's snub, his smile remaining warm and friendly. "A buddy from college gave me some tips," he said with a wink.

"Is that so?" the sap replied, his eyes growing vacant as he turned away from Pete.

During the first two races Pete gave the appearance of being absorbed in his report. He noticed the sap's scowl had deepened and his betting slips had been ripped to pieces. After the sap made his bets for the third race, Pete asked him if he could watch his coat and briefcase. The sap reluctantly agreed, making a face as if he smelled bad cheese.

Pete placed fifty-dollars bets to win on every dog in the third. The cashier was going to say something but held his tongue. As he sat back down, he saw the sap staring at him. "My buddy's about ninety-percent sure on this one," he said with a big grin. The sap grunted and again wrinkled his face as if his olfactory senses were being offended.

At the end of the third race the sap crumpled his betting slips and tossed them down in disgust. Pete deftly removed the winning slip from his wallet. To the untrained eye it appeared he had only a single slip in his wallet instead of nine. He made sure the sap got a good look at it. "I would've bet more," Pete confided, "but my buddy is only positive about the ninth race."

The sap studied Pete with a newfound interest. "What other tips did he give you?" he asked, showing off a good pound of denture work as he forced a smile.

"Well," Pete hesitated. "Other than the ninth, he gave me a probable winner for the sixth."

"Is that so?" the sap edged forward. "What dogs does he pick?"

Pete frowned. "I'm sorry," he said, as if he really were sorry. "But I promised my buddy I wouldn't give his tips to anyone else. It could get him in trouble. I hope you understand."

"Sure, sure." A tic caused the sap's right eye to flutter uncontrollably. Pete knew the sap was dying to tell him to go to hell, but the sap fought it back and forced a brotherly smile. "You can't let a buddy down, right?"

The sap won in the fourth and then lost big in the fifth. Before the sixth, Pete again asked him to watch his coat and briefcase, and then he placed bets on every dog in the race. After the race, Pete made sure the sap caught a glance of his winning ticket.

During the next two races the sap was squirming in his seat. Every few seconds he'd look over at Pete, trying to make up his mind about something. He'd open his mouth and then shut it tight. After the eighth race, he grabbed Pete by the arm. "Come on," he pleaded. "Be a pal. Who does your friend like for the ninth?"

"I can't—"

"I need this one." His eyes were dead serious. "If I can have one big winner I'll make up for the past month. You got to help me out."

Pete let his face show a pained grimace. "How much do you want to bet?" he asked at last.

"Five thousand." The sap wet his lips.

Pete nodded slowly. "Okay," he said. "Here's how we do it so I don't break my promise to my buddy. You give me five thousand and I'll add three thousand, and we split the winnings even." Before the sap had a chance to say anything, Pete counted out three thousand dollars from his wallet. The sap handed over his five thousand.

When Pete got up, it appeared as if the sap was going to follow him. He turned to the sap and politely asked him to watch his coat and briefcase. Any argument the sap was going to propose died when he looked at the coat and briefcase. Any sap could see the coat was worth two grand and the briefcase at least another. And the briefcase contained an invaluable sales report. The sap sat down quietly, his pasty face looking slightly flustered.

Pete whistled happily as he walked past all of the betting lines. He kept walking until he was out of the track. Subtracting his expenses, he had over ten grand and a new suit left. More important, though, he had run his first successful con since coming to Boston. To be good at the con game you had to have confidence, and Pete had been afraid he'd lost his. Now, he could feel it surging through his blood. And nothing could beat the exhilaration of leaving a sap high and dry. As he walked, he jumped up and clicked his heels.

Pete showed up at the Italian restaurant on time. Langely was there waiting for him, a sour look on his face. When he saw Pete, he approached him and asked if things went as planned. Pete nodded and held up a paper bag he was carrying. "Had to crack his skull," Pete whispered indifferently. "But I got ten grand."

The two men sat down, Langely with a hard sneer frozen on his face, Pete looking like a man heading to the gallows. A signal was given for them to head to the back room.

Carbone was sitting alone, his large face impassive as he watched Pete enter the room. Pete sat across from him. He purposely avoided the large man's eyes. To himself, he started counting down from ten. When he got to zero, the large man exploded. "You lost my money!" he bellowed. "You stupid piece of garbage!"

"I-I'm s-sorry." Pete swallowed and tried again. "I'm sorry, sir," he said, his eyes cast down to the floor.

"You think that means anything?" Carbone demanded rhetorically.

Langely had taken the paper bag from Pete and handed it to Carbone. "Please," he interrupted. "He's deeply sorry and would like to offer this as a show of respect."

Carbone dumped the money from the bag and counted it.

"This is only ten thousand dollars," he said with disbelief. "How is this showing respect?"

Pete sat quietly, trying to look as sick as possible. He couldn't help but rate the performance as poor. If he had been running the scam he would have tried to impart real fear and loathing before starting with the yelling and chest-beating. Langely argued Pete's case. "I agree he's a brainless imbecile," he implored. "But he meant no disrespect. This is all he could come up with."

Carbone had some of the money clutched in his hands. He waved it menacingly at Pete. "I look at you as garbage," he snarled. "And you know what I do to garbage? I burn and bury it!"

Pete lurched forward as if he were going to vomit and then pretended to hold it back. That sped things up. It's one thing to enjoy the last few moments of a scam, but quite another to have clothes needlessly ruined. Carbone spat on the floor. "You're not worth wasting time on," he said. "But if I ever hear of you again, I'll kill you." He grabbed a baseball bat from under the table and stood up. "I will kill you!" he yelled, reaching forward.

Pete fell back in his chair and just about crawled from the restaurant as Carbone bellowed after him. Toni was parked across the street and by the time he got to the Caddy he was laughing so hard he could barely talk. He plopped down on the passenger seat. "Boy," he gasped. "That was fun."

Slowly, his laughter subsided. He lowered himself in his seat so he couldn't be seen from the outside. Toni was looking at him with amusement. "I'm glad you had a good time in there," she said.

"Worth the price of admission." He saw Langely and Carbone step from the restaurant and he gave Toni a nudge with his elbow. The two men seemed to be enjoying themselves. Carbone's body convulsed in a wheezing type of laugh while Langely kidded around, his thin face displaying a big smart-alecky grin. They shook hands and separated. Pete nodded to Toni. "You take the large one. Will you be okay?"

Toni had already slid out of the car. She turned to him and

flashed her killer smile. "Don't worry about me, lover," she said, her eyes shining brightly. "If I have to wrestle a dozen of him to get you to the altar, I will. See you in church."

She was wearing a tight-fitting leather skirt cut only a few inches down her thigh. Pete watched the delicious wiggle of her rear end as she approached Carbone, and felt his heart skip a beat. Toni could take care of herself. He slid over to the driver's seat, put the car into Drive, and followed Langely.

He did a lousy job tailing Langely. Not knowing the Boston streets well enough to take any chances, he stuck close behind Langely's white Oldsmobile, most of the time leaving only one car between them. Fortunately, the small man was oblivious to it. He led Pete right to a small wooden colonial in East Boston. Pete noted the address and drove off, thankful that Langely didn't live in an apartment building. An apartment building would be tougher for what he had planned.

He barely got back to his hotel room when the phone rang. It was Toni, informing him that Mr. Carbone was really Mr. Carl Boronski. "I'd put him on the phone," she said, "but I'm afraid he's tied up at the moment."

"Just you and him alone, huh?"

"Just the two of us." She hesitated, and when she continued her voice had changed, sounding almost scared. "Pete," she said. "I found the briefcase. There was thirty-three thousand dollars in it. I also found five thousand dollars on him."

"I'll be over as soon as I can." Pete got the address and hung up. He then drove back to where he had followed Langely. The house lights were off, and as he left the Caddy he took with him a roll of duct tape he'd bought earlier in the day. Standing in the darkness by the front door, Pete strained himself, trying to listen for any voices coming from within the house. Finally, he heard what sounded like a man and woman celebrating. He pounded on the door, and muffling his voice with his hand, shouted, "It's Carl. Open up!"

He was grinning from ear to ear when the door opened and the redhead stood in front of him in her stocking feet. As recognition hit her, her mouth gaped open, but before she could utter a peep, he had tape covering her mouth. A split second later he had her on her belly, and with his knee digging into the small of her back, wrapped both her wrists and ankles with the tape. He grinned wolfishly, studying the sheer negligee she was wearing. "Fancy finding you here," he whispered softly into her ear.

As he pulled away, he noticed she still had on the same diamond earrings. He reached down to take them and then thought better of it. Langely called down, complaining about what was taking so long. Pete moved the redhead from sight.

When Langely walked into the room, he walked straight into a hard sucker punch. Pete had put more muscle into it than he had to, and the small man crumpled onto the floor. He bound the small man's wrists and ankles, and then started searching the house.

He found the five grand he was expecting to find, and not wanting to keep Toni waiting, decided to call it quits. He used a blanket from the bedroom to transport the redhead and Langely to the trunk of his Caddy. Langely was still out cold. As he shut the trunk, the redhead glared at him furiously. For the hell of it, he hit every pothole on the way.

The address Toni had given him was for a small Colonial with an attached garage. A beat-up Volvo occupied the garage. Pete knocked on the door and gave Toni a squeeze as she let him in. She shot him a worried look. "What kept you so long?" she asked.

"Had a pickup to make. You know where the keys for the Volvo are?"

She shrugged. Pete spotted an overcoat, checked the pockets, and with a big smile, held up a set of car keys. He rolled the Volvo out onto the street, and brought the Caddy into the garage. Toni watched all of it with an impatient frown. Pete opened the Caddy trunk, and with a grunt, lifted Langely onto his shoulder. The small man had woken up and was groaning miserably.

"Well, honey," Pete winked. "You want to show me our host?" Toni stared in disbelief and then started laughing. She led the way to the upstairs bedroom. There, Carl Boronski lay on the bed, his hands and feet secured by handcuffs to brass bed posts. Besides a pair of socks that were stuffed in his mouth, the only other article of clothing he head on his body were jockey shorts. Pete raised an eyebrow at Toni. "The handcuffs were his idea!" she argued defensively.

"I'm sure they were," he answered, dropping Langely onto the bed with his partner.

Pete went back to the garage and hoisted the redhead onto his shoulder. As he carried her upstairs, Toni's eyes lit up. "You got yourself quite an armful," she said with a vicious smile.

"Nothing I can't handle," he responded, sidestepping a kick she had aimed at his posterior. He carried the redhead into a bathroom and dumped her in the tub. She shot him a look of pure murder. The tape across her mouth stifled the curses she tried to unleash. Pete smiled to himself, noticing that her skin had blushed a deeper red than her hair.

Toni was waiting in the hallway. "What next?" she asked.

"I'll show you."

Pete led the way back into the bedroom, and then took out his switchblade. Langely was looking awful woozy, and when he saw the opened knife, he squeezed his eyes shut. Boronski's eyes bulged as he stared at the blade. Pete walked over to Boronski and cut his jockey shorts off. He then used the knife to free Langely of his clothing.

"What's the point of that?" Toni whispered to him after he had walked back to her.

"Later I'm going to call the cops," he said somewhat spitefully. "I want them embarrassed when the men in blue show up. Payback for trying to play me as a chump."

"And they won't tell the cops anything?"

"Not a thing." He smiled wryly. "They can't afford to, unless they want to admit to the rip-off scheme they've been running. It's going to be some show later." He broke out laughing. "The cops are going to want to know why they're naked and tied up, and our friends are going to sweat bullets trying to explain it's all one big misunderstanding. Man, I wish I could watch it. Oh, well," he showed the knife. "Can't leave our redhead overdressed."

Toni snatched the knife away. "In your dreams," she muttered out of the side of her mouth. The bathroom door slammed behind her. When she came out, she carried the remains of the redhead's negligee.

"It seems fitting," Pete offered philosophically, "that they should be stripped both figuratively and literally of their worldly possessions. And speaking of which, why don't you show me the money?"

The briefcase was in the kitchen. Looking at all the money in it made Pete's palms start to sweat. He took the five grand he had found at Langely's and added it to the briefcase. "Why don't you put this in the trunk," he told Toni, handing her the money. "I'm going to give the place a quick search."

Toni nodded. Pete knew she had already searched the house, but he checked places he knew she would've missed. Like the underside of shelves, and the back of drawers, and inside of book jackets. He found three hundred dollars hidden in those spots.

Toni came back from the garage and grabbed him, pressing her slim body hard against his. She gave him a long kiss. When she pulled away her eyes sparkled. "Let's go," she said, "we got vows to exchange."

They walked to the garage together, hand in hand. Pete stopped suddenly and slapped himself against the forehead. "The diamond earrings!" he swore, shaking his head.

Toni gave him a questioning look. "The redhead's got diamond earrings that I want to give you as a wedding gift. I'll be right back." He turned but Toni stopped him. "I'll get them," she insisted. She gave him an odd look as she walked back into the house.

When he heard her on the stairs, he started up the Caddy and drove off. An uneasiness started to work its way into his stomach. He had almost left behind a few hundred dollars for Toni, but hell, he was leaving her the diamonds—wasn't that enough? If they turned out to be fake, she'd still find a way to get back to New York. With a body like hers, how could she not? And besides, Toni was as resourceful as they come.

Still, the look she gave him bothered him. It was something other than simple jealousy—almost like she knew what was going to happen. Well, what choice did he have? If he was going to use the money to run his Hollywood scam he had to ditch Toni.

With a little bit of luck he should be able to return ten times what was in the briefcase. Maybe even more. In six months, a year tops, he'd come back and make it up to Toni, marrying her on the spot. He'd give her a diamond so big she'd need a wheelbarrow to cart it around.

No, he rationalized, it was unfair to expect him to do anything but what he did. The Hollywood scam was finally within his reach. And also, he thought with a warm smile, so were all the beautiful and hopeful actresses he'd be meeting.

First he'd drive down south, maybe to Miami, and rest up for a few days. Work on a good suntan. Buy himself a flashy wardrobe. After that, he'd get rid of the Caddy and fly to Hollywood. And then . . .

As plans whirled through his head, any guilt he had been feeling faded. He drove until morning, finally stopping at a roadside motel in Virginia. Bleary-eyed and exhausted, he opened the trunk and stood confused, not believing his eyes. There was no briefcase. All there was was a note written in the cherry-blossom-pink lipstick Toni liked to use.

The note read: "You lousy creep. When you marry me you might see a dime of the money. Drop dead, Toni."

If he hadn't been so damn tired, Pete would've gotten a long good laugh from the whole thing.

Man Friday

"Man Friday" is the sequel to "Money Run", and starts with Toni having flown the coop with all the ill-gotten gains from Money Run, and our hero, Pete Mitchel, finding himself down and out in Miami. Ever resourceful, Pete will find a way. . . .

Pete Mitchel instinctively rolled to his side when he felt the wetness splash on his face. Even in the semi-dream state he had drifted into, he found himself wondering why it tasted so much like stale beer.

Before his unconscious mind could put two and two together, he found himself jerked off the park bench and kicked in the gut. As he lay on the dirt ground, dazed, gasping for air, he slipped an eight inch switchblade from his pants pocket and had it pulled open beneath him. Standing over him were two punks, both grinning. Neither of them had seen the knife.

The larger of the two punks poured more beer on Pete. He looked like a Nazi. His neck redder than a strawberry and thicker than Pete's thigh. Short thick blond hair stood up like a brush bristle from the top of his head.

"We don't like bums in our town—do we, Rat?" he jeered. His mouth was big and pink and filled with bad teeth.

Rat, his associate, chortled in response. He was a fat, sloppy punk with reddish greasy hair and bad acne. Snake tattoos ran up both arms. "That's right," he joined in with a squeaky voice, his eyes sparkling with mirth. "We smash them up, right George?"

"That's right," the blond punk, George, agreed. "It's disgusting how they come into our town expecting to sponge off of us good folk. Nothing but cheap garbage. Makes me sick to my stomach."

Pete braced himself. He sat up slowly, keeping the knife hand behind him. With a quick sweep of the blade and a little luck he'd be able to sever arteries in both punks' legs.

George edged closer. His features darkened. "Now," he said. "If they were gainfully employed, or at least willing to become productive members of society, that would be a different story."

Pete closed the knife with his thumb. "You got a job for me?" he asked in a hoarse whisper.

George nodded. "Yeah, I do. How does two hundred dollars sound?"

After thinking about it, Pete told him it sounded fine. The fat, sloppy punk, Rat, offered a hand which Pete ignored. He stood up slowly, his stomach tight and sore from the kick he took. The two punks got alongside him, sandwiching him, hanging their arms loosely around his shoulders. Their body odor was stifling. It had been two months since Pete had outwitted himself and lost forty grand to his fiancée, Toni. Since then things had gone from bad to worse. The last three weeks he had been living off the streets of Miami, unable to raise the bus fare to get back to New York. He prayed he didn't smell like these two.

The two punks led him out of the park. As they walked, George explained how he knew Pete wasn't just a shiftless lazy bum, but a down-and-out soul who was looking for a chance to pull himself up from his bootstraps. Rat found something amusing in that and broke into a wheezing laugh, followed by a coughing fit.

They walked a quarter of a mile before stopping in front of a pink and white art deco ranch in an exclusive neighborhood near Coral Gables. Rat hustled over to the front door, jiggled with the lock, and then hurried back, his face a bright red. "All set. Door's unlocked," he grunted.

George took Pete aside. "Here's the story," he said in a soft monotone. He was standing very close to Pete. His breath felt unpleasantly hot and smelled a lot like rotting fish.

"My boss has a problem with the guy who lives here," he continued. "We want to teach him a lesson he won't forget. How's that sound?"

"Sounds okay."

George nodded, handed Pete a wad of bills. "That's two hundred," he said. "All you got to do is knock off the guy's wife. And you're going to do it with him in bed with her. It will be a lesson he won't soon forget."

George explained more of the situation. Pete stood listening, his features marble hard, his eyes half closed. George took a gun from his waistband and handed it to Pete, holding it so Pete had to look down the barrel as he took it.

"We'll be waiting for you," George told him. "You better not screw up in there."

Pete looked at the gun. A thirty-two caliber revolver. He reversed his grip and then swung it hard, slashing George across the mouth with the barrel. The blond punk fell back a couple of steps and grabbed his mouth. Rat took a step forward, then stopped.

"That's for the beer bath and the kick," Pete explained softly. "And for not brushing your teeth."

"We'll be waiting for you," George said, slurring his words. He had both hands pressed against his mouth.

"As a friend I got to recommend you start flossing," Pete said with a wink. He turned and followed the slate path to the front door. Before going in, he looked behind him and saw both punks standing frozen, blood in their eyes.

Inside, he pushed aside the front curtains and watched as the two punks hightailed it out of there, scampering away like hyenas.

Pete bit his tongue to keep from laughing. He took the money out and counted it. Two hundred as advertised. Enough to run a few scams with so he could get back to New York in style. He was about to start looking for a back window when a thought stopped him. On a hunch he cracked open the revolver. There was only a single bullet in the cylinder.

As Pete stared at the gun his lips pressed into a harsh, thin smile. A minute passed before he moved and pushed the cylinder back in place. After that he turned on the lights.

The kitchen was off to the right. He rummaged through the refrigerator and found beef tenderloin in the freezer. He used the microwave to defrost it, and cooked it up with some eggs, taking his time eating. A bottle of Dom Perignon accompanied his meal.

It was almost two hours after entering the house that Pete walked into the bedroom and turned on the lights. The wife was lying on her back, her mouth open as she snored uncomfortably. Pete guessed she was drugged. The husband was lying on his side, the blanket pulled over his head.

Pete stood and stared at the husband. The body under the blanket twitched once, but other than that was completely still. Pete walked over to it and pushed the gun barrel against an indentation in the blanket that outlined an ear.

"Take your hands out slowly," Pete ordered.

There was no movement. Pete cocked the revolver. "Have it your way then," he said softly.

Two hands came out. Pete pulled the blanket off and threw it on the floor. Laying next to the husband's stomach was a .357 magnum.

The husband, a short stocky man in his mid thirties, tried to give Pete a big, wide used-car-salesman's smile. "Get out of bed," Pete said, and then he grabbed the man by the arm and pulled him onto the floor.

"What's going on? If it's money you want—"

"Shut up." Pete picked up the .357, checked to make it sure it was loaded, and then cracked open the thirty-two caliber revolver and dropped its single bullet to the floor. "Here's your gun back," he said, handing the empty gun to the husband.

"I-I don't know what you're talking about."

Pete glanced over at the wife. She was still oblivious to the world. Blond, nice shape, particularly stunning legs. Her body had for the most part slipped out of her negligee. He forced a smile as he addressed the husband. "If you want I'll call the police right now. You want me to?"

The husband stood staring at Pete, his large broad face turning a bright pink. After a long while he shook his head.

"I wouldn't think so," Pete said. "I have to admit, I'm not very happy with what you tried to pull. But we can talk about that later. What did you drug her with?"

Without any hesitation: "Phenobarbital." The husband pushed a hand through his hair, showing off a hairline that had receded severely. He flashed an embarrassed smile. "I'll give you five thousand dollars right now to kill her and then beat me up."

Pete shook his head. "I'd do the second part for free, but the first part—no. Let's go to the kitchen."

Pete let the husband lead the way. When they got there, Pete found a pad of paper and pen in a drawer and tossed it to his host. As he explained what they were going to be used for the bright pink in the husband's face faded to a queer white. He obviously didn't like it, but he did exactly what Pete asked for, writing up a confession and signing it.

When he was done, Pete read it over. The confession outlined that the husband had Pete delivered to his house to kill his drugged wife and how he had planned to then kill Pete and pass him off to the cops as a burglar. The husband sat glaring at Pete. "Cheap blackmailing punk," he smirked under his breath.

Pete shrugged casually. "You're going to find I'm anything but cheap." He took out the husband's wallet that he had grabbed earlier when he was in the bedroom, and studied the driver's license. The husband turned a paler shade of white. Pete let his teeth show through a thin smile and crumpled the confession into a ball and tossed it into the garbage. "Let's try it again," he said. "And with your next trick, you lose some teeth."

The confession was rewritten. This time the signature and the name matched the license. The husband, Brian Hurley, looked sick. "So you're going to blackmail me," he remarked glumly.

"Not really," Pete answered as he folded the confession into an envelope. "I'm going to let you hire me. Two thousand a week plus room and board. We'll call it a Man Friday type position. What it will really be is figuring a way to keep you from pulling this stunt on the next poor sap. And making sure your wife stays alive." Pete's eyes narrowed as he studied Hurley. "As far as I'm concerned, after what you tried to do to me all bets are off. If you express any moral outrage or indignation I'm going to kick your face in and then have a nice, long talk with your wife. Right now, I've got an errand to run. I'll be back in about half an hour. Make sure you have a room ready for me. Also, I like bacon with my eggs, and my orange juice fresh squeezed."

Pete found a book of stamps in a drawer and affixed one to the envelope that he had folded the confession into. He smiled congenially at the husband. "See you in a little bit, boss," he said.

The next morning the shrill, unpleasant whine of a police siren woke Pete up. Or at least that's what he first thought it was. As he lay in bed and the haze around his brain lifted he realized the noise was actually human and coming from Mrs. Brian Hurley. She stood in the hallway with her hands on her hips as she yelled at both Pete and her husband, demanding to know who the hell Pete was and what he was doing in her house.

Pete sat up and rubbed his eyes. She was wearing a yellow, translucent robe. Sunlight streaming in from behind her showed the only thing underneath it was the same flimsy negligee from the night before. Her body had nice curves, sagging only slightly from what had to have been a hell of a hangover. Even hung over Pete guessed she would make a better than decent living as a stripper. He smiled graciously and introduced himself as Pete Michaels. "Brian and I go way back," he said. He turned to Hurley who was standing off to the side, looking sick to his stomach. "Hey buddy, remember what I told you last night about the airline losing my bags? How about getting me one of your robes?"

Hurley left without a word. Mrs. Hurley stood staring at Pete, her face a hard white, like a cat's just before the kill. "Who the hell are you?" she demanded.

Pete ignored the question. "Brian's told me a lot about you. Real great guy, your husband, inviting me to spend the next few weeks here. Of course, after all we've been through together, what choice did he have?"

Hurley arrived with a bathrobe. Pete slipped it on. Mrs. Hurley stood glaring at her husband, her mouth moving as if she were chewing food.

"All right," Pete announced, clapping his hands and swinging himself out of bed. "What's for breakfast?"

Mrs. Hurley got in his way. "I want you out of my house," she insisted, her voice trembling slightly.

Pete glanced over at Hurley who was standing quietly with his hands in his pockets. "Okay," Pete shrugged. "But first let me—"

Hurley rushed forward and pulled his wife away. "He's staying," he said. "Understand, Gloria?"

She shot him a withering look, was about to say something, but swallowed it back. Pete led the way to the kitchen. Hurley prepared breakfast, bacon and eggs and fresh squeezed orange juice. Pete did most of the eating for the three of them, Hurley mostly just played with his food while his wife sat opposite Pete, studying him, her eyes having a tough time with the light. Finally she smiled. Only with her lips, nothing in her eyes.

"You and my dear husband go way back, huh?" she said with a laugh. "Forgive me then for getting so upset before. Let's start over.

Hello Pete, call me Gloria." She held out her hand to him, and when Pete took it she held onto him longer than she should've.

"It will be nice having a good-looking man around the house for a change," she said. Hurley muttered that she better shut up. There was a slight sparkle to her eyes as her smile finally reached them. "As you can tell," she continued. "Brian has basically gone to pot. He now looks more like an ape than a man. I think he's got more hair on his back than his head."

For a moment it looked like Hurley was going to strike her. Slowly he got his control back, stood up and mumbled under his breath that he was heading off to work. Pete stopped him.

"I think I'll accept the offer you made last night," Pete said. "You know the one you made after accidentally spilling beer over my suit—about buying me new clothes to replace my lost bags. Just leave a credit card and your car keys."

Hurley stood frozen. Gloria let out a short laugh. It brought him back to life. He took a credit card out of his wallet and dropped it and his car keys on the table. "Give me your keys," he demanded from Gloria.

"Screw you. Walk to work," she said, then broke out laughing. A shrill, high-pitched laugh. It followed Hurley out of the house.

Pete took the last bite of his eggs. "It's good to see someone who finds pleasure in the little things," he noted.

Gloria got up, walked over to Pete, and sat in his lap. Her arm went around his shoulders, and her body twisted so her front pressed against him. It felt firm. "When I first saw you I was furious," she told him. "I thought dear Brian was up to something. But after watching you handle him, it's obvious he doesn't want you here. Which means I do. What do you have on him?"

Pete grinned. "If I told you I'd have nothing."

She ran a hand along Pete's cheek. It felt as cool as ice. "I think I know what it is, but why don't you tell mama anyway?" She had stuck out her bottom lip and pouted while asking Pete the last question, over exaggerating the baby talk mannerisms. Her hand had left his cheek and was caressing his chest and moving downwards. He grabbed it. "Sorry," he said. "I don't have time for this now."

"What's the matter—scared?"

"Always when handling dynamite." Pete pushed his chair back and stood up, dumping Gloria onto the floor.

She sat stunned, eyes wide open. "You dirty bastard!" she spat out.

"At least there's no misunderstanding what we both are," Pete agreed.

After taking a long, hot shower and shaving, Pete found some of Hurley's clothes that were wearable. They fit poorly on him, too short and too wide in the wrong places, but the material was rich and expensive. Can't have everything, Pete sighed to himself sadly. Gloria sat on the sofa and watched as Pete called friends in New York trying to find his fiancée, Toni. Charlie, Toni's boss, didn't know where she was. "She took off two months ago. Business ain't been the same since," Charlie said before sighing mournfully. Pete offered his sympathies. Toni worked as a hostess at Charlie's strip joint and was the club's biggest draw. Customers would come back night after night hoping to convince her to take her clothes off and join the dancers on stage. She never did, but that didn't stop them from trying. And they had good reason to try. Toni was a knockout.

Pete got a hold of Bernie Madress who had heard that Toni lost a bundle at Aqueduct six weeks earlier. That was all he knew, though. Pete had better luck with Dmitry Horowitz. He had run into Toni at the Meadowlands and thought she'd had a good day, up a few thousand. He reported that she seemed less than enthralled with Pete, repeating a few of the disparaging comments that were made about what Pete could do with parts of his anatomy. Dmitry thought it had been about a month since he had seen her. He asked if Pete could be a pal and ship him a couple of cases of Florida grapefruit. They helped with his constipation.

Pete struck out with Sal Pinini, Angie Slotnick, and "Whiplash" Joey Binder. Frankie Marzone, though, had seen Toni two weeks earlier at Pimlico. Word was she was throwing money around like crazy. Frankie didn't know whether she was winning or losing. While Pete waited to speak to a bookie he knew in Baltimore, Gloria jumped off the sofa and grabbed the phone away from him. She demanded to know who this Tony guy was. Her eyes had turned small and angry, her face livid.

Pete tried kidding with her, but it was useless. She had been stewing inside while Pete had made his phone calls, and the low simmering anger had boiled over. She was out of control, screaming at him, demanding to know what he had on her husband. Pete made the mistake of ignoring her, and as he turned a deaf ear he saw the agate book end out of the corner of his eye and narrowly dodged it, feeling it scrape past his ear, and then took a Hummel figurine off his forehead. He stepped out of the way of a flung Erte sculpture and slipped out a side door with Hurley's car keys. As he drove off in a green Mercedes convertible, Gloria ran after him, screaming bloody murder, her robe flapping open. Pete noticed she was no longer wearing a negligee under it.

A block away he looked out the rear view mirror expecting Gloria to still be legging it after him. He was a little disappointed to see that she had quit. Before turning back, his eyes focused on a rusted out Monte Carlo creeping along behind him. With a hard grin he recognized the two punks, George and Rat. George was behind the wheel, his face bright red, a thick bandage covering his upper lip.

Pete drove towards the airport, got onto Flagler and pulled up to one of the seedier bars lining the road. He was sipping a beer when George came in. Beads of sweat lined the blond punk's forehead. His face appeared grossly puffed out under the bandage. He got very close to Pete, his breath oppressive.

"You think you're a funny guy?" George asked out of the corner of his mouth that was showing.

"Funny's not the word," Pete said, nodding casually. "As you found out I usually leave them in stitches."

George spat on the floor. "Real funny guy." Then, low and mean, "I paid you to do a job and you're going to do it."

Rat was coming around from the other side. Pete smiled at the two punks and took a long swallow of his beer.

George spat again on the floor. His face had turned a bright red. "You cost me ten grand," he forced out. "You lousy piece of crap. Ten grand. Now Hurley ain't going to give me shit. But he will after you finish the job!"

Pete looked at the blond punk and then broke out laughing. He couldn't help it. When he was done, he wiped a few tears from his eyes and took another long swallow of his beer, draining it. A big grin had broken over his face.

"Let me see if I got this straight," he said. "You're mad at me because I didn't end up dead last night like you planned. Hey man, my heart bleeds for you. On your way out why don't you drop dead."

Rat took a step closer. Pete swung around and broke the beer bottle against the bar and showed the jagged edge. George moved back a foot, his face mottled pink and white. The bartender reached down beneath the bar.

"If you want," Pete said, a grin frozen on his face. "We can go out back and I'll finish the job I started on your face. But just the two of us. You send ratboy home."

George stood staring, and then jerked his head quickly, nodding. "Sure, sure. Just the two of us." He signaled to Rat to leave, winking and telling him they'd meet up later. He turned back to Pete. "Sure, just the two of us. Why not? We'll go out back behind this dump."

"I ordered a ham sandwich," Pete muttered indignantly. "After I finish my lunch I'll meet you."

"Sure thing," George agreed. "No rush. Take your time. I'll be out back, punk."

George left through the side door. Pete ordered another beer. The bartender asked if he wanted a ham sandwich.

"No, thanks," Pete said. "You got a phone I could use?"

The bartender pointed out a pay phone in the back. Pete got up and called the police. He gave the officer the address of the bar, and told him there were a couple of punks in the alley behind the bar dealing heroin. He described George and Rat. "They got guns," Pete warned. "And the greasy red-headed one is hiding behind the dumpster."

Pete took his beer back to the bar and sipped it slowly, waiting. Three minutes later he heard the sound of car tires screeching. Then from out back shouting, followed by garbage cans being knocked over.

Things quieted down after that and through the front window he saw a police cruiser roll by with George and Rat sitting in the back seat. Rat was slumped down, but George could be seen plainly. A long gash ran down his forehead and his left eye looked pretty bad.

The bartender shook his head slightly and cackled. Pete shrugged. "My mom always told me the policeman's our best friend," he remarked and finished his beer.

When Pete got back he found Gloria dressed in a pair of pink hot pants and a blouse, at least sort of. She had only bothered with two of the middle buttons of the blouse.

"I'm so sorry about before," she said, pouting slightly. "Can't we be friends?"

Pete swallowed hard as he glanced at her legs. He had to admit they were gorgeous legs. "Sure," he said, struggling to keep from staring at her waist.

She led him into the living room and sat next to him on the sofa. "Let's level with each other," she said. She held his right hand with both of hers. They had warmed up. "My dear hubby's trying to kill me, isn't he?"

Pete stared into her light blue eyes. "You're way off base," he said.

"Sure I am." Her eyes hardened, becoming more like ice crystals. "That's why I woke up this morning with my head feeling like it was going to split open. That sonofabitch drugged me. Guess what? I know about the three million dollar policy he took out on me, but what my dear ape-husband doesn't know is I added the same coverage for him."

She licked her lips. "You're going to help me kill him."

Pete shook him head. "You two consider marriage counseling?"

That just caused her to laugh as she tightened her grip on his hand. "You will help me," she insisted. "Then you can have a hundred grand from the insurance. And me also." She lifted a leg and ran it over his lap. "You want me, or don't you like girls?"

Pete swallowed hard. He was beginning to feel light-headed. "I like them fine," he said, forcing a grin. "It's snakes I'm not too fond of. Cold-blooded, deadly ones. They give me the willies."

"Good," she laughed. Her head tilted backwards, showing the soft curvature of her throat, and then came forward again and her eyes met his. "For a minute I had my doubts." She pushed herself closer to him. "As you can feel I'm warm-blooded. Maybe hot enough to burn." Her lips found his. The smell of her made him dizzy. He heard the front door and he pushed her off him. Hurley walked in, looking like a whipped dog.

"Hello, darling," she greeted him. "Just getting to know your good friend, Pete."

The next five days were tough ones. One minute Gloria would be trying to seduce him, the next she'd be enraged, demanding that she help her kill her husband. She wouldn't let up. Hurley, meanwhile, walked around like a zombie, his large broad face forlorn and haggard. He reminded Pete of someone whose time on death row was quickly running out.

Then it all changed. At least with Gloria. She inexplicably cooled to Pete, barely uttering a word to him the whole day.

The next day, Friday, Pete tried calling Charlie again, who hesitated and then gave him a tip for Hialeah Park. "Little Sweetheart in the first," Charlie croaked. "Can't miss. At least if you're half as smart as you like to think you are." Pete thanked him.

He checked the paper and saw that Hialeah Park opened at seven in the evening. Gloria walked into the living room as Pete put down the paper. She hadn't bothered wearing a robe. All she had on were a pair of panties.

She told Pete she needed to see him.

"Go right ahead," Pete said. "What's fair is fair."

"Tonight," she said, her eyes coldly distant. "Five o'clock. I'm leaving him. I'm going to do it tonight and I need your help. Promise me?"

Pete shrugged. He felt his heart pound as he watched her leave the room. After waiting a minute or so, he got up and splashed cold water over his face, and then got the hell out of the house.

He spent the day drinking beers and thinking about his situation. Hurley had tried playing him worse than a sap and he wanted to bleed him bad. So far he had gotten four grand cash and another two grand and a half in clothing, plus the two hundred from George. It wasn't enough but it would have to do. With Gloria moving out it was over and for the most part he was glad to hell it was.

He got back a little after five. As he entered the house, Gloria shouted from the bedroom, asking him to join her. The bedroom door was partially opened. As he started to walk through it a smell stopped him. A faint smell of rotting fish. . . .

Pete threw all his weight at the door. There was a dull thud and then a moan from behind it. He pulled the door back and slammed into it again. The door cracked. George fell from behind it, his nose spread out across his face like chopped meat. On his way down his chin collided with Pete's knee.

A quick glance showed the room was a mess. Bookcases, a nightstand, and a dresser had been knocked over. Gloria had been watching from the bed. She jumped off it. The little clothing she had on was torn.

"You son of a bitch!" she screamed as she charged Pete.

There was a sound from behind. Pete turned and saw Rat rushing at him, swinging a lead pipe. He ducked the pipe, grabbed at Rat's feet, and lifted the punk, sending him over his back and crashing into Gloria. The two of them fell hard to the floor, their bodies doing a complete somersault. Gloria ended up pinned by the fat punk against an overturned dresser. She thrashed underneath Rat, screaming hysterically for him to get off of her as she tried to push his belly away from her face. Pete watched as the two tried frantically to get to their feet. He waited until they just about made it and then put his foot to Rat's backside and sent them both back to the floor. As he left, he couldn't help smiling as Gloria screamed bloody murder at him.

Pete got to Hialeah Park a little after seven. Toni was by the starting gate checking out the horses.

"You got any of my forty grand left?" he asked her.

Toni's body stiffened when she heard his voice. She was wearing a halter top and shorts. Pete felt his heart skip a beat as he looked her over. She was only a little over five feet and at most ninety-five pounds, but she was the most gorgeous woman he had ever seen.

Toni sniffed the air and made a face. "Phew! What smells around here?" she asked.

"I've missed you, baby." Pete said softly. He reached over and ran his hand through her thick brown hair. "Did Charlie get my letter to you?"

Toni nodded slightly. She took a letter out of her pocketbook and handed it to him. "Pretty interesting reading," she remarked.

As she looked at him, her face softened with concern. "Are you okay?"

"How much of the forty grand do you got left?"

Toni gave him an embarrassed smile. "Five thousand."

Pete didn't say anything. He just stood staring at her.

"Don't give me any of your crap," she stated defensively. "I had some bad days at the track. And besides, if you didn't try to double-cross me in Boston—"

"How in the world could you throw away thirty-five thous—" Pete stopped cold as he glanced at the betting board and caught the listing of horses for the first race. "Give me the five grand," he said, his voice oddly weak. The hand he held out to Toni shook.

"Yeah, right—"

"Look," he interrupted, his forehead all of a sudden shiny with sweat. "I've got a sure winner on this one. Baby, it's a sign from God."

"Which horse?"

Pete wet his lips. "Gloria's Insurance Policy."

Toni laughed. "It's a thirty to one loser, Pete."

"Look, baby—" Pete took a deep breath and forced a smile. "If it doesn't win we get married as soon as we leave here. Promise."

Toni stopped laughing and studied Pete carefully. After a short while she nodded and handed him money from her pocketbook.

"You won't be sorry," Pete told her as he counted it. "We're going to win and then—" He stopped and stared at Toni. "There's only thirty-five hundred here," he stated incredulously.

"I'm saving the rest for our honeymoon."

Pete started to argue, saw it was useless, shook his head and beat it to the betting window. He added his forty-two hundred to what Toni gave him and put it all on Gloria's Insurance Policy to win. As he picked up his betting slips he felt lightheaded and had to steady himself against the betting counter. He heard the clerk mutter something about fools and damn fools.

Toni watched Pete with a sly Cheshire cat smile. She moved in close to him and squeezed his arm.

"You're lucky you made that deal," she whispered. "I decided to start saving myself for marriage."

"Uh huh."

"The best thirty-five hundred I ever spent," she added as she squeezed his arm tighter.

The horses were led into their gates. Pete glanced at the betting board and saw that Gloria's Insurance Policy had crept up to thirty-five to one odds. His mouth felt so damn dry, like he had swallowed a handful of sand.

The horses flew out of their gates. At least all but one did. Gloria's Insurance Policy sort of stumbled out, moving in an embarrassed gait. It was barely trotting by the time it reached the finish line. More than eighteen lengths back of any other horse.

It was a long time before Pete could move. He stood frozen, a hard grin etched on his face, his eyes narrowed to thin slits. Toni took the betting slips from him and ripped them up.

"Come on, lover," she said, a warm ripple in her voice. "It's a sign from God."

As she led him away, Pete broke out laughing. "Forty thousand thrown away."

"Well, sort of."

"Sort of?"

Toni smiled. "After a really good day at Saratoga I bought a new Cadillac. At least we can drive back to New York in style. And married."

Hurley looked dazed as he answered the door. "What happened here?" he asked.

Pete clapped him on the shoulder as he pushed his way by. "Gloria gone?"

Hurley nodded. Pete walked past him to the guest room. Hurley followed.

"My guess is she won't be coming back," Pete said as he folded his clothes into one of Hurley's suitcases.

"What happened in my bedroom?" Hurley asked weakly. "There's blood stains on the carpet and—"

Pete cut him off. "Your friend George is a little accident prone." Pete closed the suitcase and headed towards the door. He glanced back at Hurley and stopped.

"Were you supposed to be home around five today?"

Hurley nodded. "I promised Gloria I'd be home at five-thirty. I was held up at the office."

"Lucky thing you were. Otherwise, they still might have tried to go through with it. When you didn't show up they probably thought I tipped you off."

"What the hell are you talking about?"

"George and Rat made a deal with Gloria. I guess they figured a cut of her insurance money was as good as yours. I'm not sure what they planned, at least not exactly, but I'm pretty sure it was something where we both ended up dead."

Hurley started to look a little green around the temples. Pete took Hurley's confession from his inside jacket pocket and handed it to him.

"Consider this my letter of resignation," Pete said with a grin. "I quit."

The Dover Affair

After the hell I dragged Johnny Lane through in Fast Lane, I figured I owed him at least one chance to play the Lew Archer-type hardboiled PI, even if it's in something as sordid as the "Dover Affair".

I arrived at Tom Morton's office at nine o'clock as we had agreed, but Morton wasn't in yet and his secretary had me wait in the reception area. I wasn't happy with being kept waiting, especially since Morton had set the time, but I was willing to put up with it. Morton was Richard Dover's attorney. Richard's fiancée, Susan Laem, had been found strangled in a motel room five days earlier, and Richard was being accused by the State of Colorado of her murder. What made this such a big deal was that Richard's mother, Margaret, was wealthy and a well-known Denver socialite. Richard himself had several million in a trust fund. When I told my editor at the Denver Examiner, Eddie Braggs, that it looked likely that I would be able to write about this case for my monthly "Fast Lane" column, he was thrilled.

After about ten minutes of waiting, Morton's secretary brought me some coffee and shot the breeze with me for a few minutes, telling me how much she enjoyed my column and asking what it was like to be a private detective. Around nine-forty Morton came huffing in. He thrust his square jaw in the direction of his secretary and ordered her to bring us both some coffee and bagels, a smug expression on his face. He always seemed to have a smug expression on his face. His old man had bought him his law partnership when he was thirty-five and that only made him all the more smug. Morton, still huffing, told me to join him in his office.

As Morton got behind his desk, he put his briefcase away and then looked at me. "Damn traffic," he complained. "Denver's getting so damn congested these days. Lane, what do you know about this Richard Dover business?"

"Only what's been in the papers," I said. "They seem to be hinting that there's physical evidence against your client."

Morton's secretary knocked and came in with the coffee and bagels. After she left, Morton asked, "Before we get into that, I'd like to know if you plan on writing about this for your column."

"I'd like to."

Morton seemed satisfied, took a bite of his bagel, and stared at me as he chewed it slowly. "Richard's mother, Margaret, is going to be here at ten. She has a few concerns, but don't worry, I'm sure we can work past them." He glanced at his watch. "Shit, we only got about ten minutes."

"What concerns does she have?"

Morton waved the question away. "I said don't worry about it. Now about the physical evidence; forensics found skin and traces of blood under the dead girl's fingernails. An initial test matched Richard's DNA. Blood samples have been sent to Washington for more precise DNA testing and I guess we can pray for a miracle." Morton paused for a moment and showed an uncomfortable smile. "Police also found fresh scratch marks on Richard's arm," he said.

"What's your client saying?"

"Nothing that makes any sense. Only that he's being framed. But he is being adamant about it, and you know, I almost believe him. Lane, I'm counting on your column to sway public opinion. That's my only chance with this case."

There was a knock on the door and then Margaret Dover walked in. She was a tall woman, about six feet, but a better word to describe her would be long. She had long legs, a long torso, and a long neck. Kind of a Greta Garbo type. She was probably in her early fifties, but her hair was already more gray than blond. Until recently she probably would've been considered attractive. Now, though, she only looked worn out.

"Your secretary told me to come right in," she explained.

"That's fine," Morton said. He shook hands with her and introduced her to me. "Johnny Lane's the best we have here in Denver," he said. "I've worked with Johnny a number of times over the years."

Margaret offered me her hand and then sat down to my left. She seemed ill at ease. "Mr. Lane," she said, "I have to tell you, I am not comfortable with the idea of hiring you and having my family's private matters publicized."

"Well, now," I said, trying to hide my disappointment, "I respect my clients' privacy and only use cases for my column if I'm given permission up front. If you would like me to keep the matter private, I will certainly honor that. But Tom feels that my column could help your son."

Morton jumped in. "Margaret, the newspapers are going to be digging up and printing every piece of dirt they can. It could help us tremendously to have a forum where we can get our version of the story out. Especially with all the physical evidence going against Richard. Johnny's column carries a lot of weight in this town."

She still seemed undecided. "Mrs. Dover," I said, showing my most sincere smile. "What I am going to try to do is find evidence to exonerate your son. You believe he's innocent, don't you?"

Margaret nodded. "I know he's innocent, Mr. Lane. He was home with me at the time Sue was murdered. I don't understand why the police won't accept that."

Morton shrugged. "If it wasn't for the physical evidence

against him, they probably would. But you're his mother so they're going to take the alibi you're providing him with a grain of salt."

"I'm not lying," she said.

"I know you're not," Morton said.

She turned to me. "You've had your clients' permission for all of the cases you've written about?"

"That's right," I said. I was mostly telling the truth. There were a few times where my clients had lied to me and tried using me. In those cases all bets were off.

"And you think you can help free my son?"

"If he's innocent, I'll do my best."

She wavered for a moment, but agreed to hire me and also agreed to let me write about the case for my monthly column. My daily rate was four hundred dollars and she wrote me a check for eight thousand dollars. It was a lot more that I was going to ask for. She got up to leave, shook hands with both of us, then hesitated at the door.

"Mr. Lane," she said, "if you can exonerate my son, I'd like to pay you an additional ten thousand dollars."

Morton got up so he could escort Margaret out of the office. When he came back he informed me that he had arranged a twelve o'clock conference with Richard at the County Jail. I asked him if he had any photos of Susan Laem.

He took a folder from his desk and handed it to me. Inside were several photos of the victim while she was still among the living. One was a studio shot and a couple had her posing on a tennis court. She was so young in these pictures, barely looked twenty, and was a knockout. Long red hair, green eyes, peaches and cream skin, and a toned near perfect body. I studied her pictures and felt something funny in my throat. There was so much life in her eyes. They seemed almost to sparkle on the photographic paper. And this little smile she had like she was the only one on our little planet who knew the joke, and maybe, just maybe, she'd let the rest of us in on it someday. I put her pictures back in the folder.

"The one they've been running in the papers doesn't do her justice," I said.

"Yeah, her murder was a hell of a waste," Morton acknowledged.

I got up to leave. We agreed to meet at the Denver County Jail at a quarter to twelve. On the way I stopped at my bank to deposit Margaret's check. I also called Eddie Braggs at the Denver Examiner to tell him things were all set.

Morton was waiting for me at the County Jail. We were both given perfunctory searches and then taken to a small interview room. It had already been a long morning and I guess neither of us felt much like talking. Morton sat quietly and worked on his nails with a small manicure file. I just sat with my eyes half closed, squinting against the sunlight. I glanced at my watch. It was a few minutes before noon.

The door opened and two guards brought Richard Dover into the room. He was a slight but good-looking man. Also on the short side, no more than five foot six. He had some of his mother's features, her nose and her high cheekbones, and maybe it made him look a bit effeminate. He waited until the guards removed his ankle and wrist chains and nodded to Morton. The guards left, closing the door, and he sat across from us. Five days in county jail and his skin was already showing an unhealthy grayness to it.

Morton introduced me. Dover's eyes brightened. "You're the detective in the newspapers," he said, smiling slightly. "I read your column sometimes. It's good stuff."

"Thanks," I said.

"I didn't kill her," he told me plainly, his smile turning a bit sour. "The blood evidence is a frame."

"You think the police planted your blood?" I asked.

Morton cut in to score some brownie points by showing he was paying attention. "It's not like it never happens," he offered, jutting out his square jaw.

Dover's smile had turned more sour. "It's a frame. There's a lot of money behind this."

"And what about the scratches?"

"Just lousy luck. I got them in a barroom altercation. Sue had nothing to do with them."

"What was she doing in that motel room?'

"I don't know."

I sat back and considered him at length. His story seemed far-fetched. The scratches and his blood found under her fingernails. But he was far from stupid and he was showing a damn good poker face. "You think you know who's framing you?" I asked finally.

He shrugged. His smile was gone. He looked away for a moment before meeting my eyes. "This is a bit awkward. I'm going to have to admit to some bad behavior. I don't see any way around it. This thing with Sue could end up screwing me."

"You're taking your fiancée's murder awful hard."

"Sue wasn't my fiancée," he said.

"No?"

For the first time Morton looked like he was paying attention. Dover leaned forward, "Sue was, uh, more of a business associate," he said quietly. "She was, well, how should I say, helping me raise money from some of my mother's friends."

"Shit," Morton said.

"And how was that?" I asked.

Dover tried to show me a smile but it didn't stick. "Sue was a prostitute when I met her. Very high end. She was very good at what she did. I'd introduce her around at parties. Later, as far as they were concerned, they were screwing my fiancée behind my back. Sue would make them pay to keep things quiet."

"You were blackmailing your mother's friends?" Morton moaned.

"How much would you take them for?" I asked.

"Sue was expensive. Usually between ten to twenty thousand."

157

"And would this be a one-time deal or an ongoing concern?"

"As far as I knew it was a one-time payment. Maybe Sue was going behind my back and double and triple charging them. I don't know. Maybe that's why she was killed."

"So you think one of them killed her and set you up for it?" I asked.

"Yeah," Dover said. His lips had compressed into a harsh smile. "I'm pretty sure of it. It's the only thing I can come up with that explains why my blood was supposedly found on Sue. These guys have the money and the political weight to fix something like this."

"Jesus," Morton said. "What a goddamn mess. Even if I get you off for murder, blackmailing is still going to cost you at least ten years."

"Maybe. Sue always played it as if I didn't know what was going on."

"You're sure of that?" I asked. "You're sure she never told any of your victims that you were involved?"

"She wasn't supposed to, but who knows?"

"Jesus Christ," Morton said.

I had a pad of paper in front of me. I gave it to Dover and asked him to write the names and addresses of the family friends they had blackmailed. He worked on it for a little bit and then handed me back the pad. There were six names on it, three that I recognized. I couldn't keep from whistling.

"Pretty impressive list," Dover said.

"Sure is," I admitted. "You like any of these more than the others?"

Dover thought about it and shook his head.

"I've got to ask you," I said. "Your mom is wealthy, you've got a nice trust fund and all the opportunities in the world. Why have you been doing this?"

Dover stared at me before showing a slight smile. "Why not?"

Our interview was over. There was a knock on the door and

then two guards entered. One of them nodded to me and told me how much he liked my monthly column. I thanked him and shook his hand. They then put the shackles back on Dover's wrists and ankles and led him out of the room.

Morton seemed preoccupied as he gathered up his papers. As we walked out of the interview room, he swore a few times under his breath.

"Jesus Christ," he swore a little louder. "You see the names on that list? Jesus fucking Christ."

"You think he's telling the truth?" I asked.

Morton was scowling. "I don't know," he said. "But I sure as hell need you to find out. I'm not going to depose any of them unless I know for sure they've been blackmailed. This is going to be a goddamn mess!"

We separated in the parking lot. Morton looked upset. I didn't blame him much. These were rich and powerful men. It wasn't going to be much fun embarrassing them. I sure wasn't looking forward to it either.

If Richard were lying about the blackmail, it was a clever lie. His trial would turn into the biggest media circus Denver had ever seen. Six rich and powerful men—including one CEO and two state politicians—would have to take the stand and answer questions about whether they had illicit sex with Susan Laem and whether they paid her to keep quiet about it. At least one juror would be swayed by the whole thing. Yeah, it would be one hell of a clever lie, except I didn't think it was a lie. There was a look on Richard's face when I asked about the blackmail. The look told me not only did he do it, but that he'd do it again in a heartbeat. That he got off on it.

I was going to have to look into whether some rich and power-ful men had sex with Susan Laem and were later blackmailed. I knew the whole thing was going to get messy. And I knew I could end up making enemies that I just couldn't afford to make. The smart thing would be to drop the case. That would be the smart thing. But as my poppa always said, there were fools and there were damn fools. And I guess I fell into the latter. And there was also the money. I hated turning down the type of money Margaret Dover was offering. More important than the money, though, I needed a good case for my monthly column. The last couple of months, Braggs had to reprint past columns and I knew he wasn't too happy about it. I had a feeling that if I asked for too many more reprints I could lose my column, and then I'd be no different than any of the other private dicks working Denver.

I got in my car and headed towards East Colfax.

East Colfax is a street that the Denver Chamber of Commerce probably doesn't like to brag about. You can find streets like it in most urban cities. A street littered with pawnshops, strip clubs, massage parlors, and adult bookstores. Any time of day you can find your share of hookers, drug addicts, and runaways loitering along there.

Rude was standing at the corner of Nineteenth Street smoking a cigarette, his black eyes staring distantly into some godforsaken world. Rude works as a bouncer for a strip club a few doors down from where he was standing. He did two tours of duty with an elite force in Vietnam, spending most of his time hunting Vietcong in the jungle. The way he explains it now is he can't stay cooped up inside for too long, he needs to get out every half hour or so for some fresh air—even if all that's available is the brownish smog we get here in Denver.

I pulled up alongside him. He slowly moved his gaze towards me.

"If it isn't Denver's poet laureate, Johnny Lane," he said.

"It sure is nice to be recognized," I said. "As my poppa always said—"

"Cut it out, Lane," he interrupted. "What do you want?"

"I need to find out about this girl." I handed him one of Susan Laem's pictures.

Rude's eyes narrowed to thin slits as he studied the picture.

"She's the girl who was strangled by her rich boyfriend," Rude said slowly.

"Maybe, maybe not," I said. "I think she worked as a prostitute. If she did, I need to find out if she had a pimp, who she hung out with, or anything else you can find."

Rude didn't say anything. I handed him two hundred dollars, which barely made a dent in the retainer Dover's mother had paid me. Rude seemed satisfied with it. He told me he'd call if he found out something. He then shifted his gaze from me and stared back into his own private godforsaken world.

I turned down Nineteenth Street and headed towards downtown Denver. It was already past one and my stomach was feeling empty. I parked behind my office building and walked the two blocks to the Corner Diner. Carol was working the booths and I was glad to see her. She was a cute little thing, blond, blue eyes, her body fitting nicely in a size four waitress uniform. I kidded with her a bit and in no time at all had her blushing a nice red. When she brought me my food, though, I realized I didn't have much of an appetite. I guess the idea of tackling this blackmail business and stepping on toes that I just didn't want to step on was bothering me. But there was the money. And there were several monthly columns I was going to get out of it. I forced down a few bites and then headed back to my office.

Once I got behind my desk, I took out Richard's blackmail list and looked it over. As I mentioned before, three of the names were familiar. I recognized all the addresses, though. They were all in wealthy, exclusive neighborhoods. I got on the phone and after a little while filled out the rest of the list. One of the names was that of a judge in Colorado Springs, another was big in real estate, and the third was just plain wealthy.

Even though I operate a one-man agency I subcontract out quite a few of my cases and usually have a small mountain of paperwork that needs to be chipped away at. The last few months had been slower than usual, but I still had a good deal of paperwork to go through. I put Richard's list down and picked up one of the case reports from my desk. I tried to concentrate on the report, but had a tough time with it. My mind just kept wandering. At times I thought about Dover, about his blood being found on the dead girl, and other times I thought about the six men he claimed he had blackmailed. Then I started thinking of the dead girl, Susan Laem, wondering what the joke was that she had had on all the rest of us.

At four o'clock Rude called. He had a girl down at the club that he wanted me to meet. I asked if he could put her on the phone, but he insisted that I meet them there. It was four-thirty by the time I parked across the street from Rude's strip club.

Business was light in there. There were a few guys sitting around the stage and a few more at a couple of tables. A thin dark haired girl wearing a cowboy hat was moving slowly around the stage to Bob Seger's "Against The Wind". She already had her top off and was teasing some with her G-String. Rude was sitting at a table in the back, about as animated as a block of granite. I joined him at his table. He shifted his eyes sideways for a moment and then moved his gaze back to the dancer on stage.

"That's the girl you want to talk to," he said. "Gina. Her set's almost done."

We sat and waited until she was finished. A few dollar bills were slipped into her G-String, a few more were thrown on stage. She picked up the bills and slipped on a tight fitting sleeveless shirt. Rude waved her over to us.

Gina gave me a big "Hello, honey" and sat down next to me. Rude stopped her. "This is the private dick I was telling you about," he said to her. Then he shifted his gaze to me. "I think you're going to want to hear what Gina has to say, Lane," he said. "It's going to cost you a hundred bucks."

"I already paid you two hundred," I said.

"You paid me, you didn't pay her," he said. He started to look annoyed—one of the few times in all the years I'd known him to show any emotion on his stone hard face. "You know, Lane," he continued on, "it pisses me off that guys like me run around and do all your work, and you just write it up in your shitty little newspaper column and take the credit for it."

"Well, now. If you feel that strongly about it, Rude, I'll make sure to include you in my next column."

"You will?" he asked, sort of surprised.

"Sure will," I said. Of course I didn't mention how I'd include how he pimps for half the girls working at his club. I turned to Gina and paid her a hundred dollars. I knew Rude would take his cut later.

"You want to know about Susie?" she asked.

"That's right, darling. Do you know if she worked as a prostitute?"

Gina nodded. She took a deep breath. "It was kind of a shock to hear about what happened to her, but it also wasn't. Susie was so beautiful. She could've been an actress or a model or really anything she wanted, but everything was a joke to her. As far as she was concerned, life was nothing but one big joke. Yeah, Susie used to dance and she also used to turn tricks."

"Did she have a pimp?"

"No. Susie arranged her own business."

"Did you know Richard Dover?"

"No. I stopped seeing her before she met him. That was about a year ago."

I gave her a long look. She had a brittle smile and was nervously pulling on her fingers, but she was being sincere. I asked her whether she thought Sue Laem would be up to blackmailing her sex partners. Gina gave it some thought and told me she thought she would. "It would probably be just a big joke to Susie," she added.

It was what I had expected to hear. I started to thank Gina when Rude interrupted me.

"You haven't heard the best part, Lane," he said.

"No?"

"Gina, tell Lane about the videotapes."

Gina took another deep breath and let it out slowly. "Me and my boyfriend were in a store and we came across some videotapes Susie had made."

"Lane, ask her what type of tapes they were," Rude offered, a thin smile etched on his face.

Gina didn't wait for me to ask. "She was making amateur voyeur tapes," she said.

"What are those?"

"You got videos where one of the partners doesn't know they're being taped. There's a big market for them now. Susie had several tapes. I think the label was 'Bedroom Eyes'."

I could feel my heart skip a beat. I was pretty sure who her partners were going to be. Those tapes would create havoc in the courtroom, and just about guarantee Dover's acquittal. I wondered why he didn't tell me about them. I wondered if he even knew about them.

"I told you it would be worth your while," Rude said.

I agreed with him. I thanked Gina, and she gave me the name of an adult bookstore on East Colfax where she had found the tapes.

Things went easy at the adult bookstore. The clerk recognized me from my newspaper column and seemed to be a fan of mine. I showed him Susan's picture and told him that I thought she was in some videotapes under the "Bedroom Eyes" label. He helped me find them. There were three of them. He told me that he had sold a few of them lately.

When I got home I went through the tapes as quickly as I could. There was something disquieting watching Susan Laem, knowing that she now lay dead in the morgue. She was certainly beautiful, though. You could see why these men couldn't turn her down. There was so much passion in her, so much life in her eyes. At times, though, I could see a little smile playing on her lips.

The action seemed to take place in a motel room. My guess it was the same one that she was murdered in. The video camera must've been hidden directly across from the bed. Richard made a guest appearance on one of the tapes. From his body language it was obvious that he was aware of the camera. That answered my question of whether he knew about the tapes. Her other partners were men in their fifties and sixties. It didn't seem that any of them knew they were being recorded.

As I went through the tapes, I wrote down the track numbers where each new partner appeared. There were actually eight different men, not six. Richard was one, but I wondered who the other unaccounted for man was.

I phoned Margaret Dover at her home and told her that I had found some new evidence and that I needed her help. I didn't tell her about the tapes, or that I needed her to identify the men on them. I figured that could wait. I asked if we could meet. She sounded tired, but agreed to see me. I made sure she had a VCR and we arranged to meet at her home in an hour. There was an errand that I wanted to do before that.

The motel Susan Laem died in was off the interstate. It took about twenty minutes to drive there. The building was an eyesore: a one level concrete structure built sometime in the sixties. A sign out front advertised that adult films were available.

The desk clerk was a thin pockmarked kid with greasy stringy hair. I asked him if I could see the room Susan Laem was murdered in. He told me that I couldn't, that the police had the room sealed off.

I put the videotapes on the counter. "Listen, son." I said. "Do the police know you've got hidden video cameras in those rooms?"

His eyes dulled a bit, but other than that no reaction. "We don't secretly tape anyone here. If there are video cameras in the room they're there for our guests' private use."

"Well now," I said. "That's awfully damn accommodating of

you. I need to see her room. If I need to get the police involved, that's fine."

He thought about it for a moment and then got me the key. "If there are any tapes made, they're made by our guests," he offered sullenly.

I took the "Bedroom Eyes" videotapes from the counter, and then walked across the parking lot to Susan Laem's room. The video camera was hidden in some paneling opposite from the front of the bed. I checked to make sure that the camera was empty.

I guess it was wishful thinking on my part that a tape had been left behind waiting to play back Susan's murder to me. In a way I was glad there wasn't; it would've been a tough thing to sit through. It was tough enough sitting through the tapes I had. I returned the key to the desk clerk and headed off to meet with Margaret Dover.

The Dover home was in a historic section of Denver, just a mile or so from downtown. A big stone structure, big enough to be a small hotel. Margaret met me at the door. She looked a little more tired, and maybe more haggard around the eyes than when I had seen her earlier.

"Please come in, Mr. Lane."

She led me through a hallway and into the living room. There was a full-sized bar in it. I guess she saw me looking at it.

"Would you like a drink?" she asked.

"Well, now," I said, "right now bourbon straight up would do me a world of good."

She went to the bar and made me a drink and also poured herself some scotch. After she handed me a glass, I gave her a quick rundown on what I'd found so far and what I needed from her. She took it all in without saying a word, almost as if she were in shock. While I played her the tapes I would just show her enough of a participant so she could identify him, then I'd turn off the picture and fast forward the tape to the position where the next participant would appear. I tried to show her as little of the tapes as I could. I skipped her son's performance altogether. Through it all she looked ashen. The seventh man on the tape was identified as Chase Powell. He was married, wealthy, and owned a large accounting firm in Denver. He was a longtime family friend. Now all the men were accounted for on her son's list.

When we were done, Margaret sat quietly for a long moment. Then she asked whether I was sure that her son was involved. She wanted to know whether it was possible that that girl had arranged things without her son's involvement.

I shook my head. "Your son told me about the blackmail," I said, "and I'm certain he knew about the tapes. He seemed to enjoy the whole idea of it. He did, though, try to make it look as if he wasn't involved with any of it."

"And that girl wasn't my son's fiancée?"

"No."

She didn't say anything else for a good minute. As I looked at her it seemed as if she were aging before my eyes. Finally, she asked if there were any other tapes. I told her there weren't.

"These are good friends of mine," she said after a while, her voice sounding odd and distant. "It's bad enough Richard had to bring that girl into our lives, but to blackmail my friends and to make those tapes? My son went too far this time, Mr. Lane, he just went too far. I don't want you showing those tapes to anyone else."

I was taken aback by that. "Your son believes one of those men murdered Susan and fixed it so his blood would be found at the crime scene. I have to tell you, whether or not that happened, those tapes would create plenty of reasonable doubt."

She was shaking her head. "None of those men murdered that girl and the police did not plant Richard's blood on her body. I was lying before. Richard was not here the night that girl was murdered."

"Any idea where he was?"

"Richard was probably in that motel room murdering her. Who knows, maybe she had tried blackmailing Richard herself. Maybe she threatened to tell my friends about Richard's involvement. What I do know is I'm not going to make excuses for my son's behavior anymore."

She stood up and walked over to where her pocketbook was lying. She picked it up and took out a checkbook and a pen from it and then sat back down.

"My husband committed suicide when Richard was only four," she said. "Maybe it was my fault, but my son never adjusted to it. He was always acting out. He never showed any concern with who he hurt. I'm through protecting him, Mr. Lane. I'm not going to continue ignoring the awful things he does."

She tore out a check and started to fill it in. "You were promised a bonus if you exonerated Richard," she said. "As far as I'm concerned, you've done everything that I could've asked of you. I'm paying you in full, including the bonus. I also expect this matter to be kept private."

She handed me a check for twenty thousand dollars. I guess it was worth it to her to keep the matter out of my "Fast Lane" column. I thanked her for the check and left, leaving her the tapes.

When I got home there was a message from my fan at the adult bookstore. I called him back and he told me he had found another tape with Susan. "It's a different label," he said, "something called 'Naughty Girls', but it's really wild."

I was already paid in full and off the job. As much as I didn't feel like it, I headed off to East Colfax. I was too curious not to check it out. The clerk at the store had the tape waiting for me. "This one is really something," he promised.

When I got back home, I plugged the tape into my VCR and turned the set on. I was about to play the tape when I caught the tail end of a breaking news story, and it stopped me cold. The body of Denver businessman, Chase Powell, had been found in the mountains. The police believed he was killed elsewhere and had his body dragged to where it was discovered.

It finally clicked why Richard had left Chase Powell's name off the list and why he didn't tell me about the "Bedroom Eyes" tapes. I called a few police detectives that I was friendly with and was filled in with what they knew so far. Powell had had his head bashed in with something heavy and was last seen Friday, the same day Susan was murdered. The medical examiner now had Powell's body. After five days of being exposed to the elements the body was kind of ragged and it was doubtful how much they'd find. The last cop I talked to was out of homicide. He asked if I had anything. I told him I wasn't sure, but I'd let him know in a few days.

I tried to think it through. It seemed that Richard was involved with Chase Powell's death, but it didn't answer how Susan ended up strangled with Richard's blood on her fingers. I tried to work out different scenarios where he ended up killing both Sue and Powell, but nothing quite made sense. Most likely Powell found out about the videotapes and confronted Richard, but I couldn't connect that with Richard then killing Susan.

The thing of it was, I still felt Richard had told me the truth—that he really believed he was being framed for Susan's murder. After a while the whole thing started to give me a headache. I gave up on it and played my new videotape.

The clerk was right. It was wild. The tape had Susan in the same motel room with yet another middle-aged man, the guy being somewhere in his fifties or early sixties. He was thin and tall with gray hair and a thick gray mustache. And he was wearing an old-fashioned suit and the type of derbies they made thirty years ago. Susan got out of her clothes and then started to undress this guy—except it wasn't a guy. By the time Susan got the suit jacket and shirt off it was obvious her companion was a middle-aged woman with a fake mustache. By the time the pants were taken off I realized who she was and I just started laughing. It wasn't really funny, but I just couldn't help it. I just kept laughing until my sides ached. Because the thing of it was I now knew the big joke Susan Laem had over all the rest of us. And I knew why the preliminary DNA test matched Richard Dover's blood.

The other woman in the video was Margaret Dover. I watched for a while the pure amusement that sparkled in Susan's eyes as she positioned Dover into different sex acts. Dover moved awkwardly, her own eyes reflecting at times lust and at other times unadulterated shame. After about ten minutes of it, I started to fast-forward through the rest of the tape. There were a total of five segments with Susan and Margaret, all with the older woman initially in disguise. Each segment was wilder than the last. And with each one, I could tell it was getting harder for Susan to keep her joke to herself.

I stopped the tape. The segments must've been recorded over several weeks. I wondered what went on in the motel room that last time. My guess was Sue tried blackmailing Margaret. Or maybe she just couldn't keep her joke to herself anymore. Anyway, it ended with Susan having her life choked out of her.

I doubted Richard had any idea of what Susan and his mother were doing. If he did, he could have simply been patient and waited for the more accurate DNA test results to come back from Washington. No, he believed he was being framed which is why he was so anxious to have me hired. Of course Margaret had to go along with it. It would look damn funny if she didn't. And who knows, maybe she thought I could corroborate an alibi for him. But the blackmail and the videotapes spooked her. She couldn't get me off the case fast enough after that.

I thought about the whole thing and then wrote a letter detailing what I knew and what I suspected. I put the letter and the videotape in an envelope. After the twenty thousand dollar check cleared, I would deliver the envelope to the police. It only seemed right that I earn the money Margaret paid me. I was going to exonerate her son of Susan Laem's murder. Of course, it's a hell of a thing to have one murder be your alibi for another.

The police still had plenty of work to do to tie things up, but I was sure if they stuck at it they'd get it done. Richard was arrested the same night he had murdered Powell. He probably didn't have time to clean the trunk of his car. I was sure there was forensic evidence to find there. And I was sure there was other stuff to find. Richard would end up convicted for Powell's murder. And there was no doubt that the blood found on Susan would match Margaret's DNA.

I took out a bottle of bourbon and had a few drinks. I then started writing about mother and son Dover for my "Fast Lane" column. When I was done I read over my column and decided there wasn't a chance in hell I could use it. It wouldn't do my business a bit of good. The whole thing was just too damn unseemly. As much as I hated the idea of disappointing Braggs, the only thing I could do with my Dover column would be to line the bottom of my desk drawer with it.

It was almost midnight. I poured a few more shots of bourbon and thought about the day I had just finished.

Forever and Ever

When I originally sold this story to Hot Blood, I thought it would be an interesting contrast for them to have something as devoid of eroticism as a story could possibly be. Well, they wanted sex added, and I shoehorned it in as best I could, but it never really fit the story. Here's the original version as it was intended to be—pure noir with a bit of a nasty streak.

I noticed Morrisey eyeing the fudge brownies Luanne had sent me. "Anything I can help you with?" I asked.

Morrisey, the weasel, tried to give me a friendly smile, showing off badly formed, yellowed teeth. He scratched behind his ear and asked if he could have one.

"Of course." I held the box out to him. "Three dollars. Cash up front."

He kept the smile going. "Come on, be decent, man. You're not going to eat them all anyway."

"Probably not," I agreed.

"You'll end up throwing them out."

"No, I won't," I corrected him. "Not after waking up a few nights ago and watching you pick through the garbage for my last leftovers. When I'm done with these, one way or another, they get flushed down the toilet."

The smile drained from his face. He shrugged and moved back to his bunk. I put the brownies down and picked up Luanne's folder and took out her picture. It had been sprayed with a flowery

172

sweet five-buck perfume. I felt a lump form in my throat as I studied it. She was a doll. Big brown eyes, long flowing black hair, soft full lips. I knew her lips had to be soft. I tried to imagine how they would feel.

Morrisey said something. I carefully put Luanne's picture back in her folder and turned and stared at my cellmate.

"I'll pay you fifty bucks if you let me use your photo," he said, repeating himself.

I kept staring at him.

He shifted his small black eyes away from me. "Seventy-five," he offered weakly.

I shook my head. "I'd like to take your money," I said. "I'd really hate to pass it up, especially how my picture wouldn't help you one damn bit. But I've got a reputation to think of."

"Come on, man, you don't need it anymore. You're out of here in three weeks."

"That's not the point."

Morrisey started to argue. The way he saw it the only reason I brought in the money from the personal ads was because of my looks and if he had my picture he could do just as well. I tried to explain the obvious to him. "No matter what you convinced the ladies you looked like," I told him, "you still wouldn't be able to squeeze a dime out of them. You want to know why?"

A shadow seemed to fall over his small black eyes, darkening his features. For some reason it annoyed the hell of me.

"Because it comes down to intelligence," I said. "You should quit deluding yourself and stick with what you do best, sniveling and sneaking through the trash."

Morrisey's eyes glazed over as he looked at me. Then he lay down on his back, hands clasped behind his greasy little head. I had to fight back the impulse to get up and kick the crap out of him. Most of the cons in the joint regarded my accomplishments with awe, but there were a few, like Morrisey, who acted as if it were all nothing but luck. Like they could do the same thing.

I pulled out from under my bunk the cardboard box I used as a file cabinet and put Luanne's folder back with the others. Morrisey wouldn't have a prayer of running the type of operation I run, juggling thirty-seven women at once. My success was partly due to treating it like a business instead of just a quick score. Being organized, keeping folders on each "client", running credit checks on them. But again that's only part of it. The way I played them was the key. Squeezing every last dime out of them. Having them all hocked up to their lonely little necks. All but Luanne. . . .

I found Marge Henke's folder and took out her picture. She was blond, a little overweight, plain. For the most part a typical patsy except for one thing. A credit check showed she was worth three million, and I had her hook, line, and sinker and dangling from the end of my line.

A low convulsing sound came from Morrisey. His black eyes sparkled as he stared at me. I watched as he shook uncontrollably and his Adam's apple bobbed up and down.

"And what do you find so funny?" I asked.

"A joke," he said. "Ha ha."

He was smirking at Marge Henke's picture. I felt a hotness flushing my cheeks. "She certainly isn't much to look at, is she?" I asked, forcing a smile.

He didn't say anything. He just kept laughing. A soft, raspy, wheezing laugh.

"I guess not," I admitted. "But three weeks from now I'll be marrying her and thanks to California's community property laws I'll be worth a million and a half. And we both know what you'll be doing in three weeks. Same as usual. Rotting away. And you'll still be ugly as a stillborn weasel."

"I'll be laughing my ass off," he snickered. "Because it's a pretty funny joke. Ha ha ha."

He kept laughing. I felt the hotness spreading, tightening the veins in my throat. I closed my eyes. I had two choices, ignore Morrisey or kick his teeth in, and I knew if I started I wouldn't be able to stop. And if that were to happen I wouldn't be marrying Marge and her three million net worth. I squeezed my eyes shut, squeezing tighter until I could hear the blood rushing through my head. Until the sound drowned out Morrisey's soft, convulsing laughter. After a while I was able to ignore him completely.

Luanne visited me twice during the next three weeks. My heart ached just to look at her. She was so young and sweet and fresh. So damn beautiful. She knew I was getting out but the way I explained it to her was I needed time alone on the outside to find myself, but we would continue to write and after no more than a year we would be together. She pleaded with me to live with her right away. I almost broke down and agreed. I had eighty-two thousand in a bank account thanks to my enterprises and I weighed it and Luanne against the million and a half Marge Henke offered. Watching Luanne's soft brown eyes moisten with tears almost did it for me. I came within a hair's breath of throwing away Henke's money when common sense kicked in like a mule. After all, it would only be a year, maybe less. Then Luanne and I would have all the time in the world together. And we'd have the money to enjoy it.

I thought about Luanne a lot my last three weeks. About whether I could go a year without seeing her. Of all of them, she was the only one to have ever visited me. Twice a month, as allowed by prison policy, for the last two and a half years. None of the others had ever seen me except for the photos I sent, not even Marge Henke. At times some of them would suggest coming to the prison, but it would be easy enough to talk them out of it. Deep down inside they wanted me to talk them out of it. It was safer that way than to risk having their fragile make-believe worlds shattered by the hard cold truths of a con.

On my last day, as I was being led out of my cell, Morrisey made some crack to me about kissing my new bride for him, and then he broke out laughing. I told him to go to hell and that only made him laugh harder, his ugly face twisted in mirth.

When I was let out the front gate I found Marge standing there waiting for me. The sight of her made me instinctively step back towards the prison. The picture she had sent me was a bigger fraud than anything I'd ever attempted. It had to have been taken decades earlier and even still had to have been doctored. She was blond, or at least the stuff on her head had been dyed blond, but that was about all she had in common with that picture. The woman in it was a plain, slightly overweight, thirtyish year old. What was standing before me was closer to fifty and more than double the size. But it was the expression on her face that freaked me, though. Like I had caught her in the act of twisting the heads off puppies. And I don't know how I could've possibly been prepared for that smell. There was nothing in the pen like it.

"Marge, darling," I said and forced myself forward. I caught a stronger whiff of her and somehow kept from gagging.

"Honeypie," she offered demurely. She was caked in makeup. A heavy glob of blood red lipstick had been smeared across her lips, and thick pinkish rouge was layered over her cheeks. She tilted her cheek towards me, expecting a kiss. As I pulled away, I couldn't help tasting the rancid sweetness that came off her. My breakfast started to come up. I lunged forward, grabbing my duffel bag and hurrying away. "Let's go, darling," I murmured, trying to keep the sickness down. "Let's get married."

I ran through the parking lot with her trotting behind me. By the time we reached her car, a battered nineteen seventy-eight Chevy Chevette, she was out of breath, gasping for air. After getting in the car I rolled down the passenger window. Her smell had saturated the cloth seats. After six years of prison life I thought I could deal with anything, but not that. It was like onions and garlic and dirt and sewage and sweat all mixed together. Like sickness and rotting flesh. I could barely stand it.

She drove the three hour trip to Sacramento. Every few minutes

I'd catch her sneaking a peek at me. As we approached the city, she pulled into a fleabag motel off the highway, telling me she had booked a room there and she needed to freshen up before the wedding.

After we checked in, Marge again tilted her cheek towards me for a kiss. "Honeypie," she offered coyly. "After we legally marry, I'll let you do more than just that." And then she disappeared into the bathroom.

As I sat on the bed waiting, a feeling of longing for Luanne overwhelmed me. All I wanted was to be with her. I wanted it more than I ever wanted anything. I closed my eyes and could see her the way she was during our last visit. In my mind's eye I could see her standing in the same yellow sundress she had worn. The way her hair fell past her bare shoulders, how slender her hips looked, the way the dress outlined her thighs and then ended a few inches above her knees. . . .

Marge Henke's monotone humming filtered in from the bathroom and knocked Luanne's beautiful image out of my head. I got up, found some paper, and wrote Luanne a letter expressing how much I needed her and how it was only a matter of time before we would be together and when we were it would be forever. All the pain inside drained out of me and onto that letter.

The bathroom door creaked open. I folded Luanne's letter and slipped it into my inside jacket pocket. Marge Henke stepped out and I noticed all she had done in there was apply more makeup. Her stench was as strong as ever.

"I have to put on my dress," she announced irritably.

I told her that I would go take a shower. Inside the bathroom, I put the water on full and scrubbed myself, trying to get her smell off me. After a half hour I could still smell faint traces of her on my skin.

When I got out of the shower I yelled out to her about what a lucky man I was going to be. She didn't answer. I dried myself off, dressed, and yelled out before leaving the bathroom that she'd better be decent.

The motel room was empty. Her suitcase was still on the floor, but she was gone. I looked out the window. Her car was gone, too.

I sat on the bed and took out a pack of cigarettes and turned on the TV. At first I was sort of relieved but after an hour I started to get annoyed. As I stared at the set I decided I was going to take more than a million and a half from Marge Henke. By the time I was through bleeding her she was going to be one anemic fat broad.

I finished the pack of cigarettes and then walked over to the front office and bought a couple of more packs. The girl working the desk couldn't tell me anything about where Marge had gone. There was a liquor store next to the motel. I bought a six-pack of beer and a quart of bourbon from it and then went back to my room to wait.

I woke up at four a.m. with my head pounding and the set blaring away. Marge Henke still hadn't come back. I finished off what was left of the bourbon and then paced the room and kicked at the bed. I couldn't understand what had happened. Then it came to me. I checked my suit jacket's inside pocket. Luanne's letter was still there, but I could also pick up Marge's smell on it. There was nothing else to do so I turned off the set and went to bed.

I was woken up the next morning by her smell. It was stronger than ever. I lifted my head and saw Marge Henke standing over me, hands on her hips.

"Look at the mess you made!" she exclaimed. Her eyes were bloodshot and her skin looked even paler than before.

"Where were you, darling?"

"I don't know what you're talking about!"

I sat up slowly, trying not to move too fast. I had gone six years without touching any alcohol and the bourbon and six-pack had hit me hard.

"You don't have to talk about it," I said, squinting against the light. "I guess you needed time alone to think things over."

"I still don't know what you're talking about." She narrowed her eyes and peered at me, her large, doughy face expressionless. "My lord," she cried out as she glanced at the clock. "It's eight-thirty already. You better get up if we're going to get married!"

We drove into Sacramento, found city hall, and a half hour later were man and wife. The J.P. involuntarily grimaced as he told me I could kiss the bride. I managed to give her a little peck on the lips, and fortunately only tasted the lipstick that had been smeared over them.

Marge had a house in Davis, which was about a two hour ride from Sacramento. During the trip I started to doze off and was jostled awake by her.

"You must've gotten letters from a lot of girls." Marge said, a sly look on her face.

"I guess so."

"Why don't you tell me about them?"

I looked over at her. She still had that sly look on her face, like she knew something I didn't. "There's not much to tell. It took a lot of letters before I found the right person."

"I bet some of the girls were real pretty."

"One anyway." I smiled at her and squeezed her knee. I got no reaction, just the same sly, calculating look. "Most of the ladies were lonely and pathetic. A couple were nuts."

She didn't talk after that and I went back to sleep. I dreamt about being trapped in a sewer.

When she woke me and I caught sight of her house I almost broke out laughing. The car was bad enough for a woman with three million dollars, but that house? It was nothing but an ugly little clapboard shack.

"We're home, honeypie!" she announced.

Inside was worse than anything I could've ever imagined. The smell almost knocked me over. There was dirt and clutter and garbage everywhere. And that smell. . . .

Marge pushed me aside and went straight to the telephone. I overheard her talking to someone named Henrietta, telling her about how we got married this morning instead of yesterday. "He just took off yesterday afternoon," she said. "That's right, he left me waiting in the motel room all day and night. I don't know where he went. But he came back this morning and we got married." After that she called someone named Irma and gave the same story.

"Why'd you say that?" I asked.

"I don't know what you're talking about." She stood up, made a sour face, and ran her hands over her rumpled dress. "I have to go to the bathroom."

As I stood alone, a sickish feeling began to work its way into my stomach. I called my credit agency and asked for another credit check on Marge Henke, giving them her address and phone number. I then took my duffel bag into the kitchen and found Marge's folder.

As I read it, a cold chill ran through me. Her file had been tampered with, mixed with the file of another woman, Mary Henderson. I pulled Henderson's file and found Marge's earlier letters hidden in it. They were the rambling of a deranged mind.

In my mind's eye I could picture Morrisey laughing hysterically. I could almost hear it.

The phone rang. It was the credit agency, letting me know that Marge Henke was a bad risk with less than three hundred dollars in savings.

Marge walked out of the bathroom, peering at me expressionlessly. "What you doing, honeypie?" she asked.

I didn't bother to answer. I walked back to the kitchen and packed away my folders, then grabbed my duffel bag and started past her. "A big mistake was made, lady," I said. "Don't wait up for me."

"You ain't leaving me!"

"Oh no?" I started laughing. "What do they use to get rid of a skunk's scent, tomato juice? Well, as soon as I'm out of here I'm buying a case of it. Wish me luck."

"You heard me tell my friends about how you went away yesterday. Unless you want to end up in big trouble you better just read that copy of the San Jose Examiner I brought back with me. Page fourteen."

As I stared at her I felt a weakness in my knees. Luanne was from San Jose. "What the hell are you talking about?"

"You just better read it!"

I found the newspaper laying on the sofa. On page fourteen was a story about a young, pretty girl who had been strangled to death in her apartment. The girl was Luanne Williams.

"You killed her," I heard myself saying.

"I don't know what you're talking about."

As I looked at her, her large bloated body dissolved into a sea of redness. Before I knew it I was clawing at her, pushing her head into the wall, choking her. There was a surprising hardness to her flesh as she fought back. Her face inched its way towards mine. The harsh, fetid smell of her breath assaulted me. My senses were reeling. The ground seemed to be slipping sideways away from me.

I collapsed onto the floor, weeping uncontrollably. "You killed her," I sobbed.

"Look at the marks you left on my neck," she said in a calm, almost indifferent voice. "I'm going to show Irma and Henrietta these marks." As she stood over me, a horrible smile formed on her face. Like when I first saw her.

"Who do you think the police are going to believe, an ex-convict or a woman like me who's never had any problems with anybody? Especially after I show Irma and Henrietta what you did to my neck.

"Now, honeypie," she added coyly. "Why don't you get up

181

and lie down with me. You might as well because we're going to be together for a long time. Forever and ever."

Somewhere in the distance I could hear Morrisey laughing his head off. Laughing like there was no tomorrow.

The Manny Vassey Stories

In Small Crimes, *Manny Vassey is a ruthless mobster dying of cancer, and his willingness to give a deathbed confession sets everything in motion. In some of my early stories written in the 90s I had a prototype for Manny, a vicious, ruthless mobster also named Manny Vassey. This earlier version isn't as fully fleshed out as the* Small Crimes *version, and is also somewhat more of a caricature, but I thought it would be fun for people to see where Manny evolved from.*

Triple Cross

Here's the first appearance of Manny in a nasty noir story featuring a set of murderous triplets, appropriately titled, "Triple Cross".

The phone rang. No one should've known I was in Boston. I picked up the receiver and listened.

There was a pause. Then, "Hello, Hugh?"

"Hello, Lewis," I answered. My throat began to feel dry. "How'd you find me?"

There was a slight laugh that could've been confused for static. "You should know better than that, Brother," he said.

I did know better. There was a connection between us. I forced myself to concentrate. I pushed harder until I could hear the blood rushing through my head, and at last I knew that Lewis was in New York. It had been two years since I'd last seen him and the connection was as strong as ever. "What'd you call for?" I asked.

"The same as usual. How does twenty grand sound?"

My throat became so dry I could barely talk. I wanted to hang up. I knew I should. Instead, I told him it sounded fine.

"Good. Check in tomorrow at the Tower Plaza. I'll see you at six." There was a hesitation. "Have you heard from Dwight?" he asked at last.

"Not in years. And yourself?"

"The same. Good night, Brother." And the phone went dead.

Hugh, Lewis, and Dwight. Huey, Luey, and Dewey. We were

our mother's identical triplets. Her three peas in a pod. Her three pieces to a puzzle. There were other things, but it all amounted to the same. We were an oddity to her. Things to be held up as trophies, to be bragged about, but never to be considered as individuals. In her eyes, we were only parts to a whole.

Of course, later, after she caught us with the Hennesy girl, we became something else to her. Monsters. Sickos. Filth. That was what she called us, and kept calling us up until the moment she fell down the cellar steps and broke her neck.

Dear old Mother.

The next morning I packed a suitcase, carefully placing a thirty-two caliber revolver between shirts, and then took a bus to New York City. After checking in at the Tower Plaza, I called room service and had them deliver a bottle of Dewar's scotch and a bucket of ice.

A minute or so before six there was a soft knock on my door. I opened it and let Lewis in. I could've been looking in a mirror. We were forty years old, but we were still physically identical. Slim, baby-faced, with golden brown hair, and almond-shaped cat's eyes. Lewis was dressed better than me though, wearing a cashmere coat that matched his hair, and a brown silk suit matching a pair of Italian shoes.

"You're looking good, Brother," he said, more as a compliment to himself than to me.

"Thanks." I walked over to the service tray and poured myself some scotch. "You want one?" I asked, showing him the glass.

He shook his head. "Not quite my cup of tea."

"You should learn to enjoy the finer things in life, Brother."

"Maybe someday I will," he said, chuckling. "My latest girl-friend." He handed me a picture of a small moon-faced girl with an almost deathly pale complexion.

Lewis moved across the room to an easy chair, brushed off any possible dirt, and sat down crossing his legs. "Her name's Gloria Carlson," he said. "Her address is on the back. You'll be meeting her at nine o'clock at her place. I'll be setting up an alibi at ten, so wait till after midnight before dealing with her. That will give us a two-hour window with whatever forensics comes up with."

I nodded, still studying Gloria Carlson's photograph. "And what about the twenty grand?"

"She has over a hundred grand in jewelry, stuff she inherited. It's hidden on the top shelf of her bedroom closet. I've already lined up a fence who'll pay forty cents on the dollar."

"Why don't we swap?" I offered weakly. "I'll set up the alibi."

Amusement sparkled in Lewis's eyes. "Now, Brother," he scolded me. "You know we take turns. You don't want to be unfair, do you?"

"No, of course not." I turned over the photograph and saw Gloria Carlson had a Greenwich Village address. "How long should it take to walk there?"

"No more than twenty minutes." Lewis stood up, took off his coat, and folded it on the easy chair. "She gave it to me as a birthday present," he said, "might be a good idea if you were to wear it." He walked over to the door and stopped. "Remember, wait until after midnight. And try to do the job quietly."

I lay down on the bed and thought about the moon-faced girl who was going to die.

I met Gloria at her door. She was as moon-faced in person as she was in her photograph, but she had nice curves and a narrow waist. She greeted me with an uneasy, jerky smile.

"Hello, sweetheart," I said.

She took a step back as if she'd been slapped. "What's wrong?" I asked.

"Nothing," she said, her voice tight and brittle. "It's just that you never called me that before. It surprised me."

I laughed, I couldn't help it with the way she was looking, and the laugh triggered something in her. A shadow fell over her eyes.

She turned from me and walked into the living room and I

followed her, neither of us saying a word. There was a tension between us which indicated the state of her and Lewis's relationship. Finally, she broke the silence by asking if I wanted a drink.

"Not right now, sweetheart," I said, trying to smile warmly. "Maybe later."

"It would be no problem. Let me go make you one."

She started to get up, but I stopped her. "I'm not thirsty now," I told her.

We sat some more, neither of us talking. Maybe because of the boredom, or maybe because she did have nice curves, I reached over and made a play for her. She let me go on a little and then stopped me dead. "I'm too uptight right now," she offered as an excuse, her face reddening. "Maybe after I have a drink and relax a bit. Let me get you one too?"

She gave me an anxious look. I shrugged and she got up and hurried out of the room.

She was gone for at least ten minutes, and when she came back she was carrying a highball glass.

"I brought you your favorite," she said, handing me a glass, "Dewar's scotch."

I had the scotch warming my lips all ready to drink it when a thought stopped me. Lewis couldn't stand the stuff.

A nervous smile wrecked Gloria's face. Her eyes jumped from me to the glass. I shifted the glass away from my mouth and sniffed it. Nothing, at least nothing I could smell. "Alright," I asked, "what did you put in this?"

"What a-are you talking about?" Her smile was pulled apart by a facial twitch. "What's wrong?"

I tossed the drink in her face. Then, low and mean so she knew I meant business, I demanded again what she put in it. She didn't move. Her face became one big massive tic, jerking her mouth this way and that but not a damn sound came out of it. I slapped her hard on the side of her face, leaving a redness on her skin and a sharp crack resonating through the room. Still nothing. I took her pocketbook and emptied it on the floor and scattered the contents with my toe, but didn't find anything.

I walked into the kitchen. It didn't take me long to find the bottle of sulfur tablets hidden in the sugar bowl. I have a violent allergic reaction to sulfur, the one thing that physically separates me from Dwight and Lewis. Two tablets crushed and mixed into a glass of scotch would kill me. There were enough tablets missing from the bottle to do the job several times over. I took the bottle back to the living room and tossed it at Gloria, catching her flush on her nose. She reacted to that, her head snapping up and her mouth twisting into violent rage. I showed her my gun and it calmed her down.

"So what's the story?" I asked, as nicely and politely as I could.

She stared at me and then back at the gun. The blood had drained from her face. She didn't say anything; she didn't have to. I had smelled the setup when Lewis called me in Boston. I didn't have any idea what it was about, but it didn't really matter.

I sat down across from Gloria, letting the gun rest on my knee. There were several ways to play the hand out and I studied each one before making up my mind. Finally, I looked up at Gloria and told her to get out.

She didn't move. Her soft pale face was queered in a look of befuddlement. "Look," I said, waving my gun lazily at her. "I'm going to count to ten and if I see you after that I'm going to kick your face in. Get the hell out of here! One . . . two . . ."

All of a sudden she came to life. In a flurry of tears and bitterness words poured out of her, damning me to the worst kinds of hell. But by the time I reached ten, the door was closed and she was on the other side of it.

I searched the bedroom where the jewelry was supposed to be. There was nothing. I turned off the lights in the apartment and waited in the dark by the front door.

Eventually, a key sounded in the outside lock. I held my breath and pushed myself flat against the wall. As the door opened, I shifted my gun from my jacket pocket to my right hand. Light from the hallway filtered in, outlining Lewis as he stepped into the room. The door closed behind him, and in one motion I flicked the lights on and pushed the barrel of the thirty-two into the small of his back. At once I could sense his body tightening and then relaxing.

"Hello, Brother," he said, his voice controlled, his tone soft and lyrical. "The job successfully completed? Gloria cold and stiff and the loot all accounted for?"

He had started to turn around and I pushed the barrel harder into his back, freezing him. "Don't move, Brother," I ordered. "Why am I honored with your presence?"

"I thought I'd drop by in case you needed any help," he answered with only a slight hesitation.

"That wasn't what we planned. And there's nothing of value in her bedroom."

"No?" he mused. "That's odd. The jewelry should be there. It would be a shame to walk away from this with nothing. Let me see what I can find."

He took a soft gliding step away from me and as he did I pulled the trigger. The bullet sliced his spinal cord, causing his legs to buckle under him and his body to collapse like a sack of bricks. As he fell, his body twisted and his eyes caught mine. Not long after that those eyes became glassy and lifeless.

It was disheartening watching him die since it was so much like watching myself die, but it was also exhilarating. No more Huey, Luey, and Dewey. With Lewis's death part of me had been reclaimed.

A giddiness took me over and I had to sit down to keep from blacking out. My heart felt like it was going to explode. What I had wanted most for so long, at least part of it, had finally happened. I was no longer sharing an identity with two brothers. I was no longer split into three pieces. Now it was just Dwight and myself.

The giddiness faded. It was still Huey and Dewey. I still wasn't whole.

I got up and searched Lewis's pockets and had my first real surprise when I found Dwight's wallet. It had his license, some credit cards and a small amount of cash. I pocketed it, along with a hotel key I found for the Winston.

Before leaving I checked to make sure Lewis was really dead. It may have seemed foolhardy of me to have shot Lewis before trying to talk to him, but I knew my dear brother as well as I knew myself, and I knew I wouldn't have gotten anything from him. I said a silent prayer over his corpse and nodded farewell.

It was two in the morning before I got to the hotel room that matched Lewis's key. I stood outside trying to listen for anything useful. Finally, I sucked in my breath and opened the door. The lights were on and sitting facing the door was a round soft-looking man. He nodded at me, "Hello, Lewis," and then squinted and shook his head. "My mistake," he acknowledged, amused. "How are you, Hugh?"

I moved closer to him. I have a full head of hair and he was practically bald, but other than that he seemed to be almost a caricature of myself. His features were similar to mine, but were bloated and heavy. "Hello, Dwight," I said. "Looks like you put on a few pounds."

"More than a few," he corrected me. "And what can you tell me about our brother, Lewis?"

"I'm afraid he's no longer with us."

"I see," he said. "Could you please give me a minute?" A single tear appeared in his eye and started to snake down his cheek. He brushed it away with a finger.

"Maybe, Brother," I said, "you could tell me what's going on?"

Dwight had my eyes, but being buried within the extra flesh made them seem dull. A thin smile pulled his lips up. "I've run into some trouble," he began, his hands fluttering in front of him as he talked. Like the rest of him, his hands were bloated and exaggerated. I couldn't help noticing they were the whitest hands I'd ever seen.

"About a year ago," he continued, "I had the opportunity to take some money from an associate. Unfortunately, he's been entirely unreasonable about it."

"How much money?"

"Six hundred thousand dollars," he said without any change in expression. "To tell you the truth, Brother, I wish I had never taken it."

"Go on."

"I was working in Chicago," he explained. "Laundering money for Manny Vassey. A very nasty individual. I've come to believe he's insane. What I took was only a small chunk of what he had, nothing he should've gotten upset about."

Agitation had pushed his lips into a bitter frown. "He's been after me ever since, Hugh. I'm really quite worried about it. His boys almost picked me up in Los Angeles and I'm afraid they're still on my trail."

"So you've been trying to get them off your trail, huh?"

"I've been trying, Brother," he sighed. "I've had my hair removed with lasers and I've been eating myself sick, but I haven't been able to shake Manny." He lowered his voice into a tone of confidentiality. "I'm afraid to see a plastic surgeon; word's out on the street he's watching for that. The only way to stop him is to give him what he wants."

I stared at him until he shifted his eyes from me. "Pretty convenient," I said, "to have identical twin brothers."

"Very convenient," he agreed. "You have to look at it from my point of view. I can't sleep at night. I've been getting the most godawful migraines. Have you ever had one?" I shook my head. "Well, you should thank Jesus you haven't," he continued, his face shiny with perspiration. "Nothing's worse in the world, Hugh."

"So why was I the one chosen to be sacrificed? I'm deeply hurt. You obviously like Lewis more than me."

"That's not fair." A softness flushed over his face. "Lewis had a close call with Manny in Philadelphia and immediately saw the urgency of the matter. He also had an issue with Ms. Carlson that needed to be dealt with. And of course, he wanted a part of the six hundred thousand dollars, so we worked out an arrangement. But I didn't play favorites. It was my idea for her to put the sulfur in the Dewar's scotch. If you caught the tip off, which you did, Lewis would die instead of you. I gave you a fifty percent chance."

I could feel my lips stretching into a tight grin. "Much obliged," I forced out. "Tell me about Gloria."

"Now don't act hurt," he admonished.

"I'm not hurt. Tell me about Gloria."

"There's not much to tell," he shrugged. "Probably pretty much what you've already guessed. She had been making life miserable for Lewis for about a year now. A very obsessive, high-strung individual, and in my opinion, borderline schizophrenic. For the past three weeks, I have been convincing her to murder Lewis."

There was a bathroom off to the side from where Dwight was sitting. I walked into it and started to wash my hands. Dwight's voice droned over the water, explaining how he had approached Gloria and filled her with dreadful stories about Lewis, most of which were true. He had her so worked up she didn't know her ass from her elbow. She was convinced if she didn't get Lewis first, he'd kill her. Dwight had planned every detail of the murder for Gloria.

I took a towel and walked back to my brother, carefully drying my hands. He asked me how I handled Gloria.

"I had her beat it. I figured she'd be as good as anyone else to take the murder rap."

"I suppose she would. How did Lewis die?"

"I shot him."

"Not in the face, I hope?"

"No, not in the face."

"Everything should be fine then." His face melted into a broad smile, but it failed to reach his eyes. They stayed as lifeless as a mannequin's. "I had given Lewis my wallet to plant on your body. Instead, the police will end up finding it on him. Of course, I'll send Manny copies of the newspaper accounts, anonymously."

"I took your wallet from him," I said.

He stared at me, his mouth opening slightly, his eyes widening but staying lifeless. "I wish you hadn't done that," he said at last. "Do you think anyone heard anything?"

I didn't answer him. He continued, a desperation pushing his voice. "This isn't good, Hugh. I need the wallet on him. Most likely no one knows about the shooting yet. You could go back and plant the wallet. Of course, I'm planning on splitting the money with you."

"You have the six hundred thousand here?"

"No," he answered hurriedly. "I've got about ten thousand cash with me. Why don't we talk about it later when you come back, okay?"

I was still holding the towel. I took a step towards him. "Sorry, Brother," I said, "but there's something I want more than money."

A mix of annoyance and confusion flooded his face.

"Are you crazy?" he sputtered. "What's wrong with you?" But at the last second he had an idea of what was coming. He tried to get out of the chair, but I shoved him hard back into it and jammed the towel into his mouth. His arms flailed weakly at me as I choked the life out of him. During it all, I explained myself to him, and at the end, I'm sure he understood.

When it was all done, I fell to the floor exhausted. I couldn't move. Slowly the realization hit me that I was all alone. It made me dizzy, understanding that I was no longer split apart. I looked over at Dwight; he was nothing but a sad mockery of me. But he no longer existed. I was really all alone.

The adrenaline pumping through my body was too much to bear. I had to get moving. I had to celebrate. It was three in the morning, but hell, I was in the city that never sleeps, right?

I gave the hotel room a quick search and found forty thousand dollars in a briefcase. So Dwight had lied to me. I couldn't hold it against him; I was feeling too good for that. I took the briefcase and headed to Times Square.

Out on the street thoughts started rushing at me. A buzz ran through my body, almost like I was electric. There was no one in sight. As I got nearer to Times Square, I could make out people scurrying to different establishments. I went into one place and ordered champagne all around. I had to keep moving. I couldn't sit still. The streets seemed to be alive now. I had to step aside to let two people pass. But they stepped right into my path.

"Excuse me," I said, trying again to step out of their way.

"That's all right," one of them remarked. But they again moved in front of me. All at once I felt my breath pushed out of my body. I couldn't move. They were holding me up.

"We've been looking for you, Dewey," one of them whispered into my ear.

"You got the wrong guy," I tried to explain between gasps.

"Sure we do," the other one chuckled. Out of the corner of my eye I caught the glimmer of brass and then felt the second blow to my kidney.

Nausea welled within me, forcing a flood of hot tears. "We've been looking for you for a long time, Dewey," one of them was saying. "We had given up for the night and was having ourselves some relaxation when who do we see?"

I tried explaining to them what had happened but I was breathing too heavily. The words weren't coming out. Through the tears I could make out their hard marble features. The one who had hit me had taken out a hypodermic needle. The other one was still talking.

"I'm mad at you, Dewey," he was saying. "You had us running around the whole damn country." I felt a needle jab into my neck. Then I couldn't feel anything. Sounds started to fade away. Then darkness.

•   •   •

I woke up hog-tied and gagged. It didn't take me long to figure out I was in the trunk of a moving car. I didn't know how long I'd been under, but the muscle cramping within my body was unbearable. Whatever stuff they had shot me with left my head pulsating like a raw nerve.

I knew I had to figure out where the rest of the six hundred thousand was. That was the only chance I had. I tried to concentrate and get into Dwight's mind and was shocked to find I couldn't. With Dwight's death the connection was gone.

They stopped once during the next two days. I was left hog-tied as they poured water down my throat. "We don't want you dehydrating on us," one of them told me.

The next time they stopped, they untied me and pulled me out of the trunk. We were in a small private garage. "Welcome back to Chicago," one of them laughed. My muscles were cramping too much to walk. They dragged me through a steel door and then down cement steps into a small windowless room. Most of the room was taken up by a furnace and a butcher's table. The butcher's table had steel rings attached to its side.

They tied me to the table, securing the wire through the steel rings. They then left me alone. Shortly after that, a wide heavyset man entered the room. He was wearing a purple running suit and about five pounds of gold chains, and had a broad smile stretched across his face. His complexion reminded me of chipped glass. The other two men joined him. One of them was carrying a large metal case. I heard the heavyset man addressed as Manny Vassey.

"Hello, Dewey," Manny Vassey crooned in a high tenor's pitch. "Whatsa matta? You don't look so hot."

"I'm not Dwight. I'm his twin brother and—"

"Yeah, you're his twin brother." His top lip curled up. "That's why you're carrying around a license saying you're Dwight Jones." He reached into his running suit and pulled out Dwight's wallet and flung it at my face. "And the forty grand in the briefcase you were carrying is mine!" he exploded. "It's got my mark on it! You don't remember that I mark all my money?"

"If you check in New York, you'll see that—"

"Shuddup!" he barked, his face livid. "You always trying to take me for an idiot, huh?" He gave a nod, and one of his men turned the furnace on, the other opened the metal case. I couldn't tell what was in it, but it glimmered.

"Look," I tried to explain, "I'll tell you where the rest of the money is—"

"I'm sure you will," he interrupted. "I'm sure by the time I'm done you'll tell me everything you know. But you know what? I don't care. I don't want the money. You know what I want?"

I tried to talk but I couldn't. My tongue felt like it had swelled up to the size of a salami. One of the men forced my fingers apart. The other handed Manny Vassey a meat cleaver from the case. In one easy stroke, Vassey brought the cleaver down against the table, sending my little finger dancing away.

He moved his face inches from mine, leering at me. I could see the furnace fire reflected wildly in his eyes.

"What I want," he said softly. "Is to cut you into pieces. Hundreds of tiny pieces."

And I screamed through it all.

Next Time

"Next Time" is a riff on the Cab Calloway song, "Kickin' the Gong Around", and is Manny's second appearance. I just liked using him too much in "Triple Cross" not to bring him back.

There was a soft knock, silence, and then a frantic banging. Bill opened the door and saw his brother Joe standing in the hallway. Joe's face was so pale and shiny wet with perspiration it looked as if he was wearing a plastic mask.

Joe said, "Where's Jeanie?"

"What?"

"Jeanie ran out on me."

Bill stared at his brother and then moved aside. "Come on in," he sighed. His brother moved slowly, sluggishly into the room and collapsed into a chair. His hands were noticeably shaking.

"She ran out on me," he moaned. "She took all the junk and split."

Bill shrugged. "Maybe it's for the best. You got to get off that stuff, Joey."

Joe rubbed a thick hand across his eyes. "Man, you don't understand. I need to find her. Oh, man, look at me shake. You got anything?"

"No. You know I'm not a user."

"How about a drink?"

Bill nodded. He walked to the kitchen and poured a glass

three-quarters to the top with gin. When he handed it to his brother, Joe spilled some of it on his shirt, then gulped down the rest of the gin before coming up for air.

Wiping a dirty jacket sleeve across his lips, Joe offered a sickly smile. "I don't know why she did it. I always treated her right."

"What about that shiner she was wearing a couple of weeks back?"

"That wasn't me," Joe said, shaking his head. "We're in a biker joint and Jeanie walked right up to this ape and smacked him in the face with a bottle. Before I could do anything, she's sitting on the floor with a black eye. Did she say I hit her?"

Bill shook his head.

"I never hit her." Joe squeezed his eyes shut and moaned heavily. "If I don't find her I'm a dead man."

Bill looked around uneasily. "Come on, it's not that bad."

"Yeah, it is. I didn't tell you how much junk she took. Or who it belongs to." Joe looked away from his brother and stared instead off into the distance at nothing in particular. "I'm distributing for Manny Vassey. She took his stuff. Eighty grand worth."

Bill sat down across from his brother. Joe started crying, a soft, whimpering type of cry. "He'll kill me. If I don't get the stuff back I'm worse than dead. You know anything? She say anything to you?"

Bill shook his head. "Vassey's bad news. We have to get you out of town, maybe out of the country. How much money do you have?"

Joe smiled sadly, showing yellowed, cracked teeth. "She grabbed everything, man."

The two brothers sat quietly. Bill got to his feet, left the room, and came back soon afterwards. "I had a big score last week," he said. "Here's ten thousand. It's everything I have. Go to Mexico. I'll try to find Jeanie and Vassey's property."

Joe stumbled to his feet and took the money and embraced his brother. His body had a sickly dampness to it.

"I loved her so much. I always treated her right. She shouldn't've done this to me."

Joe turned and moved slowly to the door, dazed, unsure of his footing. Before leaving, he turned to his brother.

"When I find the guy she's doing this with I'll kill him," he promised, and then he closed the door behind him.

Bill stood silently. He reached into his pocket and pulled out a pack of cigarettes. He lit one and puffed at it slowly, his hard blue eyes staring into space. He lit another one. The bathroom door opened and Jeanie walked out.

She was thin, and the robe she wore opened to reveal long, sensual legs. She lay down on the sofa and her eyes transfixed to a spot on the wall. Her eyes had a glazed, vacant look.

Bill put down his cigarette, and slowly looked her over. Her face was oval, cat-like, fringed by red frizzy hair that went past her shoulders. Her lips were large and soft. His stare lingered at her narrow waist and then followed her long legs down to her bare feet. He gulped involuntarily on thinking about what that body had done to his over the past three months. He turned away from her and picked up the phone and called Manny Vassey.

Jeanie listened vacuously, then took off her robe and left the room. When she came back she was wearing jeans and a t-shirt.

Manny Vassey sat in the living room sifting through a large purple vinyl suitcase. He was a short, heavyset man with black oily hair and a complexion that looked like chipped glass. A jagged white eight-inch scar ran down his left cheek. Standing behind him were two of his employees, thick-necked wise guys with frozen, humorless smirks.

Vassey smiled, showing off two solid gold front teeth. He said, "So tell me again what happened."

Bill tried to smile back. It didn't exactly work. "Just like I already told you. Joey was real hopped up, kind of crazy like. He wanted to sell me your property. When I tried talking sense into him he just got more nuts and told me he was going to sell it somewhere else. I thought if I bought it and gave it back to you, maybe you'd go easy on him, you know, give him a second chance. He's my kid brother."

One of the wise guys behind Vassey chuckled. Vassey's grin widened. "You paid ten grand?"

Bill nodded. His throat felt so damn dry. He needed a drink bad.

Vassey pursed his lips, his eyes soft and thoughtful. He motioned towards Jeanie. "Hey sweetheart, come over here."

She obeyed, moving mechanically, and sat down next to Vassey. He grabbed her jaw with one hand and turned her face towards his and peered into her eyes.

"Just seeing if anyone's home," he said, his thick lips stretching into a nasty grin. "You're Joey's sweetie, right?"

She nodded, her face expressionless.

"Why ain't you with him?"

"Because I'm not stupid," she said, angrily. "I told him I'm not double-crossing you. That he could choose between me and the money."

"Yeah, is that right? I think you're lying. I think you just couldn't bear to walk away from all this crack." He broke out laughing. He let got of her jaw and let his fingers linger as they fell across her chest. "You're not bad looking," he acknowledged. "I got a position for you if you want it. Sweaty work, but no heavy lifting. Give me a call."

She stood up and walked over to a corner of the room, hugging herself tightly across the chest.

Bill exhaled uneasily. "What about giving Joey a break?"

"We'll see."

The two wise guys chuckled softly. Vassey busied himself with the contents of the suitcase. Bill and Jeanie both stared into space. It seemed a long time before the phone rang.

Vassey answered it and spoke softly. He hung up and

addressed Bill. "We found your baby brother. He had ten grand on him."

He took out a wallet and counted out fifteen thousand dollar bills, stood up, and shoved the money into the front of Bill's shirt. "Something extra for being smart," he said.

Vassey paused and then peeled off two more thousand dollar bills. "This is for the funeral," he said. "As a personal favor there will be a body for you to bury, but you're going to have to have a closed casket."

Vassey and his two wise guys headed to the front door. Before leaving, Vassey turned and told Bill he had an opening for a distributor, for Bill to call him on Monday.

After they left, Bill collapsed onto the sofa, holding his head with both hands. Jeanie broke out laughing and then fell on top of him, lying with her thighs around his neck. She pulled two crack pipes and some crystals from her pants. She put crystals in both pipes and forced one of them between Bill's lips.

Bill watched as she lit hers and as her eyes reacted to the drug, softening and becoming dilated. She had been right about everything, even how much Vassey would give him. He knew next time she'd set him up. He tried to think who she'd do it with.

His hands shook as he lit his pipe. It was only a matter of time before she double-crossed him, but for the next sixty seconds he couldn't care less.

Nothing But Jerks

The third Manny Vassey story. I wrote this as a way to work out some of my anger at my work mates when none of them called while I was recovering from surgery.

Lou Johnston felt worse than lousy. He had been shot in the gut three weeks earlier while robbing a bank, and although Doc Wilson had fixed him up for ten grand, the pain killers he was taking weren't helping a hell of a lot. To make matters worse, his feelings were hurt.

As he lay in bed staring at the television, a scowl formed on his face. He'd had nothing but liquids for three weeks and it left what had been a large beefy face looking shriveled, like a tire gone flat. The scowl added to the deflated look.

"Norma!" he bellowed.

A weary-looking blond in her late thirties walked into the room. There was a haggardness about her eyes and mouth. "Yeah, Lou?" she asked.

Lou stared at her sourly. "Get me a beer," he ordered.

"You got one sitting on the nightstand."

"It's warm."

"It's not warm. I got it for you only ten minutes ago."

Lou picked up the bottle and threw it at her head so she had to duck. The bottle spewed beer as it flew past her and bounced off the wall.

"Get me a beer," he demanded. "And clean up the goddamn mess!"

Norma stood frozen. After about a minute the muscles in her jaw relaxed enough so she could spit out what she had to say. "Just 'cause you're mad at other people don't mean you can take it out on me!"

Lou mimicked her, repeating exactly what she said.

"Go screw yourself," she snapped.

"Go screw yourself," he mimicked.

Norma stared at him, and as she did, her hard blue eyes softened. She walked over and sat on the bed and placed a small delicate hand against his cheek. "I know you're upset, baby," she said, a genuine tenderness warming her voice. "But your friends care about you. It's just that they know you're okay and they're probably afraid of being tied in as accessories."

"That's a lot of crap," Lou grumbled. "There are plenty of times I stuck my neck out for them." Then under his breath, "Goddamn lousy stinking bunch of jerks."

The phone rang. Lou and Norma looked at each other, anticipation tensing both faces. Norma got up and left the room. When she returned she was grinning. "Harry Lansome called," she said. "He's coming by later for a visit."

Lou pursed his lips. "At least one of them's not a total jerk," he noted with a childish smugness.

Harry Lansome was a slight man with a long face and heavy basset hound eyes. He shook hands with Lou, then handed him a box of Cuban cigars and pulled a chair up to the bed. Lou took one of the cigars out and sniffed it, a large broad grin breaking over his face.

"Norma will give me holy hell if I smoke this now," he said with a wink.

Harry smiled softly. "Wait 'til you're on your feet. They'll keep."

"Of course they will. So why'd you wait three weeks to visit? I could've been lying here dead for all you knew."

"Aw, come on." Harry shifted uneasily in his seat. "You know how things are. And word's out you're okay."

"Yeah, all I did was take a thirty-two in the gut. Why wouldn't I be okay?"

"I'm sorry, Lou—"

Lou interrupted him. "Just giving you a hard time," he said, his eyes playful. "Pal, I'll tell you, this thing hurts like a mother. Ever been shot in the gut?"

Harry shook his head somberly.

"It was so fucking stupid," Lou said. "All because I'm too nice a guy."

"Yeah, I heard—"

"That sonofabitch bank guard is begging me not to hit him. He must've been at least sixty and he's crying his eyes out how he's got a family and all that shit. And then all on his own he falls to the floor. Just like that. I should've whacked his fucking head. But I'm being too nice a guy."

Lou's features darkened as he thought about it. "The goddamned sonofabitch. He had a gun strapped to his ankle. Lying on the floor he pulls it out and shoots me in the gut. That after being such a goddamn nice guy and all."

"Pretty lousy, Lou."

"Sonofabitch. I hope they're still scraping his fucking brains off the wall." Lou smirked angrily. "Pal, I got to tell you this thing really hurts like hell."

"Hey, a few weeks from now and—"

"Yeah, I know, I know." Lou sighed, and his eyes hardened as he showed a nasty smile. "You should've seen the look on the sonofabitch right before I blew off the top of his head. What the fuck did he expect?"

"Who knows with these things?"

Lou nodded in agreement. He closed his eyes and placed a hand palm up against his forehead. "I better get some rest. Doctor's orders. You know, this is about as serious an injury you can get."

"Sure, of course." Harry started to get up, hesitated, and then sat back down, his slight frame hunched over. "I got big troubles, Lou."

Lou slowly opened his eyes.

"I wouldn't bring it up now with how you're feeling and everything." Harry scratched nervously at his nose, his mouth sliding to one side as if a fishhook were pulling at his lips. "But Jesus, Lou, I don't know what else to do. I need you to talk with Manny Vassey."

"That's the only reason you came here, huh?"

"Jesus, no. Of course I wanted to see how you're doing, but I thought I'd kill two birds with one stone—"

Lou raised a hand to shut him up. "Yeah, sure. I understand. You want a beer?" He yelled out for Norma. When she brought them her smile faded at the sight of Lou.

"Harry needs a big favor from me. That's why he came here," Lou said. He took the beer from Norma and drained half of it with a long swallow. Harry sipped halfheartedly at his.

"How are you in trouble with Manny?" Lou asked sincerely.

Harry gave an embarrassed smile. "Could Norma leave the room?"

"No reason for her to. She's gonna hear it anyway. So what are you doing, ripping Manny off?"

"Not me," Harry protested. He edged forward, his face very pale, almost greenish. "You know I've been running numbers for Manny. I just found out my shithead brother-in-law's been skimming off it for the last six months."

"How much?"

"Fifty grand."

"Does Manny know yet?"

Harry shook his head vigorously. "No, thank God, not yet. I want to pay him back everything plus interest plus anything

206

else he think's fair, but I need you to tell him I knew nothing about it."

"If he thought you did, you'd be dead. After a very long while."

"Come on, Lou," Harry said. "Don't joke about this."

"Who's joking? You know what Manny did before he got into the rackets?"

Harry nodded, a deeper and more sickish green coloring his face. "I heard something about it."

"He was a butcher," Lou said. "It's something he's always liked. I think it has to do with chopping things up."

"Come on, Lou," Norma cut in, "Harry doesn't want to hear about this."

"Sure he does," Lou corrected her. He turned back to Harry and smiled fully. "He still has a butcher's table. But he uses it only for special occasions. I got to watch a couple of times."

"You're making me sick," Harry said. His skin had become very pale, clammy, making it almost look like his face had been molded out of wax. "Don't joke like this."

Lou broke out laughing. "What's wrong, can't take a joke? Harry, I'm just playing with you. Don't worry about anything, okay? I'll speak to Manny and straighten him out."

Harry closed his eyes as if he were saying a silent prayer, then he got to his feet and grabbed Lou's hand so he could thank him profusely. He said something about having to meet some business associates. Lou watched vacantly as the slight man turned and left the room.

"Lou, honey, he really did come to see how you were doing," Norma said. She took a step towards the bed and stopped. Lou continued to stare vacantly straight ahead, his face expressionless, phlegmatic. He turned to her slowly and asked her to get him the phone.

"Please, Lou, don't—"

All at once his face was chalk white with rage. "Get me the goddamn phone!" he yelled, blood boiling in his eyes.

• • •

Manny Vassey stood in the bedroom shaking his head sadly at Lou. He was a short, heavyset man with black oily hair and a complexion that resembled chipped glass. A jagged white scar ran from his left eye to his mouth. Standing next to him were two of his employees, thick-necked humorless wiseguys.

"You got careless," Manny said.

"Maybe so." Lou shrugged. "But only for a minute. Not for six months."

"What do you mean?"

"Why don't you ask Harry Lansome?"

Manny Vassey pushed a thick hand through his black oily hair. The two wiseguys standing behind him were smirking. Manny looked down and regarded Lou with a thin smile. "This isn't funny. What are you trying to tell me?"

Lou propped himself up. "You're goddamned right it isn't funny. It isn't funny when you got some little shitbag like Harry Lansome ripping you off for fifty grand. Why the fuck didn't you ever check to make sure that little piece of puke was collecting what he was telling you he was collecting?"

Manny's thin smile pulled tighter. He turned to one of the wiseguys and whispered to him softly. The wiseguy left the room smirking. Manny turned back to Lou and told him he was going to have some company for a bit longer. He then pulled a chair up to the TV set and sat down. The remaining wiseguy picked up a newspaper and smirked at the comics.

It was over an hour before the first wiseguy returned. He nodded at Manny. "Fifty-two grand," he said.

Manny's face darkened. "It don't make sense," he said. "Harry's smart enough to know what that fifty grand will buy him."

Lou propped himself further up in the bed. "He was laughing about it, Manny. It was like it was one big joke to him." Lou's voice shook angrily. "If it wasn't for being incapacitated by my wound, I would've grabbed him by his greasy neck and smashed his skull in. I was never so mad in my life, Manny, sitting here and listening to that shitbag brag about fucking you."

Manny moved his head slowly up and down. "Thanks, Lou. I owe you one."

"Hey, what else am I going to do?" Lou lowered his voice. "About owing me one. Maybe there's something you can do to help me out." He turned to Norma and told her to get the mask that he used in the bank job. Then turning back to Manny, "How about leaving Harry with a thirty-two in the gut?"

"There won't be enough of him left for that."

"Yeah, well, it wouldn't work anyways." Lou rubbed a hand across his large rubbery face. "He's got a brother-in-law, Tommy Malone, who's a big bulky guy, about my size. It would probably work with him. And it would sure as hell let me sleep easier."

Manny smiled and the light reflected off his two solid gold front teeth. "I'll get the mask from Norma on my way out." They shook hands. After Manny left, Norma came into the room. "Are you okay, baby?" she asked.

Lou lay staring at the TV, sulking, his face embroiled in a petulant frown. "Three weeks and not even one of them calls to see how I'm doing," he complained. "Nothing but a bunch of lousy, stinking jerks."

The Brutal

The Plan

This is a mind bender of a crime noir story. You'll see.

As I drove to work I listened to the radio about the latest murder. I tried paying attention to the details, but couldn't. I had too much on my mind.

At the coffee machine all the talk was about the Broadway Butcher. I stood around and listened. The latest victim was a thirty year old librarian from Tampa, Florida attending a library conference in New York. Donald Vicks brought over the front page of the Boston Examiner which showed a picture of the victim while she was still among the living. She was small, pretty, had medium length brown hair and slightly almond-shaped eyes. Like all the other victims she looked a lot like Louise, my wife.

I left the discussion and sat down behind my desk. I forced the Broadway Butcher out of my mind. There were too many other things to worry about. Like the stack of sales inquiries I had to follow up on. And Louise. . . .

I couldn't get any work done. I was dead tired and I was worrying about Louise. About our fight. It had been a bad one, maybe our worst yet. And to top it off she had threatened to show up at the office to continue it.

And Louise, bless her black heart, is a woman of her word.

I had asked Jack in security to keep her out. At about ten past eleven Jack called to tell me my wife was on her way to see me.

His voice sounded hurt as he apologized. "I tried to stop her, but well, you know—"

"Yeah, I know." I hung up and pushed myself away from my desk, hoping to catch Louise before it was too late.

As I turned I saw her enter the Sales office. Donald Vicks flashed me a sympathetic smile and then buried himself into his work. I ran to Louise and grabbed her by her elbow.

"Come on," I pleaded under my breath. "Let's take this outside."

She pulled away, freeing herself. "What's the matter?" she asked, her voice rising to a high pitch. "Afraid your coworkers might find out about you? Is that it, Mr. Innocent?"

Bob Harrison, my manager, had opened the door to his office and was staring out, his pale blue eyes not at all happy. I looked at him in a pleading sort of way and then back at my wife. I felt sick to my stomach. "Louise, please," I said. "This is not the place—"

"No, it isn't, but no place is, huh?" she challenged, her mouth convulsing as if she were about to spit up phlegm. Then she started bawling, all at once like a switch had been thrown. As tears streamed her face they left black traces of mascara. She looked so damn ridiculous. The thought of carrying her to the window and throwing her out head first overwhelmed me. All I wanted was to watch her fall the five floors to the cement below. But all I could do was stand there and let her humiliate me.

Through her sobbing she asked where I was the previous night.

"I already told you—"

"Where were you?"

"Look, Louise, what do you want me to say?"

"Tell me the truth!"

"Honey, please." I took a step towards her and she moved with a surprising quickness, slapping me hard across the face. At first all I could hear was that slap echoing in my ears. After a while I could hear her calling me a dirty bastard over and over again.

Finally she stopped. As she stared at me her eyes shrunk to

small black points. The office became deathly quiet where only Louise's breathing could be heard. Then she started laughing.

"You're pathetic. Nothing but a pathetic lying bastard." Her laugh died away. "And," she added, weakly, "I guess I must be pretty pathetic too. I'd have to be to stick around as long I did. Maybe we should give each other a break and call it quits?"

I felt like I had been smacked full in the face with a sledge-hammer. My mouth dropped open and all I could do was stare at her. She was serious. Dead serious. After a while I could talk. "No, honey," I heard myself begging her, "we can work this thing out. We got to. It's too important." My voice choked off. Louise was studying me intently. She could tell I was dead serious, too. She opened her mouth, paused, and then she called me a bastard one last time. Before she left she addressed the office, hoping that everyone enjoyed the show.

When I returned back to my desk I was shaking like a leaf. I couldn't let her move out on me. Not now. Not after everything I'd been through. As I was trying to sort this out in my mind, Bob Harrison called, asking me to step into his office.

My knees were still wobbly as I entered Harrison's office. He looked uncomfortable. It's not easy firing your best salesman.

"I'm sorry, Russ," he started. "But—"

"Yeah, I know." I dropped into the chair across from him and met his pale blue unhappy eyes. "It's a shame about the Mullin deal. I was so damn close. Well, maybe if I push it a little I can turn it around."

"That's not what this is about."

"No? What, about Louise? Well, I don't blame you for being upset, but I wouldn't be too hard on Jack if I were you. I'm sure he tried the best he could to keep her out but I doubt that she—"

"Stop it." His voice was just above a whisper. He paused and then looked away from me. "I hate doing this, Russ, but I can't tolerate her disruptions to the office. I've warned you about her."

"She's not coming up here again. I promise you."

"You've promised me that before."

"I know. Christ, I know." I tried to smile. "I can't afford to lose my job now. Not with the recession. I'll work it out with her. I'll do whatever I have to." I swallowed hard. I had to fight to keep from sobbing. "Damn it, Bob, give me one more chance!"

He studied me. His pale blue eyes looked miserable. There was a slight crack to his lips as they formed a smile. "You never got home last night?"

I met his eyes. "I was out late trying to close the Richmond contract. Afterwards, I didn't feel I could stomach Louise and all her craziness so I spent the night in a motel. When I stopped off this morning to change into something clean she went nuts. That's all there is."

I stood up and told him I still had some details to iron out about the Richmond contract. He nodded and watched as I left. We had an understanding. One more visit by Louise and I was unemployed.

When I got back behind my desk I was shaking. I couldn't afford to lose my job, not now, not with Louise going to New York in two weeks. With Sales you're always traveling. I was going to need the alibi the job gave me when Louis met the Broadway Butcher.

I don't know what happened between Louise and me. For the first few years it seemed like we had the perfect marriage. I don't think either of us could've been happier. Then it changed. She changed. Everything with her became a battle. Everything became twisted and ugly. If I said it looked like rain, she'd mutter something under her breath about hoping I'd drown in it. One night I woke up to hear her swearing at me. It was four a.m. and she was sitting up in bed, her knees pulled to her chest, and in a barely audible whisper she was calling me every hateful thing imaginable. It went on for over an hour and during it all I pretended to be asleep and in my mind pictured ripping every limb from her body.

For a long time I thought about divorcing her, but it didn't seem right. She had to suffer. She had to suffer as bad as she made me suffer.

And just as important, I had to be able to get away with it. I wouldn't be able to stand it otherwise. Not after what she'd put me through.

I knew for six months about Louise's business seminar. For the last three months I'd made seven trips to New York. One trip every two weeks. My next trip would coincide with Louise's seminar.

For a while I was puzzled about how the newspapers were reporting the murders. They left in some of the details, like about the teeth and the fingertips, but they left out so much more. Eventually I realized what was going on. They were purposely misleading the public, trying to protect against any copycat murders. And in doing so they made my plans for Louise all the more perfect. Because no copycat murderer, like a husband, could possibly do it. At least not if they were going to match all of the Broadway Butcher's grisly details.

The newspapers were wrong about a lot of it, though, especially their psychological profiles. I got no thrill out of any of it. In fact, I wish I could've made it fast and painless for them. But I couldn't. They had to die the same way Louise was going to die. And Louise's death had to be pure horror.

When I arrived home that night Louise had a suitcase spread out on the bed and was folding her clothes into it. I just stood and watched. It was all for show. If she was serious about leaving she would've already been gone.

"You almost got me fired," I said after a while.

She looked up from her packing. The skin around her mouth tightened, and for a second it looked like she was going to let loose with something nasty, but as she looked at me a softness melted into her face.

"You were serious before?" she said in a tone I hadn't heard in years. "About me leaving? You really don't want me to leave?"

The fragility in her voice almost floored me. I had to blink to make sure it was really Louise standing in front of me. When I was able to compose my voice I told her I wanted her to stay.

"I think you mean it," she said.

I shifted my eyes away from her. "I do. I realized how close I was to losing you and it scared me. I don't think I could stand it."

"Where were you last night?"

"I wasn't with anyone. Does it matter?"

"Yes. Where were you?"

I looked her straight in the eyes. "I met yesterday with a client in Connecticut. I was tired. I didn't feel like driving home so I stopped off at a motel. By myself. That's the whole story."

"You didn't go anyplace else?"

"Like where?"

Louise stood staring at me. As she did, her eyes seemed to grow larger. I had forgotten how big they could be. "I don't know," she murmured. Her bottom lip began to tremble. "You really think we can work things out?"

I moved my head up and down an inch. Her eyes were quickly becoming moist. It's funny, but I had forgotten they were brown. For the last few years I had thought of them as nothing but small black holes.

She bit her lip. "I'm sick of hating you. I'm sick of what's happened to us. I can't take it anymore."

She started bawling and then stumbled to me, burying her head into my chest. She felt so small in my arms. Her tears so hot. The last few years she cried a lot but not like this. Always out of hatred or anger or frustration. Usually a smoldering combination of the three. This was different. As I held her, as I tried to soothe and comfort her, all I could think of was good. Let her think things were getting better. That we could actually be happy again. Later, when the time was right, she'd find out the truth. And her last few hours would be all the more unbearable.

We made love that night. Afterwards, she fell asleep in my arms, her head resting under my chin. I felt too exhausted to push her away. About all I could do was let my eyes close. . . .

I could see myself in an alleyway. I'm bending over something. Maybe a dead dog. I can't tell. From behind, my hair is a mess, sticking out and streaked with dirt and sweat. I'm watching as I move away. What I was bending over wasn't a dog. It was the last victim, the librarian from Tampa. Her face looks like raw hamburger. What's left of it. . . .

I woke up in a cold panic. At first I thought I was back in that alleyway. Then I remembered. I looked over at Louise. She had rolled over on her side and was still sound asleep. I collapsed back onto the bed.

It was the first time I had dreamt or even thought about any of the victims. It took a while before I could fall back to sleep.

The next morning at breakfast Louise was eyeing me suspiciously. "I'm afraid I'm going to wake up any minute now," she said.

I walked over and forced myself to kiss the top of her head. "You have woken up, darling. What we had before was the nightmare." As I massaged her shoulders all I could think was just wait baby, in two weeks you'll have yourself a genuine eye-popping screamer.

Louise grabbed one of my hands. "Maybe I should cancel my trip to New York?"

I stopped cold. All I could do was stare at her.

"I don't want to risk what we just got back." Her eyes were searching mine. "I can skip it this year."

"I'd feel too guilty," I said at last. "I know how important it is to you."

"We should be together now," she insisted stubbornly, her eyes still searching, still probing.

"We've got two weeks for that. And then an eternity." I reached down to kiss her forehead, but she moved and got on her toes so that instead her mouth found mine.

"You're trembling," she said.

"Because of how much I love you."

The next two weeks went by quickly. During it Louise fumbled around awkwardly, trying to do all the little things lovers do. I played along, partly to keep her in line, partly so that our final meeting would have just the right *je ne sais quoi*.

I have to give Louise credit. During those two weeks she worked hard trying to please me. Sometimes I'd look at her and find myself confused, not recognizing her. Her razor-sharp edges softened to the point of being inviting. Her eyes so damn big. So damn brown. . . .

Neither of us slept much the night before her trip to New York. She spent most of it on top of me; sometimes making love to me, sometimes sobbing silently.

I drove her to the airport the next morning. After a painfully long kiss, she burrowed her head against my chest.

"I don't want to leave you now," she said, her voice muffled by my overcoat. "I wish you could come with me."

We stood silently for a moment. She pulled away and gave me a timid smile. "Why don't you come with me?"

I looked long and hard into her eyes and found myself shaking my head. "I can't," I muttered, my throat thickening. "I'll see you when you get back."

She stood quickly on her toes and pushed her mouth hard against mine, making the kiss last. "If you get the chance," she whispered, "sneak down to New York and surprise me. You know where I'm staying."

I nodded and watched as she walked away.

I didn't go to New York. Instead I stayed home and thought about

Louise, about when things first started going wrong between us and why. I guess it wasn't as big a mystery as I first thought. If you looked at it honestly, you could say that I caused most of it. And to be even more honest, I must've, at least subconsciously, wanted it to happen. I must've been searching for an excuse to create the Broadway Butcher. The psychological profiles the newspapers came out with were a lot closer to the truth than I'd want to admit to.

Louise has come back from New York, and these days tries her hardest to please me. She senses something is wrong but keeps quiet about it, afraid to upset our newfound peace.

I would like to tell her what is troubling me. I really would, but I can't. You see, I do love her, probably always have. And if I told her, she would leave me. I don't think she'd be surprised, though. Sometimes I catch her looking at me a certain way and . . .

And . . .

At night when I try to sleep I see them. Different ones each time but they're always there. Always the same way. Louise can somehow sense the tension building within me. She tries her best to relieve it, but it doesn't really work.

Sometimes now when I'm awake I see them. It's getting harder to keep them out of my head. It's getting harder to keep from getting into my car and driving back to New York.

I tried throwing away the pliers and the other stuff. A few days ago I went to a store and bought all of it all over again. I couldn't help myself.

I know it's only a matter of time.

At least I'm no longer kidding myself.

A Rage Issue

This one's probably my most autobiographical story. Yeah, a Phil Leotardo look-alike backed his car into me while I was waiting at a light and he decided to parallel park on the street, and yeah, the guy came charging out of his car yelling it was my fault, and yeah, I had a few moments where I lost it. But that's where the stories diverge. My wife was in the car with me, and she kept me from doing something stupid. And so instead, I was able to work out my rage with this story.

The guy looked like Phil Leotardo from the Sopranos. Not exactly like him, he was thinner and had a mustache, but he had that same white helmet of hair and that same general air like he was some sort of mafiosa badass the way he popped up and down, examining the rear bumper of his red Grand Jeep Cherokee and shooting me dirty looks—as if the accident were my fault, which was total bullshit. What happened was I had stopped behind this Phil Leotardo dipwad in traffic and he decided to back up and take a parking spot on the street, along with taking a piece of my front right bumper with him, not to mention ignoring me blasting on my horn. Anyway, I tried to stay calm. It was just a fender bender, not worth anyone losing any blood over, but watching this Phil Leotardo wannabe strutting around and shooting me looks as if this were my fault started bugging the shit out of me. If my wife had been in the car with me she would've gotten me to control myself, but she wasn't. I rolled down my window and asked Leotardo why he didn't stop backing up when he heard my horn.

The guy was fucking beside himself over that. At first he was speechless with indignation, then he came charging towards my car, his index finger making short jabs in the air with each step he took.

"Didn't you see I was trying to park?" he bellowed, his face red and veins bulging on his forehead. "Why'd you have to pull up so close to me? What the hell is wrong with you?"

Whoa.

Before I go on any further, let me give you a little background about myself so you'll understand why I ended up reacting to "*What the hell is wrong with you?*" the way I did. I have a bit of a rage issue, something that was passed on to me by my dad. It came from the way he'd wale on me over any little thing. Before he'd beat the hell out of me he'd first have to get in my face, screaming "*What the hell is wrong with you?*" until I was soaked with his spittle and the world would start slipping away. It would happen a few times each week, every once in a while breaking bones, sometimes knocking me unconscious but mostly just leaving me seething. When I was fifteen he died, but yeah, it left me with a bit of a rage issue.

Some more about myself. I'm decent sized, not the biggest guy in the world, not the smallest either. About six feet, a hundred and ninety pounds. I'm also deceptively a lot stronger than I look. When I was twenty-four I started studying martial arts, first taking Kempo-Karate. I thought that kind of discipline would help me deal with my rage. Wrong. It was probably the worst thing for it because what you're learning how to do is beat the fuck out of someone. All that training and sparring just made me want to beat the fuck out of people for real. I should've quit, but I enjoyed the classes too much, especially the subtle way it fed my rage. So I stuck with Karate for six years, earned my black belt and two additional stripes past that, then moved on to Tae Kwon Do. Tae Kwon Do is kind of a funky martial art. While Kempo-Karate is basically geared toward street fighting, Tae Kwon Do has some really bizarre and complex kicks, some of them very deadly, especially if you're going against some shmuck who doesn't know how to fight. Anyway, I did Tae Kwon Do for three years, then switched to Kung Fu, the Tiger-Crane style. I've been doing that for the last seven years and have been getting pretty good at it, learning lots of ways to hurt someone really bad. The big difference between Kempo-Karate and Kung Fu? With Karate you're learning how to fight and spar, with Kung Fu you're learning how to kill.

Getting back to Phil Leotardo.

I didn't exactly black out when he yelled what he did at me, but it brought me to a pretty bad place; a place where while I was aware of what I was doing, I really didn't have much control over it. So I was out of my car yelling back at Leotardo, calling him a fucking cocksucker and letting him know that he caused the accident and if he thought any differently then he had fucking shit for brains (another thing good old dad used to like to scream in my face). Leotardo was flustered. He almost took a step away. Almost. But then he had to glance back at his jeep. There was a woman sitting in the passenger seat—she was about half his age, around thirty, either his daughter or a date; I'm not sure which but from the way she was dressed, I'd guess date. Anyway, instead of doing the smart thing, he decided to put on a show for her. He tried poking me in the chest with his index finger. I swatted it away with a tiger-claw move, really as basic a kung fu move as you can do, and without any real conscious intent, followed through with a tiger claw strike. You can think of it as kind of a slap to the face, except I hit him in the jawbone with the heal of my hand and drove with my legs, putting all my weight and power behind the blow. It happened so fast. Blink of an eye. A normal person hitting someone like that might stagger them, maybe even knock them off their feet. Someone like me, as strong as I am and with sixteen years of intensive martial arts training behind them, I'm going to minimally shatter their jawbone into dozens of tiny pieces. In other words the person is fucked. As it turned out with Leotardo, I did more than that. I killed him. Maybe it was his head hitting the curb when he fell that did it, but it didn't matter. Looking at him with his eyes glazed and half-opened, I knew he was dead.

The white-hot rage that had been driving me was gone and replaced by something very cold. It was like ice cubes being pushed into my eye sockets and hard into the back of my skull. Like I had the mother of all ice cream headaches. With a clarity of thought I turned to the woman in Phil Leotardo's car. She hadn't quite connected yet what had happened, but she knew something was seriously wrong. Her mouth had formed a small "o", like she wanted to scream but couldn't quite remember how. I didn't give her a chance. I moved quickly to Leotardo's Jeep, broke the passenger window with my elbow and grabbed her by her hair and pulled her head out the broken window. In the brief instance where the street light caught her face like that, I knew she had been Leotardo's date—there was no physical resemblance. Just lousy luck on her part and all because of a stupid fender bender. But what the fuck else was I going to do? I don't have to go into the gory details, but she was dead pretty quickly.

I took a couple of steps away from the car and looked around. It was dusk out. The whole incident took maybe a minute, no more than that. Miraculously no one drove by, and no one left the bar we were in front of. It was possible no one saw what happened. I scanned the surrounding buildings and didn't see anyone, didn't see any security cameras either. I started towards my car and that's when I noticed the police cruiser parked two cars up. As if on cue, the cop left the bar at that moment with a takeout coffee in hand. He gave me an odd, almost embarrassed kind of smile, then noticed my car and the jeep, saw that there had been an accident, and his smile faded as he realized he was going to get stuck doing paperwork. Then he saw Leotardo's dead body. He was a little slow on the uptake, and to be fair to him this was a quiet white bread suburb fifteen miles from Boston, the type of place where a double-murder like this never happens, and he probably never dreamed of dealing with something like this. Still, he should've moved faster. By the time he had dropped his coffee and was fumbling with his service revolver I had swept his feet out from under him. He didn't have a chance to put up much more of a fight than Leotardo or his date. As quickly as with those other two, he was dead and I was driving as fast as I could away from there.

At first my mind was buzzing, wondering if anyone saw me and if I was going to come home later and find cops waiting for me, or worse, have police sketches of me plastered all over the news, and how Carol would react to that. I wasn't quite panicking, but I was close to it.

Then I thought of my car. The broken molding, the dented bumper, Leotardo's red paint on my car. If no one saw me then that was going to be how they caught me. Garages would be on the lookout for that type of damage, and the police would be called as soon as they saw a car like that. I turned around, took some back roads so I wouldn't have to drive by the murder site, then headed back to Boston.

It hadn't fully hit me yet that I had murdered three people until I started driving back towards my office. Maybe I could say Leotardo was an accident, that I was too caught up in my rage, but as hard as I hit him I was minimally going to be putting him in the hospital. No, he was no accident, not if I was honest with myself. The other two, they were cold-blooded murders. I was in full control and clear-headed when I killed Leotardo's date and then that cop. Whispering in the back of my mind was the last thing Leotardo's date said to me before I struck the fatal blow which nearly decapitated her. *Please, mister*. Jesus, what a sad final two words. Thinking about it made me feel funny inside, but I forced myself to put it out of my mind. I had other things to worry about.

Once I got back to my office, I started driving the back streets of Boston looking for a red Jeep in traffic. When I found one, I got behind it, then angled my car towards the left as if I were trying to pass it, and clipped his rear bumper, making sure the damage to my car was in the same place where Leotardo had hit me earlier. Both of us pulled over. The driver of the jeep was a big guy and he was livid.

"What the fuck . . ." he started.

"All my fault," I cut in, smiling, pleading in a way, because I couldn't afford to let my rage loose again, not after what had already happened.

He stood staring hard at me, but his moment of fury had passed. His eyes glazed over, showing his disgust, which was okay, I could deal with that.

"Let's just exchange papers," I said. "I'll even buy you a beer if you want."

"Why don't we just exchange papers," he said stiffly.

We did that. After he left I called Carol on my cell and told her I had an accident, but that no one was hurt, just some dented fenders.

"Where are you?"

"Still in Boston."

"I thought you left work two hours ago?"

"Something came up."

There was a pause on her part. I could picture her brow furrowed in confusion. "But you told me two hours ago that you were leaving work."

I took a deep breath. I was starting to feel a little hot under the collar, a little of my rage resurfacing. Not that I thought Carol was calling me a liar, but that's the thing with rage, once you let it out it's hard to keep contained.

"Yeah, I was leaving the office, but an idea popped into my

head, and I had to work on it, you know, see it through," I explained as patiently as I could.

"Oh. Okay," then her voice taking on a tinge of excitement, maybe some fear, "Have you been listening to the news?"

"No."

"Dave, three people were killed right in front of Maguire's."

"Really?" I felt a sickness in my gut. "What happened? Some sort of shooting?"

"No. They were beaten to death. Right in front of Maguire's! That's only three miles from our house. Can you believe that?"

"Wow."

"I know."

"Well, I'll see you soon."

I cut off the call. I had to.

That night I was distracted. My thoughts kept drifting on me. Carol thought it was because I was worried about the accident, and she kept trying to console me, telling me that accidents happen, that I'd get the car fixed, and yeah, my insurance rates would probably go up, but we'd be able to deal with it. She was good about it. Coming over to me rubbing my neck and shoulder, trying to ease my worrying. I'd smile up at her, but then just as quickly lose my train of thought again.

The three murders were the lead story on the eleven o'clock news. It turned out Phil Leotardo's real name was George Conly, and the woman with him was Elaine Halprin, and described as a female companion. The cop was Joe Sullivan, a six year veteran on the force who was leaving behind a wife and three kids. I felt bad about that. Carol noticed the way I reacted to that part of the story and rubbed my back and gave me an understanding smile. Kind of like: *isn't that sweet that you feel so much for other people.* I didn't bother correcting her.

It didn't sound like the police had anything, but that didn't really help me much. Maybe they were holding back information. Maybe any minute now cops were going to be breaking down my front door. That was what I kept thinking. But at least they didn't plaster any police sketches of me over the airways.

That was a hard night. I didn't sleep for a second, just kept tossing and turning while I waited for the cops to show up. Again, Carol thought it was because of my worrying about my fender bender. She knew I hated car accidents. The next morning the newspapers had more about the killings—at least about the victims. It turned out George Conly had mob ties, and the police suspected that that might have had something do with the killings. In any case, no sketches of suspects showed up and nothing about any witnesses.

It was a hard day at work also the way everyone gossiped about the murders, and it made me feel like crap hearing all of it. I survived the day, though, and over the next week things got better.

It was a week after the incident that I took my car to a body shop to get the bumper fixed. The town cops where the murder happened called me at work to ask if I could come down to the station to answer some questions. I was prepared for it so it didn't phase me. I brought my insurance paperwork with me, and after they spoke with the guy in Boston who I hit, and probably also had someone check his car, they were satisfied. The lead detective apologized for any inconvenience they caused me, and I told him I understood given the circumstances. I was just glad they didn't call me at home. I couldn't help feeling that Carol would've suspected something, maybe even guessed that I purposely got into the second accident to cover the first one.

It was over three weeks after the murders when I had my big scare. Saturday morning the doorbell rang and two cops were standing on my doorstep, both looking like they could spit nails. One was a square-looking guy with a big bushy mustache that hid his upper lip, the other was a young guy, his face pinched and angry. I was sure they were there to arrest me, and was silently sizing them up and trying to figure out if I could take them if I had to. It turned out they were there to collect money for a fund set up for Joe Sullivan's family. I dug deeply, not too deeply so they'd suspect anything, but deep enough to make a difference. The cop with the bushy mustache thanked me.

"It's hard having to do this," he told me. "Joe was a good kid. Jesus, what a world we live in."

I nodded and watched them leave.

Over the next six months things started to get back to normal. I'd still find myself jolted awake at times, thinking the cops were on to me, but for the most part I was able to put those murders behind. I also knew I had to do something about my rage. I thought about seeing a therapist, but the problem was I was afraid I might let something slip—and not just about these last murders, but about some of the others that had happened over the years. Yeah, these weren't the first. You see, I just have this rage issue. It was still hard to believe I had gotten away with as many as I have, but somehow there were never any witnesses, at least none that ever slipped past me. I don't think about them much; just sometimes late at night, and that would usually be nothing more than a flash of worry that somehow the cops were going to discover me. Anyway, I had all that buzzing through my mind and was trying to figure out how safe it would be to see a therapist, and I just wasn't paying enough attention to the road and ended up hitting a BMW as it was backing out of a parking space. Maybe it was my fault, maybe it was the other driver's, I wasn't sure. The other driver was a woman, in her seventies, shit, old enough to be my mother. I didn't say a word to her, but maybe I had an angry look on my face. I don't know. Whatever, something set her off and her little prune face became rigid with anger.

"Didn't you see me backing up?" she complained, her voice sour, her body seeming to bristle. "What is wrong with you? Well? Well?"

Whoa. . . .

Adrenaline

This is a violent story, not for the fainthearted, and in some ways it's a story about violence. It's also a story about one man being tied up with razor wire and tortured by four desperate criminals, and either that man or those four criminals are getting out alive, and it's even money which way it ends up.

The elderly couple who owned the house lay dead upstairs in their bedroom. At least I was assuming they were dead. I heard them crying out earlier, then silence. Victor made an offhand comment to Al about how he held them down while Benny cut their throats. Maybe he was lying. Maybe Benny screwed up and they were still alive, but if they were they weren't making any noise.

We were all now in the basement. The whole gang. Me, Benny, Victor, Tony and Al. They had me tied to a wooden chair, my ankles secured tightly with razor wire to the chair legs, my wrists tied with rope to the chair arms. Benny had already used pliers to pull off three of my fingernails. He'd spent the last two hours sticking pins into the exposed flesh, now he was lighting matches and burning the tips of my fingers. He was trying to make me tell them where I had hidden the eight hundred grand—I guess he was doing what he thought he had to, but it looked to me like he was enjoying it too much. The last time I passed out I caught glimpses of the rest of them when I came to. Victor's face a blank slate—he couldn't care less what was happening to me, just like he didn't give a shit what happened to the old folks upstairs; Tony smirking, maybe looking a little queasy; Al staring at me with big soulful eyes as if what was happening to me pained him greatly. As far as I was concerned, not a peep. Let them do whatever the fuck they wanted, they weren't going to get word one out of me. Fifteen years ago when I was a member of the US Army's special forces, I spent a year and a half in Iraq and I'd find myself wondering then if I'd be able to stand up to torture if I was caught. Now I knew. They could've done anything to me and they wouldn't have cracked me. The pain might've brought tears to my eyes, and at times made me pass out, but I wasn't talking.

After I left the army I bounced around a lot and worked everything from construction to private security to fisherman. It was hard staying in one job for too long. I had done too much killing and too many missions, and missed the adrenaline rushes from my time in special forces. It got to the point where I was antsy all the time. I couldn't sleep or do much of anything. Five years ago I started putting my training to use, doing a string of bank jobs up and down the East Coast. I didn't kill anyone; I don't think I even hurt anyone badly—I also didn't make nearly as much money as I'd expected, but it gave me what I needed, especially the rush. At least then I started sleeping better.

Sixteen months ago I met up with Al. He was putting together a gang to knock over high-stake poker games and they needed someone like me—someone who could plan out the operations and was as fearless as the rest of them, maybe even more so. They had enough muscle already with Victor and Tony, and plenty of psycho with Benny, but while Al was a smart guy, he didn't have the operational skills that I had. Without someone like me, every job would end up a massacre.

We pulled five jobs without incident, at least nothing more serious than Benny slashing people's faces with the barrel of his 9 mm. The sixth job all hell broke loose. It was bad news from the start. First Al's info was all wrong—instead of it being a group of medical professionals, it was mafia—high end guys, big shots. Then Victor wasn't watching carefully enough and let one of them pull out a gun, and before you knew it bullets were flying everywhere. While everyone was being shot up, I grabbed the money and ran. It was a lot more money than we were expecting—at least ten times as much. Maybe Al didn't screw up with his info, maybe he just didn't want to tell us who we were really hitting. Either way, it didn't matter to me. I kept running all the way to Los Angeles.

Earlier today a car pulled up to me on the street for directions. The window rolled down, and when I leaned over to help there was Benny in the driver's seat leering at me. Before I could react I was jolted from behind with a stun gun. Christ, I'd thought they were all dead, but it was still damn careless of me. Right before I dropped to the pavement in convulsions I couldn't help wondering how many of them had survived. It turned out they all did. They might each have taken some bullets, but they were all still living and breathing. I didn't bother wondering about how they'd found me. It wasn't as if I was being all that careful the last four months. It made me think that maybe there was a reason for that. That maybe I had gotten bored and was looking for a big-time adrenaline rush. That I was hoping one or more of them had survived and would find me and put me in this situation. . . .

Or maybe I was just overanalyzing the situation, trying to do anything to keep my mind off what was happening to me.

Fuck if I knew.

Except . . . I had to keep my mind spinning on other thoughts than what was being done to my fingers.

How long ago did they snatch me? Ten hours ago? More? Less? I don't know. I was losing track of time.

More matches were lit. Benny showed a hard grin as he pressed the burnt ends against the exposed flesh where my fingernails had been, his expression turning somewhat demented—partly from the way his face had caved in when one of the Mafioso's bullets took out a chunk of his cheekbone, and partly from how bright his eyes had become. Yeah, he was enjoying this way too much. I decided then I was going to see him dead. No matter what was in store for me, he was going to die first.

Spiteful sonofabitch, ain't I?

At least it gave me something to focus my mind on.

Benny tried to give me a sympathetic smile, but the craziness shining in his eyes made it a joke.

"Joe, why the fuck don't you just talk?" he said.

"I think it's 'cause he's enjoying it," Victor offered from somewhere behind him.

Benny took hold of my jaw, his fingers digging hard into the bone. He forced my head upwards so our eyes would meet, but I kept my focus somewhere around the middle of his skull as if I were staring straight into his brain.

"Is that it?" Benny asked. "You one of them sick masochistic fucks who gets off on what I'm doing to you?" He increased the pressure with his fingers, squeezing harder into my jawbone. He studied me like that for a good thirty seconds, then to Victor, "I don't think that's it. I think he's just a stubborn fuck."

"You ask me he's getting off on it," Victor said, half-teasing.

"Nah, I don't think so. He's just too fucking stubborn for his own good." Benny shook his head sadly. Then he turned sideways and asked, "What do you think, big guy?"

Al, disgusted, said, "Just get on with it, okay?"

Benny focused his attention back to me.

"You going to make me hurt you real bad first, is that it?"

I kept staring through him, refusing to say a word.

He made a *tsk-tsk* noise.

"Joe, so far I've just been fooling around. You really going to make me get serious? Shit, I hate having to do this to you. Before you fucked us on that last job, I liked you, thought you were a good guy."

Sure, I could tell he hated every second of what he was doing.

Sonofabitch. I ignored it when he picked up a nutcracker. Fuck if he was going to see fear or anything else in my eyes. Victor helped him pull my fingers apart, and then my middle finger was clasped between two metal bars. Benny twisted the nutcracker until the bone in my finger cracked like a dry stick. A satisfied smirk showing, he kept twisting.

"You're crying, Joe," he said, his voice more of a grunt from his exertion. "Fuck, just like a little girl. Why don't you just tell us where our money is so we can get this over with?"

He kept twisting. Out of the corner of my eye I could see the skin separating on my finger. I could see the broken bone sticking out of the gaping wound. Damn, it hurt like a mother. I had been concentrating like hell to welcome the pain and become one with it, and for the most part before it had worked. This time, though, fuck. One more hard twist and the world ebbed violently in and out like a wave crashing over me, then everything just disappeared.

I don't know how long I was out. I had passed out a few times before this, but those times it seemed like I was only gone for a few seconds, this time I knew it had been much longer, maybe as long as a half hour.

Gradually I became aware of a tapping noise. My eyes were being forced open and as they focused the grayish blur in front of me transformed into Al's round sorrowful face. He was slapping me lightly, trying to bring me to consciousness. Once he realized he had succeeded he stopped his slapping.

As he stared at me, his eyes were as sad and soulful as ever and he even let them turn a bit moist.

"Fuck, Joe, it doesn't have to be this way," he said. "If you do the right thing, we can all walk out of here happy."

The two of us were alone. I guess the plan was to play good cop, bad cop. Or good torturer, bad torturer. My finger was throbbing as if it were being pulled apart in a vise. I didn't let on, though. A quick sideways glance of it showed they had wrapped a bandage around it, probably hoping I'd forget that the bone was popping out of the skin.

Al's thick eyelids lowered a bit as he tried smiling at me. He was maybe fifty and had a heavily-lined face and dark curly brown hair. A big man, bigger than the rest of them, but also softer than any of the others. Kind of a teddy bear-type. At two-sixty, he probably outweighed Benny by a hundred pounds, but then again, Benny was as hard as a blade of steel.

"You'll still get some money out of this, Joe," he said. "Not a full share, not after what you put us through, but something. I'll try to get them to agree to fifty grand. How does that sound?"

I let that sit between us for a while, his sad soulful eyes ever hopeful, then I asked him if he thought I was a fucking idiot. It was the first words I'd spoken since they'd snatched me. He seemed surprised I had bothered to respond to him, then he manufactured some hurt in those soulful eyes of his over the fact that I didn't believe him.

"I don't think that at all, Joe. If you can just trust me, you can walk out of here alive and with some money in your pocket. By the end of the day we can all be happy. Now what would be wrong with that?"

"One more time," I said. "I'm not an idiot. I know I'm a dead man here so quit the fucking act."

Al was frowning, his large brow heavily creased.

"I don't know why you're saying this. There's no percentage in us killing you. If we leave your body here, you'll connect us to the couple upstairs. If we take your body with us, then we have to worry about how to dispose of it. It's just so much easier for everyone if you walk away on your own—"

"Shut the fuck up." I waited until he closed his mouth, then I went on. "Here's the deal, and I'm only offering it once. I accept the fact I'm a dead man, and to be honest about it, I don't give a shit. You can have Benny fucking cut me open and pull my intestines out inch by inch and I'm not talking. I have nothing against you, Al, and not much against Victor and Tony, but I'm not too happy with Benny right now. If you want to know where I hid the eight hundred grand, you have to kill that psycho bastard in front of me. I have to see him die. You do that and I'll tell you where the money is. I know I'm going to die today, but I want to see that cocksucker go first. One more thing. I lose any part of me—a finger, a tooth, anything, and the deal's off. The money will disappear with me."

When I was mentioning the part about Benny cutting me open and pulling my intestines out inch by inch, I could see the idea of that flash in Al's eyes, but he quickly dismissed it, realizing it wouldn't do the trick. It wouldn't get me to talk. Once he dismissed it, his eyes went back to being soulful and hurt. What a bunch of fucking hogwash he tried selling me about the difficulty in getting rid of me. Benny would have no trouble cutting me into pieces. Put those pieces in some garbage bags, and it would be no problem leaving me scattered along the highway. Or use a few gallons of sulfuric acid to melt off my face and fingerprints. Getting rid of my body would be easy, and I was sure Benny had already thought up a dozen ways to do it. Jesus, it was one thing to torture me, another to insult my intelligence.

Al's face darkened as he thought over my proposal. Finally, he shook his head.

"I can't do that, Joe. For chrissakes, let's be reasonable."

I'd already tuned him out. When they snatched me they had emptied my pockets. I knew they had searched the motel room I'd been staying in. There were no other clues where the money might be. I knew as well as they did that without me talking they were never going to have any idea where the money was. I couldn't help smiling at the thought of that. Al took hold of my face and moved it so we were again looking at each other. He could see the reason behind my smile. He let go of me and tugged absentmindedly at his lip as he regarded me.

"Joe," he started, his voice weak, awkward, "if you don't start cooperating with us it's going to get ugly. You know that don't you?"

I didn't bother answering him. I didn't have to.

We sat together for a few minutes with Al wringing his hands and trying to think of something to say to me. Then he got up and left. When he came back, it was with the rest of them. Benny stormed to the front and hit me hard in the ear, knocking me to the floor. I could feel a trickle of blood leak from my ear. Victor and he righted my chair, then Benny got in my face.

"You stubborn fuck," Benny said, his breath sour and smelling like cat food. "We would've given you some money and let you walk out of here mostly in one piece, but fuck you! You had your chance. When I'm done with you—what's left of you, anyway—is going to be begging to tell me where the money is." He slid a switchblade from his pocket and opened it, making sure I got a good long look at the six-inch blade. "You're going to start losing slices, Joe, and whatever I cut off you're eating, even if I have to shove it down your throat. So what'cha in the mood for first, a nose or ear?"

I just stared through him. If he was expecting fear or anything else, fuck him. Let him whittle away at me all he wanted. This was the ultimate test, and I knew I was up to the challenge. The adrenaline now was pushing through me, making me dizzy. And as far as Al went, let it eat away at him for the rest of his miserable life that he might've found out about the money.

"No preference, huh?" Benny was saying, his breath now smelling more like a toilet than cat food. "You want to make it look like you ain't fucking listening to me, is that it? Fuck you then. You want to act like a deaf man, might as well make it your ear."

I didn't move. I sat as still as stone. Benny, furious, his face crimson, moved quickly and grabbed my ear, bringing the edge of the blade against it. Before the blade could be pushed upwards, there was a blur of motion, then Benny was being pulled away from me. Tony had him in a bear hug. Benny looked startled as all hell as he looked at Al moving towards him holding out a piece of the same type of razor wire that was biting into my ankles. Victor looked confused also.

"What the fuck . . ." Benny started.

Before he could get another word out, Al was on him, wrapping the razor wire around his neck and pulling it tight. He had prepared for this, both ends of the razor wire attached to makeshift wooden handles so he could pull tightly without cutting his own hands. The shock in Benny's eyes was really something to see, but he wasn't going down gently, his legs kicking spastically like they had a life of their own. Not that it was doing him much good.

"What the fuck are you doing?" Victor sputtered out. He tried to pull Al away. Al turned and barked at him to step back, his eyes dead black holes, any soulfulness from them long since gone.

"If I don't do this, Joe doesn't tell us where the money is. Now back the fuck away!"

Victor hesitated for a moment, but took a step back and watched Al's round face purpling from his effort as he pulled the wire tight and just about decapitated Benny. Benny's legs were still kicking, though, making me think of a chicken with its head cut off. The stench of his bowels emptying filled the room.

"He'll tell us. We just need to keep working on him," Victor argued, his eyes jumping from Al to Benny's head that was now nearly sliced off. His feet had stopped kicking. Another few pulls on the razor wire and his head would be completely separated from his body. Al realized that and let go of the wire. Benny's lifeless body slumped to the floor.

"He wasn't going to tell us shit. Not with the military training he's had." Al was clenching and unclenching his fists, then rubbing his hands. He slowly shifted his eyes to mine. Ignoring Victor, he addressed me. "I did what you wanted. Now where the fuck is the money!"

The adrenaline was pumping through him even more than it

was me. Any pretense of civility and calm were long gone. Fuck, I envied him.

"What are you talking about?" I asked as innocently as I could. I then turned and stared hard at Victor. "You've only done half the job so far."

Victor got it first, then Tony, with Al being slow on the uptake. Victor's face blanched white. "M-Motherf-fucker," he stammered out, fury raging in his eyes. He started to pull a thirty-eight automatic out of a holster. I don't know who he was planning to shoot, me or Al, but before he had the gun out Tony tackled him to the floor and the two of them were thrashing about. Slowly Al realized the stunt I pulled. At first nothing but anger in his eyes, then a begrudging admiration, and finally a cold calculating look as he realized he'd now only have to divide the money two ways. He nodded to me, then joined the fracas.

"You double-crossing motherfuckers," Victor kept repeating as he fought over the gun. It started to look like he was getting the upper hand over Tony, but Al changed the equation by kicking Victor hard in the head. From where I was sitting, I couldn't as much see the kick as hear it, as well as the dull *oomph* that came out of Victor. I heard another thud, then saw Tony crawling up and getting onto Victor's chest. The way his shoulders were tensing I could guess what was happening. When he was done, Al helped him to his feet. The two of them walked over to me, Tony looking disheveled, his breathing ragged, Al, his eyes nothing but dull black stones.

"Both of them taken care of," Tony said, his face flushed, his eyes tensed.

"You're jumping to conclusions there, pal," I said. "Victor wasn't part of the deal. It was you and Benny."

Tony took a step back, asking, "What the fuck you mean me?"

"Exactly what I said. You and Benny. That was deal Al made with me."

"He's fucking with you," Al tried to tell him. He reached for him, but Tony jerked his arm away, his eyes bouncing nervously between the two of us.

"Why the fuck me?" he demanded.

"Because I never liked you," I said as straight-faced as I could.

"Why? What I ever do to you?"

"For chrissakes, Tony, get a grip," Al was saying, "He's just fucking with you. There was no deal other than Benny."

Tony wasn't buying it, especially after Al kept quiet and let him kill Victor. His eyes darted around for the thirty-eight that Victor had dropped on the floor. "Joe, why don't you like me?" he asked, hurt, half-looking at me, half at the gun.

"I don't know. Something about the way you look. It's hard to pinpoint these things sometimes."

"You were not part of any deal!" Al shouted. He made another reach for Tony, which was the wrong move. Tony dove for the gun. Al, having no choice, followed him. I ended up knocked over onto the floor. I couldn't see them during their death struggle but I could hear them while they grunted and groaned. Where I landed, my right hand—the one where Benny had pulled off my fingernails and damn near tore off my middle finger—was only inches from the switchblade he had dropped. By tensing and relaxing my arm muscles over the last few hours I'd been able to create an inch of slack in the rope, and was now stretching my fingers, ignoring the pain in them, as I reached for the knife. The tip of my index finger was able to touch it. Working slowly I inched the knife close enough to where I could grab it. The death struggle was still going on by the time I had the knife in my hand. It was another several minutes before it was over, first one gunshot, then another, the noise only muffled slightly by a human body. My back was turned so I had no idea who had won. I lay there and waited, trying to shield the knife from view.

Whichever one it was, he sat on the floor breathing hard. It took several minutes before he got to his feet and walked over to me. I only had one chance and I had to time it right. As my chair was being pulled up, I pushed the knife blade several inches into his leg trying to sever the posterial tibial artery. From the way the blood gushed out of the wound, I knew I'd connected. I learned hundreds of ways to kill people during my time in special forces, and this was as good a way as any.

It turns out the person I killed was Al. He took a couple of steps away from me, already woozy, and then sat hard on the floor. It's amazing how fast you can die from having that artery severed. His eyes were already glazing over, and I had to talk quickly so I could explain where the money was. After all, I felt it was only right I kept up my end of the deal.

"I guess you figured out that after I took the money I headed west, but you probably don't know that I stopped off in Vegas along the way. You see, Al, as an adrenaline junkie, I had to stop there. I didn't really give a shit about the money, but taking it the way I did was a bigger rush than you could ever imagine. The problem was after a rush like that I needed another fix, and Vegas gave it to me. I put the eight hundred grand on black, and for those few seconds while that little black ball bounced around the wheel I had the adrenaline pumping like you wouldn't believe. The ball landed on black, and all I could feel was deflated. I needed another spin of the wheel, I needed to feel that rush again. The casino gave their approval for another bet, so I let one point six mil ride on black. This time I lost. If I had won I would've kept betting until I lost, 'cause the rush was more important than the money. Anyway, that's where the eight hundred thousand is, left at the Bellagio's casino."

The way his head was tilted to one side I knew he was gone. Cutting the artery like I did, without medical attention you only have about sixty seconds, and I think my explanation took a little longer than that. Eh, fuck it, I tried.

So there I was. Three fingernails pulled off, one finger badly broken, razor wire biting into my ankles, my hands tied to the chair, with maybe an inch of leeway in the rope securing my right hand, and holding a knife between my thumb and palm, my fingers too fucked up to hold it any other way. Upstairs lay a dead elderly couple; in the basement with me were the bodies of four violent criminals. If relatives came during the next few days to check up on the couple upstairs, I'd be saved, but would probably be tied to this gang and the armed robberies we'd pulled off and would be heading to jail for a long time. If no one came and I couldn't figure out a way to free myself, I'd be dead within a week.

Fuck, I'd been in tighter spots. Thinking about my situation got the adrenaline pumping.

God, I loved it.

The only problem was, when I figured a way out of here, what was I going to do to top this?

How was I going to get another adrenaline fix after this one?

A problem for another day.

Nine-Ball Lessons

This one's short and sweet about two hoods philosophizing over life-lessons that can be learned from a game of nine-ball.

Charlie "the Mole" Greco gently kisses the eight-ball into the corner pocket setting up an easy nine-ball shot in the opposite corner. As he's chalking up his stick, he asks me how playing pool is like making love to a woman.

I shrug, tell him I don't know.

"Think about this," he says. "Even though you usually get better results with a gentle touch, sometimes it just feels so damn good to slam it home."

Charlie bends over the table and slams the nine-ball hard nearly bouncing it out of the pocket, his face turning red as he laughs at his own joke. Nobody I know likes laughing at their own jokes more than Charlie. He looks up at me, kind of quiz-zical, wondering why I'm not laughing along with him, 'cause usually I do. I tell him I got too much on my mind. Which is true. I drop a ten-dollar bill on the table for the game, and he waits while I rack up the balls for the next game.

Charlie and I've been playing pool every Thursday night at the back table in Donnegan's since high school, almost twenty years now. I dropped out of school after one year, being more muscle than brains and having an open invitation to work for "Big" Tony Lombardo, but Charlie being a smart guy finished high school, then two years of college before dropping out to take the job I helped arrange for him with Lombardo. I do "muscle" work for Lombardo—stuff like breaking deadbeat's arms, busting heads, sometimes much worse. Hence my nickname, "Knuckles". Not too hard to figure out. Charlie's nickname is my fault. He doesn't have much of a neck, and has kind of a long nose and round face like a mole would, but that doesn't have anything to do with me giving him that name. And it's not because he spies on people or has any sort of facial blemishes. I started calling him "Mole" because of his bad eyes. Before he got his contacts, Charlie used to squint like a mole coming out of the ground. Probably because of the physical similarities the name stuck, but if it wasn't for me, and his eyes were better, he would've ended up with something like "Professor", or maybe "Socrates" or "Plato" or some other philosopher, 'cause he's always philosophizing about life, especially how it relates to pool.

"What the hell does a muscle-head like you got on his mind?" Charlie asks, his eyes like small gray polished stones as they sparkle with amusement.

"Just business," I say.

"You need to have your mind on the game," he tells me. "Pool is like life, focus is everything."

He breaks the rack, pocketing both the three-ball and the six, but also dropping the cue ball in the side.

"Jesus fucking Christ," he swears, his lips pulled back to show his canines. He turns, shakes his head angrily at me. "You see, Knucks, just like life a game of pool can shit all over you when you least expect it."

I now have ball in hand. If I want to try it, I could place the cue ball behind the one and take a tough cross-table combo with the nine to win the game, but it's a low percentage shot. I see Charlie spotting the combo and then trying hard not to look at it, trying hard to will me not to see it. But that's not why I place the cue ball so I can easily tap the one into the side. It's because the combo's a low percentage shot and I don't do those. I like to play it safe. After I make the shot I hear a heavy exhalation of breath coming from Charlie, a thin smile creeping onto his lips.

"You had the game, Knucks," he tells me. "All you had to do was combo the nine and you had the game."

"Low percentage shot," I tell him as I sink the two-ball and set up an easy four-ball corner shot.

"You never get anywhere playing it safe."

I give him a go-fuck-yourself look as I pocket the four and then the five. I don't set myself up as much as I wanted with the seven and I end up rattling the ball around the corner pocket, but it doesn't drop.

"Fuck," I swear under my breath.

"Pool is like life, Knucks. You gotta make it look easy. Never let them see you sweat."

I watch as Charlie takes the game from me, his shit-eating grin stretching wide. I drop another ten-dollar bill on the table.

"What's wrong, Knucks? You seem so damn preoccupied."

Preoccupied? Yeah, that was one way of putting it. I stop to polish off the pint of Guiness I've been drinking. "I told you before, just business."

"Yeah, so what does Lombardo have you so worried about it?"

I wasn't going to tell him. As I said before, I'm a guy who usually plays it safe. But Charlie and me have been buddies over twenty years, and I can see the concern spreading across his face. I shrug and tell him it's because of the Voodoo Lady business.

"Oh chrissakes, Lombardo still has that bug up his ass?"

I rack the balls up and wait until he breaks. It's a bad break. Worse than bad. Not only does nothing go in, but he leaves a quick one-nine combo to take the game. I line up my shot, taking my time.

"He lost fifty grand on that," I tell him without taking my eye off the shot. "And then you got the two hundred grand he didn't make that he was expecting to."

I sink the shot and look up as Charlie crumples the ten-dollar bill I had just given him and tosses it back in front of me. I smooth the bill out, taking my time with it before placing it in my wallet. I usually don't beat Charlie and maybe that's why I'm taking my time celebrating the victory, or maybe I'm just trying to stretch things out and avoid the unpleasantness that's coming. I'm not sure. It's already ten o'clock. But I just stand and watch as Charlie takes his turn racking the balls.

"I thought you already got that one figured out," Charlie says.

I look at him, and he looks back, mostly bored. A month ago ten grand was spent fixing a dog race, and forty grand spread out among WIN and perfecta bets. If Voodoo Lady wins as she's supposed to, Lombardo takes home a minimum of two hundred grand. The dog should've been shot up with enough amphetamines to guarantee a win, but more was used than should've been and the dog's heart exploded in the middle of the race. Left the bitch dead where she fell.

"I thought so, too," I say. "But Lombardo found out ten grand was bet on the dog that won."

Charlie strokes his chin as he thinks about it. "We were double-crossed," he says. "I paid that kid ten grand to fix the race for Voodoo Lady. He must've intentionally overdosed our dog and pepped up the one that won. And the sonofabitch bet the ten grand I paid him on the winning dog."

I nod. It could've been that way. Makes sense. But it also could've been Charlie who double-crossed us. Give the kid the hypo with enough junk to kill, then pay someone else to speed up the winning dog. You do that you get to walk away with all the money—what you've won with the ten grand bet, plus the remaining thirty thousand that was supposedly spread among losing bets. The question is why does Charlie only bet ten thousand on a sure thing? Well, I guess that's pretty easy to figure out. He'd want to set up the kid at the track in case Lombardo's able to get his hands on the betting info. That's if Charlie's the rat

247

and not the kid. Charlie looks like he's telling the truth, but then again, the kid stuck to his story when I broke each of his fingers, and kept breaking bones until he passed out. I tell Charlie what I did to the kid and the story he told. Charlie keeps looking at me straight on. Not a flinch, not a waver, nothing as he tells me the kid was simply sticking to the lie.

So there I am. If Charlie's lying to me, I can't tell. I can't read it, just like I couldn't with the kid. I shrug and tell Charlie that's what I thought but it's what's on my mind. Then I break the rack. A pretty good one sinking three balls and leaving me an easy setup for the first three shots. I peek at Charlie as I make them. He looks unconcerned, just pissed.

"Nice break," Charlie says.

I just make a face as I line up my next shot. I'm barely paying attention as I'm knocking down shot after shot before sinking the nine. I'm trying hard to get a read on Charlie, just like I did that kid.

"Sonofabitch," Charlie swears. "Two games in a row. Fuck. When was the last time you took two in a row from me, Knucks?"

"Been a while," I say.

The next game is more of the same. I hit some sort of streak where I can't miss. For the first time I see Charlie looking worried. Not a fucking drop of perspiration when he thinks I might be suspecting him of ripping off Lombardo, but the thought of losing three games in a row to me has him sweating. Fuck, I just don't know. I wish I could read him. He tries distracting me by telling me why people like nine-ball so much.

"With eight-ball you have so many choices," he's saying. "With nine-ball the order's set. You don't have to think so much. You just do what's laid out in front of you. Simplicity, Knucks. That's what people strive for in life."

He's right about that. It's when you have choices to make when you get yourself in trouble. Thinking about that does distract me, at least enough so I miss the nine-ball shot. But at least I leave him a tough cross-table bank shot. At least it's no gimmee. Still, he's grinning from ear-to-ear seeing how he psyched me out.

I stand back and watch him line up the shot. He's off on the shot. You can tell from the sound the cue ball makes when it hits the nine that it's too flush, but I watch as the damn nine-ball does a slow spin towards the side pocket and falls in. Charlie starts laughing at that. Damn near busts his gut.

"Like in life, better to be lucky than good," he forces out, still cracking up over his luck. "I was shooting for the corner."

"No shit."

His face is turning red as he's laughing harder to himself. I just stand watching trying to get a read on him. I mean, we've been buddies over twenty years. I need to know which one's lying to me, Charlie or the kid. But the thing is the kid never changed his story, even when I slapped him awake and sliced him open from neck to groin. Even as he was gurgling out blood, he insisted he was telling the truth. But there's nothing Charlie's saying to make me think otherwise either. Except he should've noticed when Donnegan's cleared out an hour ago. That was when I was supposed to do the job. He should've realized it was too quiet in there. But then again, it could be nothing more than being worried that Lombardo's falsely suspecting him since he was the guy responsible for the bribe and laying down the bets. I just don't know. But then I realize it doesn't matter. I'm just dumb muscle. I'm not paid to think. I'm just one of those guys who does what's laid out in front of him. Charlie was right. Like everyone else I seek simplicity in my life. I start joining Charlie, laughing also as I pick the nine-ball out of the pocket and start tossing it in my hand. That just makes him laugh harder.

"Charlie," I ask, "you know what a nine-ball's like?"

He's just about choking with laughter now, his face turning a bright red. Barely able to spit out the words, he mutters something about how this is going to be good.

I'm laughing hard too at this point. I catch the nine-ball and stare at it. I turn to him, a hard grin etched on my face. He's barely able to keep from pissing his pants, his round body convulsing as he laughs himself sick.

"Come on, Knucks," he forces out between tears of laughter. "What's a nine-ball like?"

"It's like a hard fucking rock," I say to him. Before he's able to connect what I'm saying I slam the ball hard into his forehead. He drops like a sack of guts. With the ways his eyes are staring open I know he's dead, but I stomp down on his windpipe to make sure. Maybe he was telling me the truth, maybe he wasn't, but it wasn't my call to make. As I said before I'm just dumb muscle. As it is, the job should've been done an hour ago. It wasn't my place to figure anything out. I call and arrange for the cleanup. I know the guy on the other end is pissed. I'd kept him waiting. I hope my fuck-up doesn't get back to Lombardo.

Before leaving I give Charlie one last look and think there but the grace of God, and realize that's as much thinking as a dumb muscle like me's entitled to.

CPSIA information can be obtained at www.ICGtesting.com
Printed in the USA
LVOW051048240612

287412LV00001B/101/P